OUT OF BLUE COMES GREEN

OUT OF BLUE COMES GREEN

M. E. COREY

PAGE STREET YA

First published in 2024 by
Page Street Publishing Co.
27 Congress Street, Suite 1511
Salem, MA 01970
www.pagestreetpublishing.com

Distributed by Macmillan, sales in Canada by The Canadian Manda
Group.

28   27   26   25   24   1   2   3   4   5

ISBN-13: 978-1-64567-932-5
ISBN-10: 1-64567-932-2
Library of Congress Control Number: 2023936745

Cover and book design by Laura Gallant for Page Street Publishing Co.
Cover illustration © stc019 (Scotty Hervouet)

Printed and bound in China

FOR MĀRA.

I hate you less than I hate all the others.

CONTENT WARNING:

transphobia, homophobia, depression, suicidal ideation,
suicide attempt (on pages 64–66), bullying

Chapter 1

WAITING IN THE WINGS IS a little like waiting to be born.

So close to the stage. Almost my turn. I can hear the crowd cheering for the dancer on stage.

I grasp the fretboard of my guitar, reciting lyrics in my head. The crowd screams some more. Soon they'll scream for me too. This is my moment to recreate myself.

The smell of my new leather jacket mingles with the dusty chalk odor of the stage while sweat trickles down my back, soaking into my black T-shirt.

I deny I ever felt so strong,
but you know I've fallen deep.
And I can't fall asleep ... anymore.

Too personal. I can't sing this. Why didn't I choose a cover song? We could've played The Cure or The Smiths, but no, I wanted to play one of my songs. Stupid.

A few deep breaths. Libby elbows me, leaning toward my ear. She has to yell to be heard over the noise. "Kinkade, when you said you were going to change your hair, I didn't know—"

My stomach drops but I force a smile, running a hand across the two inches of hair that remain, raising my eyebrows at her. My tough guy pose makes her laugh.

She yells, "Cool!" and I can tell she means it. "Just be sure you sing in your regular voice." Her dark eyes are not amused.

I know she's right. I can't hit the low notes as well. These clothes and this haircut may suggest that I'm male, but my voice does not.

Libby's fourteen-year-old cousin, Gene, extracts his bass from its case, laying eyes on me as if it's for the first time. He's wearing black jeans and his black James Jamerson t-shirt, like he's old enough to be cool. A few seconds pass before he recognizes me, and his thick eyebrows shoot up. He forces them back down.

Cheers from the crowd die out as the principal introduces our band, "Next up, we have the band Blue."

Libby shoves me toward the stage and rolls her drum set out on its wheeled platform, some drama thing they had sitting around. Leaving my last bit of confidence behind, I stumble onto the stage with her. The audience murmurs. Once Gene has plugged in his bass, he's stranded far to stage left with his short cord. He plucks out a few notes with his long, deft fingers. Beside Libby's drums, my amp waits for me to plug in my guitar. As I do, feedback reverberates through the auditorium. To distract the audience, Libby taps out a rhythm on the edge of her snare, waiting for me to get my act together. I can't panic. I'm cool. I look great in this jacket. This song rocks.

Her steady cadence quiets the crowd.

I step to the microphone as Libby continues a beat. Moving from the rim to the drum, she sets the pace for the song. But this is easy for her; she sits in the back, protected by her drum kit. Even while she plays, she's got her analytical producer's eyes. I'm the one exposed out front.

Shut up and play.

I strum the first chord to Libby's tempo, head down, eyes closed. Hearing the rush of the notes from the amp, I slip into the melody line, humming to myself. I play the opening riff and sing:

> *I can look out over this lonely road,*
>
> *but I can't get back to you.*

Libby slams on her bass drum.

> *I don't know what to do.*

Libby taps the cymbal.

> *Anymore.*

Switching chords, I sing the chorus. Gene keeps the bass line strong and even, completely in sync with Libby. My amp chooses now to crackle with static, all my notes lost. But it comes back seconds later when I jiggle the plug on my guitar.

Keep going.

When I sing the last line of the chorus:

> *Now all I can see*
>
> *You walk away from me*
>
> *Alone.*

My eyes open and my stomach turns over. The crowd stretches back into the dark auditorium. Huge.

Keep playing.

One row back near the center is a boy from my math class. What's his name? He cups his hands around his mouth and shouts, "Dyke!" which spreads through me like a plague. I hit a wrong chord but keep going.

Cheering reaches my ears as I go into the middle riff, louder than that asshole boy. Libby smacks a drum solo. Gene keeps up with it all, even though Libby's part wasn't planned.

3

As I strum the second verse, "Fucking dyke!" gets drowned out by Libby's cymbals. Then the chorus, and though we'd agreed to only do two verses, I continue into the third. Despite her glare at the back of my head, Libby keeps drumming, flipping back her long, tightly curled hair, sneaking up the tempo. She always wants everything faster, faster. I speed up, though I'm sure this will ruin my vocals.

But she knows what she's doing. We pull the last part off perfectly, the lights dim, and the crowd goes crazy. No matter what that asshole yelled at me, the rest of the crowd loved us. I can't keep my smile from spreading. This is so amazing.

Libby disconnects my amp as she shoves her wheeled drums off the stage; Gene lugs his amp and bass behind her.

I let out an audible, "Wait," before I follow. We can't be done already.

Backstage, Libby starts to break down her drums, unscrewing cymbals and her bass drum mallet. I stick my guitar in its bag, set it aside with the amp, and give her a hand. She texts her uncle to meet us, and when he arrives, the three of us lug out the drum pieces one by one to Uncle Doug's SUV. Carefully. Libby's drums are her babies. When she has any money to spare, it goes into her drums. I'm surprised she doesn't wrap them all in individual little blankets. Gene doesn't attempt to help; he fiddles with his bass strings as if he might need to replace one before sliding his bass into its case.

Uncle Doug stops us before we can take another load out. "You were fantastic tonight!" He wraps Libby up in his arms, and her smile is pleased and content at the same time. She hates when people hug her, but Uncle Doug is different because he's her mom's brother.

When he lets her go, he offers me a handshake. "You, too, kiddo. You've got a wonderful voice." He's checking out my hair and clothes, but he's not surprised in the least.

I clasp his hand. "Thanks." He hasn't called me by my name in years, just "kiddo."

I take another part of the drum kit outside.

The January air is frigid in Minneapolis, but it feels good for a few moments, a respite from the hot stage lights and the weight of my leather jacket. Libby's too cool for a winter coat too, so she freezes in her vintage jean jacket, her mom's from years ago, with frayed cuffs and eighties band buttons. It's sentimental since her mom's been gone for six years now. By the time I head back for another drum load, my skin shivers, my damp shirt icing over. I hustle through the lot, past my car, and back inside.

Once everything is loaded, Libby slams the hatch closed, leaning against it for a moment. She blows out breath like she's exhaling cigarette smoke. "We were great." She pulls black, fingerless gloves on, rubbing her hands. Then she has her notebook out, always planning changes, detailing what worked, what didn't.

"Yeah." I still feel the drumbeat pound through me. I want to be back on the stage for our next song.

She jams her fists into her jacket pockets.

"I think I'm going to stick around for a few acts." I kick an odd clump of snow into bits. "You know, see how bad everyone sucks." I cock an eyebrow at her. "We set the bar pretty high."

She laughs, bending in to give me a quick hug. "I'd like to stay and take notes on the other groups . . ." Her eyes go to her ride.

"Nah, it's almost over," I reassure her.

"All right. See you later."

I give her a manly nod.

One step away, she turns back. "You look good." Her gaze lingers for a bit so I'm clear that she means my hair, my outfit, my maleness.

I can feel my face warming. She's one of the only people who has known about me for more than the last half hour. "Thanks."

Libby gets in her uncle's car where Gene has already snuck into the back seat. Doug, who's had the engine running this whole time, sticks a hand out the window at me as they drive off. After the crunch of the tires over the snow fades into the distance, I'm left with silence. No drums. No guitar. No crowd. Only me.

The wind kicks up, blowing snow in swirls. We're supposed to have a blizzard tonight, but I never trust the weather report.

When I go back in, I don't watch any other acts. Instead, I sit on the dusty wooden floor beside my amp and guitar, surrounded by discarded school-band debris—music stands, old song books—listening with my eyes closed. The junior on stage right now thinks he's a comedian. He's not. A few freshmen do a short one-act scene that's all right. For the most part, though, it's as I expected from a high school talent show: nothing above ordinary.

I wait until the last act has finished before I leave. Maybe on my way out someone will say something nice about my performance. Unlikely. More likely I'm setting myself up for a verbal beating, but it could be different. People actually applauded.

I'm not Kayla the Freak when I play my guitar. I transcend whatever prejudice they have. For a moment. For a song.

For most of them, anyway.

I hoist my guitar onto my back and grab my amp, mingling with everyone filing out of the auditorium. It's a dangerous move that makes my neck stiffen. Anyone could be in this crowd. But I'm still on such a performance high, I can't make out the evil kids from the ordinary ones.

The crowd carries me along, nudging me closer to the wall. A few heads turn to look at me. A couple people meet my eyes and give me a smile or a nod. Then from nowhere, I'm blocked by a brawny chunk of a guy who traps me against the wall. I break to the left, but he moves at the same time, and his two cronies fill in the other escape route. JT positions his muscled forearm over my head, against the wall. "Nice singing." His breath reeks of vape, the funky mango-vanilla flavor he likes.

He has me right where he wants me, close to the crowd, but out of the main line of sight.

"Move." I slide into his man Hunter, who sets a pick like we're playing basketball.

JT grins, muscly creases in his face extending all the way to his blond military cut. "Are you trying to confuse people?"

I take a quick breath in to tell him to shut up, but hold it in. I'm not trying to confuse people; I'm trying to straighten them out.

"Come on, Kayla." He lays his meaty hand on the side of my head, playing with my two inches of hair. "What did you do to your beautiful hair? Remember that day in fourth grade when you cut your hair like right here?" He lays his burly hand where my neck meets my shoulder. "So hot."

I pull away, slamming my amp into his leg.

He swears, doubling over for a moment.

Before I can get more than two steps away, his other goon Dirk grabs the collar of my leather jacket from behind so I can't escape.

A few girls slow down to see what's going on.

JT scowls a bit. "Naw, naw, let her go." He pulls Dirk's hand off me, and calls after, "Someday you'll remember our moments together and ask why we never married."

Disgusting asshole. I throw a glare over my shoulder once I have gotten far enough away.

He blows me a kiss as he flips me off. But I know something he doesn't: I know what's coming up behind him.

Three seconds later, Principal Eckert sidles up to him. "What's going on, JT?"

Adjusting my guitar strap on my shoulder, I smile to myself and rush out the door into the bitter air and blowing snow in the parking lot. Breathe. Calm down.

Few cars besides mine remain. No people. That's good. Snowflakes land on my face and my jacket as I place the amp and guitar in the back seat, but it's so dark, I can barely see where I've put them. When I slam the door, someone's standing in front of me, and I stumble back a step.

I put my arm up to block the snow and see that it's okay; it's a girl. And not one who hates me: It's Christine Walker, who sits next to me in art class. Has a charcoal preference while I'm a straight-up pencil drawer.

Her expression is not one I've seen on her before. Sheepish? Embarrassed? "I thought you were pretty great. On the stage." She tilts her head, so she has to look up at me through her sandy blond hair. Then she, too, puts up an arm to block the weather.

"Thanks." The air around me seems to warm.

"Did you write that song?"

"Yeah."

She averts her gaze. "You have a beautiful voice."

"Yeah?" If I didn't know better, I'd say she was flirting with me.

"Maybe you could play something for me. Sometime." Snowflakes collect in her hair.

I lower my eyes. She's so beautiful. I can absolutely play for her sometime. Maybe I should write her a song. I step closer into the light.

She squints. "Kayla?"

She didn't recognize me? Shit. She thought I was some boy she didn't know.

"I didn't recognize you." Her voice flattens. "You cut your hair."

I trace the edge of it around my ear. "I wanted a change."

She nearly spits when she laughs. "I guess." She inspects me and clearly no longer likes what she sees.

I keep my chilled fingers from touching my hair again. "You don't like it."

Nervous laugh. "It's not that. It's just sort of," she searches for a word, "boyish." She pulls up the collar of her jacket. "Wait. Is that what you wanted?"

I swallow hard. That's not completely obvious? How can she not—but I should just tell her, be honest. After all, we've become art friends over the last few months.

"The jacket's cool," she says.

I smooth it down against my stomach. "Thanks." The leather is stiff with the cold. "Did you really think we were good?" The snow turns to ice pellets, stinging my cheeks.

She nods, but her smile dies quickly. Perhaps she's remembering that she thought I was someone else. That she was possibly attracted to that someone else. And now here she is with disappointing me.

"I have to get home. I think that blizzard's coming."

"You sure? I could give you a ride if you want." I follow when she takes a few steps away.

"I have my car."

"Right. Okay. Well, are you taking art next semester?" Second semester starts in a few weeks.

With a little wave, she turns her back to me, pretending not to hear.

The world around me feels so cold again.

Chapter 2

THE CAR ONLY WARMS SO much by the time I drive through the snowstorm and finally reach home, so my fingers are still icy when I go inside with my amp and guitar. I need to get up to my room so I can get warm.

"Kayla? Is that you?" Mom calls from the living room.

I don't want to talk to her right now.

She calls again, and I can hear foot thuds coming my way. I'm not fast enough to escape.

Her lips pucker when she comes into the kitchen where I am. "That's what you wore to the talent show?"

Guess you would've known if you'd shown up.

Her brow crinkles. "Where did you get this jacket? Aren't you worried what people will think?"

"What are they going to think?"

She grasps my jacket sleeve, pulling me to the stairs, pointing with her eyes. In a low voice, she says, "Go, before your father or brother see you."

God forbid Dad knows the truth about his only daughter. Of course, I'm not sure I'm ready for him to know. Based on how Mom's been handling it, I can only imagine how he will. And my brother, Sam? Also unknown.

In my room, I lean my guitar against the wall and place the amp beside it. An hour ago, riding the wave of our phenomenal performance, I would've wanted to plug it all in and practice or start on my song for Christine. Now, though, I just can't.

Mom appears in my doorway before I can change into warmer clothes. Her face has softened. A little. "Take that off." She pulls at my jacket sleeve.

I do, and now that I'm in my black V-neck, she stares at my chest. My face warms. Before I left for the talent show, I bound my chest with this stuff I found at the fabric store. It's sort of like a giant Ace bandage. I stitched up the ends so there wouldn't be any loose strings. I thought it was amazing, the way it made my chest look so flat. Mom does not seem to share my feelings.

I cross my arms.

After giving me a pitying look for far too long, she sits on the edge of my bed. I know she wants me to join her. I ensure there's enough space between us when I do and glare at the pink-painted wall across the room. Her voice is barely audible. "Aren't you taking Dr. Behmann's advice?"

Just go away, Mom.

"Well?"

I'm trying to remember what I've told her. What I said I talked about with Behmann. "It doesn't suit me."

Deep Mom sigh. "It needs to *suit* you, Kayla. This isn't a choice you can make."

My teeth clench, holding back the profanity I'd like to hurl at her.

Standing abruptly, she steps to my closet, throwing open the door. She pages through my shirts. "All of these, Kayla.

Too boyish." She holds the sleeve of a green flannel, shaking her head.

"I like that one."

She shoves the sleeve into the closet, repulsed, slamming the closet door. "You're too old to be a tomboy." She stands over me, pity in her eyes again. "What about next year? Don't you want people to take you seriously?"

With my eyes, I trace the edge of her sock, noting a tiny, frayed spot that will likely grow to a hole soon.

"College can be a time to reinvent yourself. Drop all of this . . ." She waves her arms over me as if casting a spell to remove my essence. "You could be—"

Dad's voice barrels up to us, "Honey, is Kayla home?"

Squeezing her eyes shut, she whispers a swear. "I'll be back." She signals me to stay, as if I'm her pet.

Descending half the staircase, she reassures my father that everything is all right, adding, "She needs to get her sleep now," so he won't come up to say goodnight to me.

"I heard that storm is really picking up out there," Dad says. "Glad she's home safe."

I should close the door, but instead I sit on the bed, waiting like a dutiful daughter.

When she returns, she starts in on me right away. "I just don't understand you." She closes my door to contain our conversation and her whispered yell. "I don't need you putting all of this into your father's head. He's got enough to worry about without thinking that you're—"

What am I, Mom?

"I talked to Dr. Behmann. He wants to see you again in spite of what happened between you two."

"Come on." There is no way I will ever set foot in that asshole's office again. "You have to be out of your mind."

"Just hear what he has to say—"

"I have heard what he has to say. I'm not listening to that prick anymore."

"Language, please."

"No, Mom, you don't understand. He's awful. He's the worst kind of awful. Do you know what he said to me about being trans—"

My mother scowls, shaking her head at the word.

"—gender? Any idea?"

She doesn't look at me now.

"He says I haven't given myself long enough being a girl and that—"

She raises her hands against my verbal gun. "How do you know he isn't right?" Meandering around my room, she picks at things on my dresser, my desk, touching them as if they are festering growths. "You need to accept reality." She plucks up a tiny sample of men's cologne, assessing its presence in her daughter's room. "People don't change who they are. They don't change their gender."

Why am I bothering? "I don't want Dr. Behmann's help, and I don't want yours either."

Her judging scowl droops as she places a hand on my cheek. "I might be the only one who can help you."

Squirming away from her hand, I open my bedroom door wide, leaning against it. "I need to get to bed."

Before she leaves, she returns to my closet, fishing something out of the back. As she passes me, she lays a gauzy, cream-colored, flowered shirt in my arms. "This is one of my favorites."

I've hated this shirt since she gave it to me for my last birthday. It touches my skin, but slithers down to the floor since I refuse to grab it. Then when I close the door over it, it bunches up. The more I wrestle with it, the more it wedges itself under the door. It's not until I am on my hands and knees, shimmying it out that I am able to freely shut the door.

I listen for a few minutes before I undress, stepping into my closet as much as possible as I undo the makeshift binder from my chest. The skin beneath expands in the air as if denied necessary sustenance for the past few hours. Wrinkles in the binder have imprinted magenta ridges on my skin. Running my fingers along them, I wince. One of these days I'll have the money to buy a better one—one that won't have to hurt like this.

Once in a bulky sweatshirt and athletic shorts, I slip under the covers. My anger has heated me up, all but my hands. I shove them under my thighs. Without thinking, I gently whistle to call Sasha, to have her warm me, to feel her soft fur and let her snuggle against me. But she doesn't come. Of course, she doesn't come.

Sasha died two months ago.

Chapter 3

MAYBE I DREAMT OF HER. Maybe I imagined she was here with me, that I could feel her warm fur, that her breathing was even. But in the morning, I'm alone.

I want my dog back.

Dodging Mom and Dad for the rest of the weekend is easy enough, but Monday morning is a different story. Though I don't want to sit across from Mom, I need to talk to her. Instead of saying anything, though, I continue to spoon Cheerios into my mouth. She meets me silence for silence, sipping her coffee and reading the news from her tablet. I pull my green flannel closed so she can't tell my chest is flat. Flatter. Taking a moment while she's clearly occupied, I discreetly pull at the end of the binder where it's digging into yesterday's sores. I tried to make it looser, but too much looser makes the entire effort pointless.

When she finally speaks, every word is reluctant to leave her mouth. "Be sure to wear your scarf. It's going to be below zero all day." Her eyes flick over to me.

"Yeah, all right." Now's the right time. The ice is broken. Do it. Ask her. "Mom."

She's back into her coffee and news.

"Mom, we should get another dog."

Her eyes close as she stops mid-sip of her coffee.

"There's an animal rescue not far from my school. We could get one that's already housebroken. One that's a few years old." One that already wants to be around people, one that's calm enough to cuddle.

"Kayla—"

My father interrupts her response when he comes into the kitchen. He looks cool, like he always does in the mornings, dressed in a suit and tie. Stooping to kiss Mom's cheek, he grins as he asks, "What have I walked in on?"

"Ask your daughter."

I purse my lips at the name she's called me.

He takes the seat next to me. "Well?" Then he notices my hair. Last time he saw me it was at least six inches longer. "Whoa." He ruffles it. "Quite a change." His smile looks sincere, but I can't tell if it's shock or amusement. "All right."

I poke an *O* down with my spoon. "I was asking when we can get another dog."

His face droops. "Sasha was one of a kind."

"I know."

"We can't just replace her."

"I know that. It's just the house is so empty." I pluck a tiny hair from my jeans. Sasha's. How can her fur still be on my clothes?

Dad straightens himself. "And what happens to this new dog when you go off to college God-knows-where?" He grasps my forearm, shaking it playfully as if he's kidding.

It's not bad enough that we're talking about my dead dog, now he wants to talk about my undetermined future. As if

I'll go away to college, and do what? Live in the dorms? Have a roommate who constantly questions who I am? I can't live with some girl I've never met before. And how much more scarring would it be to live with a boy?

But I can't stay here with Mom.

Dad wolfs down a bagel half, kissing me on the forehead, and says, "It wouldn't be fair to the dog, sweetheart." Then he's up and putting on his winter coat.

"Take a scarf," Mom says.

"You want a dog too." I throw these words at his back to make him give in. Though he stops for a moment, he doesn't stay and soon is out in the garage, starting the car.

Mom releases her coffee cup. Her hand makes a move to grab mine, but she thinks better of it. "You know he's right."

I change the subject. "Is Sam up yet?"

"I don't think so."

Pushing back from the table, I put my bowl in the dishwasher and slip on my leather jacket. "I have to go." I drape my scarf around my neck to keep Mom from commenting.

"Hang on, Kay." Sam comes in.

Sam pulls his winter jacket from a hook, sticks his bare feet into old tennis shoes with droopy heels, and escorts me out to the driveway where my poor car huddles in the January cold. The blizzard last night did some great work with snow drifts across our driveway. My car looks like an awkward ship tossed along white waves.

The wind bites at my fingers and head. I'm not used to this short hair. Sam, though, wears shorts and a college hoodie, holding his jacket in case Mom or Dad see him. He prefers the Minnesota winter uniform: shorts and a sweatshirt.

I have no idea why he has followed me, but it's too cold to wait for him to tell me. I duck inside the driver's door, and he takes the passenger seat. I chuckle at him. "I'm going to school, you know. I'm not driving your ass back here." The snow on the windshield and roof makes my voice hushed like we're in a soundproof room. I start the car and crank the defrost.

He gives me the serious older-brother face. "Watch your language."

"Whatever."

He laughs. Perfect straight teeth. "Look, I thought we should talk. I don't get to see you ever."

Whose fault is that? "I've got to get going." I crank up the temperature and the fan to defrost my windows.

"Hang on a second." He scowls. I'm distracted by his squared jaw and manly brow. We look so much alike, but he's clearly the male version, and in comparison, I'm clearly not. "I saw you come home the other night like you were performing at some concert."

I smile, remembering the rush of the crowd. "What about it?"

He stalls for too long. "I didn't even recognize you."

I try not to smile too much.

"It's not like you've ever been girly, Kay, but what's this?" He gestures at all of me, like I'm suddenly not a who but a "this."

I'm too aware of my chest binder. I don't want my brother thinking about my chest.

He tilts his head to meet my eyes, but I won't let him. "Tell me what's going on."

19

We had the whole weekend to talk about this, and he picks now. Outside. When I have to get going. "I have to go to school, Sam."

"Everyone will see you."

I laugh too angrily at that. "And?"

"And? I don't know. Is this how you want them to see you?"

I overthink my answer before I simply say, "Yep."

"You're going to do it, then?" He clears his throat. "You're going to be a boy."

I shrug each shoulder one at a time, awkwardly. "Yeah."

A smile spreads slowly across his face, and he hits me— sort of hard—in the shoulder. "Good for you." He opens his door. "See you after school."

I open my door, too, and call to him, "Help me clean off the car first."

On my short drive to Lakeview High, I smile. Sam is so strange sometimes. He gets it. I didn't think he would be so easy. I put on a song that I recorded with Blue and immerse myself in the memory of last night by blasting "I Don't Remember" so I can yell the lyrics along with it. My stomach flips when I recall the look in Christine's eyes in the parking lot. When I was me. Before she knew I wasn't me.

The recording isn't as powerful as what we did last night. I ought to tell Libby we should redo it. We record everything on her uncle's old laptop. The sound isn't perfect, but it's better than not recording. She brags about the software at the community college where she's taking a music production class, but we can't afford to rent it out.

I should send this MP3 to Christine.

Inside school, I hang my jacket in my locker and grab the books I need. JT and some of his jerk friends are on the stairs to my first class. I can hear his obnoxious laugh and a few words about fags. His friends spread out on the stairs to leer at a couple of girls and steal some kid's calculator. Ducking behind taller people—which isn't hard since I'm not even five-nine—I change direction, heading down the stairs. JT yells, "Was that my girl Kayla?"

I shut out their laughter. The bell will ring in a minute, so I jog to the other staircase, up two flights, and back over to the art room. Ugly sweat makes dots down the back of my shirt, which is just perfect. Exactly how I want to see Christine the day after our talk. Our moment.

Just inside the doorway by the sinks with shelves of paint brushes and empty jars, I take a few seconds to blot my forehead with crude paper towels. On the giant slanted art desk we share, Christine has her supplies arranged. Charcoal. Paper. No matter how much Ms. Horvath tells her to experiment with color, Christine sticks to black and white only.

Already her hands are shaded dark gray. Seems she's adding a second layer of charcoal to her drawing, which is clearly a palm tree.

I say hello, pulling out my stool beside her.

She blends the tree leaves to a darker gray.

"Funny running into you last night." I laugh, but it's so obviously fake.

With strands of her sandy hair in her eyes, she selects another rectangle of charcoal, darkening lines along the edge of the tree. Split second glance and a tiny smirk is all I get. Her words go into her paper. "Are you fishing for another compliment?"

"Are you going to offer one?"

Not even an eyebrow twitch in response. She grasps an art gum, blending charcoal into the tree's leaves, lightening bits of the leaves to suggest sunlight.

"That looks great." I want to take it back as soon as it's out; I'm trying too hard.

"I need to get the texture of the leaf."

"Well, if anybody can—" I stop myself, taking out my pencils instead. Before I can completely chicken out, I lean closer to her. "I was wondering . . ."

A student passes behind us, so I wait.

"I was thinking maybe . . ."

The girl on the other side of Christine asks to borrow something, so I wait.

"This Friday, I thought it might—"

"Kayla." Ms. Horvath's voice announces my name so loudly that I'm surprised every Kayla for twenty miles doesn't hear her. "This will be the last piece for your semester collection?"

I lift my arm from the desk, revealing a sketch of a round, furry creature, vaguely outlined with dozens of tentative marks.

"We're running out of time. Finals are next week, which means this has to be completed." She scowls, eyes drifting past my sloppy mess to Christine's perfectly rendered umbrella leaves. Christine can move from zero to sixty in under ten seconds when it comes to art.

Horvath gestures to Christine's paper as if it is the Second Coming. "Marvelous work. Absolutely marvelous."

Adding several more lines to my sketch, I bide my time until Horvath has moved on, only now, Christine is absorbed in her work. Lifting a hand to scratch her cheek leaves an adorable line of dark gray. I look for a Kleenex to wipe it off for her.

Her eyes narrow at me, and I realize my hand is inches from her face. "Sorry, but you've got . . ." I almost touch her before her own hand all but knocks mine away as it returns to her cheek. She uses the back, though, successfully removing some of the smudge.

"I was wondering what you're doing on Friday." It all comes out so quickly.

Christine sets her charcoal down, recrossing her legs so she's facing me. "Kayla, I think there's been a misunderstanding."

I shake my head.

She keeps going. "I really did like your song yesterday, but that doesn't mean I . . . like you." Her hands come up quickly. "Not that I don't like you." She shakes off the words, then whispers, "I'm not a lesbian."

"No, I wasn't—" I check all around us. Someone must have heard her, but only Ms. Horvath is looking at me. "I thought we could go out as friends."

Her sad smile lets me know that I sounded just as pitiful as I thought.

Chapter 4

FOR THE LAST WEEK OF the semester, right up through finals, Christine is mostly nonverbal. Sits beside me in art, silent. When I run into her in the hall, nothing. To her credit, she always makes it seem like I've caught her at the worst possible time, and she must, must, must continue on without me. Polite. Super polite. She even gives me a pretty smile with her sincere hazel eyes.

All I have to do is help her remember the me she saw after the talent show. She liked him. Flirted with him. Once she sees that he and I are the same person and forgets this Kayla she thinks she knows, she might agree to go out with me.

Still, right now there's nothing more between us other than my complimenting her work too much, especially her final project for first semester Art. A few times I try to talk to Libby about her, get some advice on how to get Christine to be interested in me, but Libby has as much experience dating as I do, and no experience being trans and asking someone out. We don't talk much about her and guys. I can only hope that Christine's in my section of drawing next semester; otherwise, I won't see her anywhere. Maybe lunch.

I should let it go, but that look in her eyes after the talent show. I would give anything to have her look at me like that again.

First day, second semester, senior year. I can't feel the cold of January as I walk across the parking lot; I can only think about what lies ahead: Strength Training, which I've wanted to take since I was born, and Accelerated Drawing. My other classes are all honors-level crap that make my transcript look good.

First hour, weight room. I can't wait to learn some new exercises and better techniques. I've exhausted all the sources I've found online and even library books. Maybe Coach Wendell can help me put on some muscle.

Strength Training messes up my schedule so I don't have Art the same hour as last semester. I just hope I don't sweat too much before I see Christine—if she's there, fingers crossed—in second hour. If she's not in second hour, I have to seriously think about dropping Strength Training.

Arriving as early as possible, I duck into the girls' locker room to change. No one's here yet. Kicking off my shoes, I take down my pants, but before I can step out of them, I hear the door open. A dozen voices or more chattering away. Shit. I slam my locker closed, rushing for the bathroom stalls.

I secure myself behind the stall door, double checking the latch, then change quickly—sweatshirt and baggy shorts—and wait, trying to get a breath in that doesn't shiver out of me.

A locker closes. Another opens. Someone says, "I hate having gym first hour."

"I know, right? It's the worst."

"What do they expect me to do about my hair?"

The air grows humid around me as I wait, my binder cutting into my side, trapping sweat beneath it. For a short time, I count in my head—one, two, three—by the time I've counted to seventy-six, the girls are still out there. Screw this. I have to get to class.

I gather up my school clothes, abandoning the stall, and keep my eyes focused on the lockers, not the girls. When I pass the first girl, the chattering quiets. Whispering begins.

One girl screams. "Oh, my God. What are you doing in here?"

A few others cover their already-clothed bodies with splayed fingers. "You can't be in here!"

I make my movements as fluid as possible, sliding open the locker, dropping the clothes inside, spinning the lock.

Someone whispers, "What is he doing in the girls' locker room?"

"Shut up. She has hips."

"It's a girl?"

Laughter springs up here and there. "Holy shit, you're right."

A short blond loudly whispers to her friend, "I've never seen a he-she before." She cackles.

I breeze out the door, clenching my jaw so hard pain shoots through my head, and quicken my steps to class. Music blasts, punctuated by clanking metal. A few guys are already pushing up weights. The guy bench-pressing grunts with each rep, and each grunt strikes me like an actual blow. JT. I clamp my teeth together. He won't ruin this class for me.

At least we're not segregated by gender. But, I'd rather be with JT than be labeled a girl. Of course, I've been labeled a girl since birth.

JT pushes the bar up one last time, setting it down with a purposeful rattle and a barbaric groan. His blond crewcut doesn't move as he sits up, charged, ready to go spear a boar. His gaze finds me before I can look away, get away.

"Kayla!" His face brightens like he's found out he'll actually graduate this year. He's on his feet, strutting up to me.

The more I back up, the more he lurches forward, so I sidestep behind a bench, crossed with a barbell. My fingers encircle the bar as I assess the weights on each end. Could I hurl this at him if I needed to?

His voice quiets. "Admit it. You're in this class for me." He puckers his lips, kissing the air and winking.

I'm in this class in spite of you. I don't need to check the room for back-up; I don't have any, even if Coach shows up now.

JT steps up to the bar, his body against the metal, nearly touching me, forcing me to take a step back. But when I move, he doesn't let me. Grabbing my shoulders, he holds me in place in front of him, a stupid grin creeping across his face. Balling up my sweatshirt in his hands, he winks. My shirt rises slowly, exposing my belly button, growing dangerously close to exposing my binder. My muscles tense.

"Dude," Hunter moves in beside him. "Coach is going to be here any minute." Hunter meets my stare. His eyes seem oddly kind.

JT inches my shirt higher so I have to stand on my tiptoes or reveal what's underneath. He flares his nostrils. "You still got the good stuff under there?" A nasty waft of mango-vanilla floats to me.

I shove him with both hands, falling backward to the ground when he lets go of my shirt.

Hunter yanks JT's arm. "Come on."

"The chicks' weight room hasn't been built yet, so you know, get the hell out." JT wipes nonexistent snot from beneath his nose. He whispers as he leans toward still-on-the-ground me, "You're too much of a distraction."

I get to my feet before JT can grab hold of me again.

Ten feet away, working her calves, Tiyana Taylor stops mid-press. She catches my eye like Hunter, then saunters over. "I don't see a Dicks Only sign on the door."

Hunter and JT's other friends howl, but JT doesn't miss an opportunity. "How do you know she ain't got one?"

Tiyana purses her lips. "Whatever. All I know is this is everyone's weight room. Dicks, chicks, and," she sizes me up, "whatever Kay is." She feigns straightening her ponytail.

My awkward smile does nothing to thaw her stare.

JT's mouth opens in a giant guffaw, but the sound is over-powered by a shrill blast. Coach Wendell blusters in, spitting the whistle out so it bounces against his rounded midsection. Thundering out commands for us to gather around him, he slams a hand down, silencing the music, silencing leftover laughter at my expense.

"Listen up. Every day I need to know you're present, and you've got a plan." He proceeds through the list of twenty-eight names, glaring up at each of us in turn.

Kayla Kinkade. Here.

He hesitates before going to the next name. He has a

comment for me, I can tell, but he stuffs it down and moves on. Is it stupid for me to hope that he wants to ask what I prefer to be called? What my pronouns are? He/him. Ask me.

When he's finished, he spends far too long explaining workout goals and setting them. We need them for each day, week, and month of the semester. Nothing about a training partner or anything stupid like that.

Once he's done, the music starts up again. I step back, waiting to see who goes where, watching the coach file in among the football players. He gives a few of them hell for standing around instead of pumping iron. After all, they've had a whole minute. The five of them have taken over the main free weight area. No one else gives them so much as a glance before they choose another location in the room.

Across the room where there's a second, much smaller free weight area, I place myself between two of the class's other misfits. I hold a ten-pound dumbbell straight up, bend my arm at the elbow, and flex my arm up and down. A boy shorter than me watches too closely. He holds a similar ten-pound weight, which he thrusts skyward, mimicking my motions. After only three reps, his other arm goes up for support.

Weak. Once the judgment fades, I recognize him. Danny. Elementary school. We were friends back when I could be a boy, and no one tried to fix me.

"Hey," he says. At first, I'm not sure he's spoken.

"Hey, yourself."

"I haven't seen you in a long time, Kayla."

I close my eyes, shutting out that name. Focus on the movement. Arm straight. Bend. Push.

"I think maybe back at Oak Grove Middle School."

His breath sputters as he presses up the ten pounds again. "You look . . . different."

I suppress my laugh. Is that the best he can come up with? The real question is why he's bothering. I don't want to let my guard down just to have him make fun of me. "Is there something you want?"

Danny struggles to bring the weight down, sputtering a bit. "I saw you at the talent show. Your band's pretty good."

"Thanks." I doubt Danny knows music at all, but I won't turn down a compliment.

"I didn't recognize the song."

"Oh, no, I wrote it." I probably shouldn't have said that. I try not to give out any personal information so it can't be used against me.

His eyebrows rise. "Wow. I liked it."

Whatever. There's not much else he could say without being an asshole. "Thanks."

"You know, my uncle has a pub. They do live music on Saturday nights."

Across the gym there's a tremendous clank of metal as JT puts down the barbell again. He has to make a show out of everything.

Halting his dumbbell, Danny runs a hand through his long dark bangs and shoots a look over at JT's group. "I don't like those guys."

I snort. "You and me both."

"At least you're an athlete."

I bite my lip.

"I mean, you were." He lets the weight fall to his side. "Why'd you quit? You were really good."

I put the ten-pounder back and take a set of twenties, then position myself on the edge of the bench.

"You could hit a three pointer every time. You were the free throw goddess . . . god."

I bring the weights to my chest. "That was junior high." I lie back to do presses. Instinctively, I pull my knees up, feet on the bench. I hate the way my shorts lie flat against my pelvis.

"I guess." Danny's eyes slide up and down my body like he's looking for something. Maybe he wonders how far my transformation has progressed.

Fuck off. Arms ready, I press the twenties skyward, my pecs straining. Jeez, it's been too long since I worked out.

"You want me to spot you?" He moves up by my head. Too close.

I sputter out, "No," feeling a little guilty for judging him before now that he's being so nice.

"Ever think about joining the team again?"

The girls' basketball team? Really? I am not explaining myself to him. Does he really want to know that changing in the locker room became utterly too embarrassing? That getting my period made everything too awkward? It's impossible to tell myself I'm a boy when I have cramps and have to account for bleeding. And the massive discomfort when I change clothes with girls whose bodies are not little girl bodies anymore. Danny can't understand that. Even Libby doesn't understand that.

I press the dumbbells upward over and over until my muscles numb.

Chapter 5

ART CLASS. CHRISTINE BETTER BE in this section of Accelerated Drawing. Though our conversations over the last week have been short, this could be a new start, a do-over. Scanning the slanted drawing desks and backless stools, I can't find her. Come on. After JT, can't something go my way?

A hand closes around my forearm. "Hey, jerk face." Libby.

"Takes one to know one." I hip check her. Lightly.

She pulls a little before releasing me. "Let's take these spots by the window."

I plant my feet.

Libby marches ahead alone, then scowls at me. "Seriously?"

I know she can read my plan across my face.

She says, "Don't you think you've barked up that tree one too many times?"

I can't explain, though. If she could've seen the look in Christine's eyes the night of the talent show, surely she'd understand I can't let that go. Whatever was there could be there again. I just have to find it. Or inspire it.

Christine whisks into the room, ignoring Libby and me completely. She takes one of the desks Libby had designated for me and her. I hear Christine ask a friend to come sit with her and the disappointment when her friend has already partnered up. She tosses her sandy hair as if it doesn't matter.

Christine's here. A smile spreads across my face. The rest of my senior year will be art class with Christine. What could be better?

And now that she has no partner, I can save the day.

Strolling up beside her, I gesture to the empty stool. "This seat taken?"

Her eyes search the room. "I don't . . ." When someone comes through the door, Christine's face lights up, then darkens. Some new girl with too many pins announcing her bumper-sticker causes, not a friend. Libby talks to the new arrival and secures her for a seat mate.

Wait a minute. Who the hell is that? What's she doing with my best friend?

Christine, gesturing toward Libby, angles her body awkwardly toward me. "Guess you should sit." In her eyes, we've both been thrown over. That could work for me.

I settle onto the stool, trying to savor the moment. Christine and me, together again. Then I hear Libby's screechy laugh, the one that makes her shade her face in horror. That new girl's laughing too. What's so funny? From what I can see of her clothes from here, she isn't going to fit in too easily. Are those all from the back end of Goodwill? Guess Libby will take her under her thrifty wing. My friend treats thrifting like it's part of her production design. How does this piece fit into her overall "concept?" Neither of them has to worry about what their clothes say the way that I do.

Focus. Art. Christine. She already has charcoal, paper, and her favorite eraser. Fingers gray and dusty. Not sure what that's supposed to be yet. A landscape? I'm sure it'll evolve into something glorious.

Taking out my supplies, I sketch an outline—four legs, a tail, short snout, drooping ears.

Horvath saunters over to my desk with a too-sweet grin on her face. "Starting off the semester well, Miss Kinkade?"

I cringe. "I was thinking about switching to charcoal this semester." I just want to catch her off guard. Or maybe solicit some help from my desk partner.

This stops her. "Switching?"

"Sure. Something new." Not really. But think of the training I could get. The time with Christine. After-school meetings, our fingers covered in charcoal as we make art together.

Ms. Horvath stoops down beside me as if this will make our conversation private. "This is not the time to switch media." She glances at my tabletop, closes her eyes for too long. "But if you want to try something new, you could try a new theme."

My pencil works at the ears, shading the curves as I keep my mouth shut. Sasha's ears were always so soft. When I'd talk to her, they'd perk up so she could take in my words, as if every sound made absolute sense to her.

Ms. Horvath's knees creak as she stands. "We've seen enough of this dog, haven't we?"

I choke when I force down what I want to say, and luckily for Horvath, she's far enough away when I find my voice again that she wouldn't be able to hear me.

Christine's fingers have slowed over the palm leaf. "I can't believe she said that." She sits a little straighter. "I like the dog, Kay."

Ms. Horvath would never call out Christine for using the same theme.

I keep my head bent over the sketch like I'm focused. I shouldn't take anything Horvath says to heart. Anyway, she must not understand dogs. How much room they take up in your heart. How much space is empty when they leave.

Christine pats my nondrawing hand briefly. "And you draw her so well."

My stupid face grins.

She reaches in her bag, handing me a tissue. Shit. She knows I'm crying. "Don't listen to Horvath. Who is she anyway? A high school teacher?" Christine snorts, or whatever it is pretty girls do when they laugh that way.

The cafeteria is a bit rowdy, but it's only noise. Too many people with too many issues having to eat lunch too quickly. I grab a tray, follow the line, select the lesser of two evil entrees, and make my way to our table. Libby's there already, cell phone in hand, putting some of her own music through an editing app. It's not exactly my taste, but it's interesting.

Before I reach her, one of my old friends from middle school basketball, Elise, steps in my way. A chill moves through me. She's standing too close. "You ought to go to that audition the school's having."

What?

"Your band is the one everyone will want." She nods knowingly like we're both in on a secret. But I have no idea what she's talking about.

As I slide into the chair across from Libby, I shake off that strange interaction and set my tray down hard. "You didn't waste any time finding a replacement in art class, did you?"

Lowering her phone dramatically slow, she licks the fronts of her teeth. "You were the one who turned your back on me for some girl."

"You don't get it. This might be my only chance." If she had been there after the talent show—

"Speaking of chances, how about our last art class together? Ever?"

I didn't think of that. I drop my façade. "Right, right. I was an idiot."

Libby nearly spits out the fry she's biting. "Are we going to design our first album's cover or flirt with some . . . ?" She thankfully doesn't call Christine one of the names she's used in the past.

My face warms.

"You need to pull back a bit." Libby lowers her voice. "You're going to scare her."

"Too late." I stab a fork into a shrimp popper. "I don't know what I'm doing."

"That's obvi—" She stops herself. "Just give her some time. Or better still, don't. Move on."

As if fate wants to test my restraint, Christine passes by our table with her friends. Choking on my water, I stifle a cough.

Christine's tall friend whispers, "Why is she staring," as she glares at me, which forces out my cough and the water. Luckily, it's the table that suffers and not my clothes. Still, the tall friend seems to find me repulsive now. Christine, thankfully, gives me a smile.

Libby reaches over and flicks my hand. "Ignore them."

"How am I supposed to—"

A lunch tray with a soy burger arrives at our table with an awkward girl. "Couldn't find you at first."

Who the hell is this?

Pushing her bobbed chocolate hair behind her ear, she sits down between my best friend and me like she's been invited.

Wait. This is the girl from art class. Libby's new partner. I note a few of the buttons on her bag. One white button has love is love is love is love written in cursive rainbow-colored letters. Another has a series of raised fists in varying skin tones. There's a peace symbol and a Planet over Profit logo.

"I hope this is okay," she says to me. When she's level with me, I can't ignore her light blue eyes. On me. Unwavering.

I look over at Libby, who chomps another fry. "It's fine. I told you my best friend would be here."

Now they're both looking at me like I should say something. I'm still processing her issues. And while I'm used to people staring, this is different. Unlike the criticism in Tiyana's eyes or the amusement in JT's, something kind lingers in the new girl's.

"This is Madi," Libby says to me.

I nod at her. "Hey." It's a guy thing I've been perfecting. Slight movement of the head. No emotion on the face. Little inflection with the word.

Madi's cheeks pinken a bit. "Hey."

I break our stare, so I don't start to think she's interested in me. That's a blunt-edged sword that stings forever after.

"I should thank you," Madi says. "For letting me be Libby's partner."

"It's not really partners," I say. "You just sit by each other."

She smiles too broadly. "Yeah, of course." She keeps looking at me.

"Anyway," I say, "we might have to switch seats."

Madi's smile disappears.

Libby leans in, ignoring my words. "Madi's new. Today."

I suppose I could feign interest—first day of the second semester of her senior year is an awkward time to start a new school—but I only want her to leave.

Libby whacks me with the back of her hand.

"What?" My skin reddens.

Libby dips her head toward Madi a few times, but I pretend I don't know what she wants me to do.

Instead, I take out the novel I got for English class this morning. Too much reading every night and unlike most of my classmates, I'm not going to skim the summaries online.

Madi grasps my book, tilting it up so I can't read. "Oh, I love *The Great Gatsby*," she says. We have to write a persuasive essay proving either that Gatsby could repeat the past with Daisy or he couldn't. "Aren't you glad we're reading it?"

I'm about to answer when I check myself. Guys don't generally answer questions like this. Too emotional. I give her a single nod.

"I thought I saw you in AP Lit this morning." Madi pushes her hair back behind her ear.

Libby kicks my shoe under the table, so I say, "Yep." That's it.

Madi taps my copy of *Gatsby* again. "It's so sad how he thinks he can remake himself as a rich man, and Daisy will love him."

"I'm not at that part yet."

Madi's cheeks pinken again. "Libby didn't tell me your name."

Shit.

"This is Kay——"

I kick Libby under the table, much harder than she kicked me, before she can say my full name.

"Kay?" Madi says. "Like King Arthur's brother?"

Libby and I both raise eyebrows at her.

"You haven't read T. H. White? *The Once and Future King*? Kay kills a griffin in one scene." Her words spill out of her mouth almost before her tongue can keep up with her.

I laugh. What a strange girl. "Kay, like in Kinkade."

Libby rubs the back of her neck. "King Arthur? Is he that guy with the Round Table?"

I mock her, rubbing the back of my neck too. "Seriously? How do you not know who King Arthur is?"

"I do. I just said he's the guy with the Round Table."

"No, you asked if he *was* the guy with the Round Table."

"Same thing."

I shake my head at her. "Not the same thing."

Madi puts out her hands, one to each of us like she's holding us back from each other. "Guys, it's not a big deal."

"We're not fighting." Libby fake-glares at me.

The color drains from Madi's face. "Oh, is he . . . your ex?"

Libby and I gawk at each other, then burst into laughter. "Oh, no," Libby says. "Not ever. Not a chance."

"You've got that right," I say. But it's hard to put words together. My whole body is tingling. She just called me "he." She thinks I'm a boy. Honestly thinks I'm a boy.

I guess I have that head nod thing down.

Chapter 6

FOR THE NEXT FEW HOURS, the head nod gets me a few reply nods as I maneuver through the hallways between my new semester two classes. I think I should try it on Christine. Show her my masculine ways.

But I'm an idiot. Not only is that a ridiculous thought, I won't see Christine again until art class tomorrow. The rest of my classes are all Advanced Placement—Christine is not exactly a Try Hard—and then I have Drama. She could be in Drama. Nah. She's not the type.

I come across Libby between classes, and she's got something in her hand. Before she gives it to me, I see that it's one of the light blue flyers that have been all over the walls around the school. Something about prom. When she shoves it into my hand, I glare at her. "What do I want this for?"

"Read it. Read it." She tries to control her smile. She's wearing that bright pink lipstick I hate, but she thinks it's perfect for her dark skin tone.

I skim the flyer until I see what she's excited about. Live Student Bands Wanted! The school wants a live student band to perform at prom instead of getting a DJ? Terrible idea, one. And nothing I'm interested in, two. But that must be what

Elise meant earlier when she stopped me in the lunchroom.

I shove the paper at her with a disdainful snort. "Pass."

She shoves the paper back. "Are you kidding? It's a chance to play every kind of music there is."

"Mmm. Classical? Reggae?"

"Shut up. You know what I mean. Pop, rock, indie, R & B. You know how much I want that."

I stop myself from rolling my eyes. She's always talking about wanting to play with different bands. Blue isn't her dream like it's mine; she doesn't want to be pinned down to one group. In fact, to be a music producer like she wants, it's better to have experience in a variety of genres. I hate talking about that with her.

"They're not going to want us." I crumple the paper into her hand.

"What? Why not? What's wrong with us?"

"We're not exactly Mr. and Ms. Popularity."

She puts an arm around my shoulder and walks me toward my class. "That's why it works. We're the edgy kids. We're rock 'n' roll."

I laugh so hard I can't catch my breath. "Pretty sure when you're the one who has to call yourself edgy, you're not edgy."

"Ha, ha, ha. Laugh all you want. But I'm right. And the school will thank us for making prom awesome for the first time."

"Nope. Not going to happen."

Libby side-eyes me. "It's our ticket in."

I shake my head. She really buys into everything she hears.

"We play prom. Bekkah thinks we rock. Tells her dad—"

"Just stop right there." Bekkah Ingram's dad is a myth.

"We could really go somewhere."

I move to go into my class, but she holds me back. Her arm still around my shoulder, she makes me reminisce. "Remember when we did the talent show. Everything so in sync. The lights bright above you. Jamming on your guitar. Gene pickin' on the bass. And I did that amazing drum riff. They went crazy for us."

As she describes that night, I feel the rush again. Singing into the microphone. Hearing my guitar fill the auditorium. And all the time Libby and Gene were right along with me. It all fell together perfectly. Then it was over too fast. Like being extracted from a dream.

I scowl at her. She's selling me on her vision. But prom cannot possibly be the same as the talent show.

I give her a little shove so she lets go of me. "I'll see you later."

Only a year ago, Blue wasn't even a band. Libby and I played music in her basement sometimes, but we didn't talk about it too seriously. Since her mom's death six years ago, she's been living with her aunt and uncle and Gene. When we'd play, her Uncle Doug kept lingering on the stairs. Then he started singing along to some of our songs, saying how good we sounded. Each time his wife, Lexi, told him to leave us alone, he came down another stair to the basement. Before long, Gene started doing the same as his dad: settling on the stairs during our rehearsals. Then he started bringing his bass, picking out notes along with the songs. Soon after, we roped

Gene into being our bassist, though I'm sure Doug wished we'd asked him. Even though he's only a freshman, Gene can actually play just about any instrument, but we don't want him getting a big head and thinking he runs the band.

Bad enough he had a say in naming it.

He didn't like any of my suggestions. I came up with some great stuff: Depressed Poets, Sedated Losers. Really quality names. But Gene acted like they sent the wrong message. "Why does it have to be so negative?"

"Depressed and sedated are negative?" Libby snorts.

He showed off a riff on the bass and said, "By definition, yeah."

I attempted a more impressive riff on my guitar, but I missed a string. "What's your idea, then?"

"I don't know. Something less negative."

"Sunshine? Rainbows? Oh, I've got it. The Galloping Unicorns. The Sunshiny, Rainbow-colored Unicorns. We could have a logo made out of glitter."

Libby ponders for a moment. "Why not something that sounds negative but doesn't have to be? Like Blue?"

Drama is in the choir room, which is odd since it's not a music class, but whatever. I only need a credit; I don't need a special room. It's a hike from my other classes to the choir room in the music hallway, far down on the opposite end of the school. Inside, I see multiple tiers to stagger the choir members, a line of eight chairs or so on each. A piano takes center stage down front. Despite my love of music, I have never taken a choir class. If I did, I'd have to admit that I'm truly a soprano. Some things I can't change about myself.

I skim through the faces of the students who are early, searching for a friend. A few people I know, of course, but there's no one I want to know better. I stride up a few tiers to a lonely corner and take the chair there. Sliding out my drawing tablet, I pick up where I left off this morning after scoring the seat beside Christine. I turn my pencil to get the curve of her nose right. (Sasha, not Christine.) Sasha's fur was so short, but still thick. Every day after school, we'd sit together in my room on my bed, and I would pet her, tell her about my day, and everything would be fine. JT and everyone else would cease to exist. Sasha was the one who always understood me.

The door clangs shut, and I start to assess each person who enters the room, determining whether I'm in danger of losing the empty chair beside me. But I don't know any of them very well. With each one it occurs to me anew that Drama could be an okay place to end the day. Most of these people look as awkward as I am. Some of them as mentally messed up as I am. Perhaps we could make a therapy group on the side.

The next person in the door is a teacher. Long black skirt, black top. "Afternoon, everyone." She flutters around the piano, grabbing a stack of papers, which she hands to a student in the front row. She waves her hands as if to say *Distribute, distribute.* "I'm Anna Sands, Ms. Sands." She enunciates the *z* sound in *Ms.*

A few people cheer for her. Members of the Theater Department.

Ms. Sands bows with a flourish. "We're going to be taking a lot of risks here, so it's important that we trust each other."

Maybe *they* will be taking some risks. Not me. I shade in the dark side of Sasha's nose.

"Consider me a friend. Someone who wants you to be in touch with your inner actor." She changes her tone as if she's reading our Tarot cards and circles her hands around, summoning magic.

Most people laugh a little.

I hold my amusement in. Getting in touch with my inner actor. If there's one thing I've had tons of practice with, it's acting. Granted I haven't done the best job of playing a girl all these years, but I have persuaded quite a number of people, even ones I wasn't trying to. Of course, my success is largely due to my supporting cast continually insisting I am a girl.

The classroom door opens to a late student. Wait. I recognize her. It's that girl from lunch. Mandy? She knocks into a chair in the first row—smooth—then starts up the tiers. I hope she doesn't think that just because we both know Libby, I want her to—

She sees me watching her and takes it as an invitation. A moment later, she fills the empty chair beside me. "Hi," she whispers. Her "Black Lives Matter" and "Free health care for all" pins clank together when she drops her bag, the top edges frayed from use.

Ms. Sands stands, paused and waiting.

Mandy—that doesn't sound right—calls down to her, "I'm sorry I'm late."

"The first thing we'll be doing," Sands continues with a tiny but not dismissive wave to Mandy, "is two truths and a lie. Work on your ability to sell what you say."

It's so hard not to roll my eyes at this prospect. I keep shading Sasha's nose.

"Is that your dog?" she whispers to me.

I'm not answering that. Cool guys who are asked questions don't reply.

She shuffles her feet. "Sorry."

Madi? That sounds right.

The stack of handouts gets to our row. I take one and pass them on, skimming to see if there's anything I really need to read. It's just a course outline.

Madi gets out a pencil and starts circling and underlining things. Listens to Ms. Sands for a minute, then circles something else. Her eyes roam up and down my body until I straighten my plaid button down to be sure I'm not giving away the truth. But she's not checking to see if I'm female; she's trying to figure out why I'm not writing anything down.

"Choose a partner and get started." Ms. Sands waves her arms, conducting our mingling.

I haven't heard the instructions, but I assume it's standard Two Truths and a Lie rules. Madi's on her feet nearly dancing. She has far too much enthusiasm for a regular teenager. "Do you want to go first?"

I never agreed to this. Whatever. "You can go." I reluctantly rise.

"Oh." Her dancing slows. "Oh. Okay. So, the first thing." She pauses for too long. "I have an older brother." She smiles like she's tricked me already. "Second. My family just inherited a million dollars." Her lips purse. "Third." She looks blank. "My family just declared bankruptcy." That feels truer than the others, especially when she shifts her gaze.

"Are you sure that's what you want to go with?" Stupid choices. Again, I'm keeping myself from rolling my eyes. Still, as the only person in the world who sees me as an actual boy and speaks to me on a regular basis, I should probably be nice to her. "So, you do have an older brother, that's pretty clear."

She rubs the back of her neck.

"And your family is either wealthy or poor."

She smirks. "Guess that wasn't too smart."

Judging from her uninspiring clothing, torn backpack, and strip-mall haircut, I make my decision fairly easily. "I'm going to go with poor. So, the lie is the million dollars." Too easy.

"You're right!" She's pleased I figured it out without seeming to consider that it means I now know she's poor. She pulls the sleeve of my shirt. "You go."

I have no idea what to say for my truths or my lie. Besides, now I'm worrying about this girl I don't know. Her family's bankrupt? Does that mean she needs money? They could be homeless. Should I ask if she wants to stay at my house? "So do you—" But I can't.

She laughs too loudly. "Go."

"Sure, okay." Two Truths and a Lie. I've always hated this game. All of my truths are far too personal. And all of my lies too. This isn't a game for high school seniors. It isn't even something we should be doing in high school. "First, this class is a joke."

This confuses her.

"Second," I say, "this school is a joke." That amuses me, but I hold it in. "Third, I'm a joke." That one hits hard, though I hadn't banked on it affecting me. It's her fault; it's that sad look in her eyes.

But the sad look fades when she realizes I'm not saying anything more. She scowls. "For real? Those are your answers?"

I raise my eyebrows.

Ms. Sands yells out, "Time's up. Switch partners. Tell the same truths, but give a new lie."

I step by Madi to find a new partner or pretend to, but she grabs my sleeve. "Hold on. I haven't guessed yet."

I whisper in her ear, "I don't know the answer."

Once we've truthed and lied to nearly everyone else in the class, we finally run out of time. Not nearly too soon. I have made up all new material for the second person, and despite Ms. Sands' directions, I use all three of the sentences with everyone every time. Each one, a lie. But it's over and I don't have to figure out what it means about me on any deeper level. I can just go home.

Sliding Sasha's picture into my drawing portfolio, I shoulder my backpack and turn right into Madi. She's packing up her stuff. Instead of apologizing—cool guys don't apologize—I say, "See ya."

I'm barely at the door when she catches me. "Wait up."

Jesus. Desperate much? But I should give her a chance.

"Did you read the syllabus? No? Did you see that we need to go to three different plays this semester?"

"Shit." I don't go to plays. Do guys go to plays? I can't remember listening to a conversation where guys were talking about a play they went to.

"One has to be professional, one community theater, and the other one has to be a college play."

"What's the point of that?"

She doesn't hear me; she just continues on. "There's this

fantastic social justice play that just opened called *Pipeline* about how Black teens end up on the school-to-prison pipeline—"

"Social justice play?"

She smiles her idea away and offers an alternative. "Or . . . there's a Shakespeare at Augsburg College. We could go this weekend."

Is she asking me out?

"It's *Twelfth Night*."

I think I've heard of that. I'm about to say no thanks when I rationalize that it might be better to just do it since I have to do it anyway. "Yeah. All right." I continue out the door.

It hits me when I'm stepping outside into the frigid air in the student parking lot: I've just agreed to go on a date with a girl. And she thinks I'm a boy. A shiver ricochets through me, but it's not entirely unpleasant.

Chapter 7

SHIT. SHIT. SHIT. THE SECOND I'm out of the building, I regret saying yes. I turn the key in my car's ignition, my ears numb because my stupid jacket doesn't have a hood. I do not want to go to a play with Madi whatever-her-name-is. Shit. If it wasn't a school assignment . . .

The engine won't start. I turn the key again. It sputters a bit but dies. Shit. I just want to go home.

I draw my shoulders in, trying to warm up. I do not need to be stuck in the student parking lot in the dead of winter. I check the side mirror. Lots of students heading to their cars, most with friends, most not wearing enough clothes for today's frigid temp. Some jock boys in shorts. Stupid. Just like me.

I turn the key a third time, and the sputtering finally brings the car to life. I lower the pedal, feeding the engine slowly so it won't die again. I glance to the side mirror, only to see it completely darkened with someone's black winter jacket. There's a pounding on my window so hard the glass could break.

My elbow slams down the lock button. One of JT's friends. Kirk. Dirk. Dickhead. Something like that. He gets too close.

"JT wanted me to check on you." He yells this as if I wouldn't be able to hear. "Your car's a piece of shit." He steps back, eyeing my wheels. "Yep. That's a real piece of shit."

My heart hammers as I shift into reverse and rev the engine.

"He wants to know what you're doing tonight." Dirk the Dickhead sneers at me. So hilarious.

I press down on the gas, the tires sputtering against the hardened snow, car lurching back. I nearly hit him as I turn the wheel. He swears at me, but I keep going out of the lot and toward home.

Once there, I shut myself in my room, shedding my leather jacket and Vans before dropping onto my bed. I press my head to the pillow, rest my arms at my sides. Everything is all right. I'm safe. Music through my headphones begins to mute everything from today. JT fades. Tiyana's glare, Danny's questioning eyes. The locker room girls. But no matter how far into the music I descend, I can't make Madi go away. Her light blue eyes implore me to go to the play, darkened cheeks and her stupidly shy smile say she likes me. And her damned enthusiasm—as if life isn't torturous.

Cold fingers wrap around my wrist, making my arms flail, knocking off my headphones. Mom. Her lips, a straight line across her face, open for too long before she says, "You need to get ready."

I forgot. Across my bedroom hanging from the top of the closet door is a gray and black dress that I unfortunately recognize. "I'm not wearing that."

My mother's sigh fills the room. "Kayla, we've been over this." She puts her hands on her hips. "Just once I'd like to have a decent family picture. Just once."

With your son and daughter. "Just let me wear this." I pull at my flannel's collar.

That doesn't warrant a reply from my mom. "At the department store, you said the colors looked cool." She flips up one of the sleeves on the dress.

Yeah, 'cause that was the only dress that didn't have pink or lavender or flowers or lace.

"You said you would wear this."

If you made me. I said if you made me.

She stomps to my dresser, then throws a ball of black tights at me. "Fifteen minutes, Kayla. Then we're leaving."

I'm not putting on tights.

"We aren't going without you." Her words are more a threat than a solution, as if she'll come back, stick me in the dress herself, and carry my ass to the car.

She probably would.

I pluck up the tights, whipping them at the pink-painted wall, wanting them to explode on impact. Instead, they bounce against my San Antonio Spurs poster and drop to the floor.

As if telepathic, my mother appears in my room again, plucks up the tights, then opens my top dresser drawer. She comes to me with tools for my humiliation: the tights and a bra. The latter she shoves into my hand, waiting until I have accepted it. Her expression communicates exactly what she wants: no binder. "Fifteen minutes."

She has lectured me about this for weeks. When Sam is home from college, we'll have a photo shoot for the family, and she'll have her manly husband, her studious son, and her effeminate daughter all around her.

I need to get out of here. Take off in my car. To hell with Mom's picture. I don't want one more photo of me looking like a fucking female.

I grab my phone, frantically typing about the dress, the tights, the hate in my mother's voice. I'm about to send it to Libby when someone knocks.

Dad inches the door open. "Hey, kiddo. This is really important to your mother. You're going to look great."

"I doubt it."

These words bring him inside the room instead of driving him away. He sits beside me on my bed. "I don't want to hear any more of that. It doesn't matter what the kids at school say. You're a beautiful girl."

First of all, no. And second, just stab me in the heart, Dad. It'd be easier.

"You know, Sam has to go back to college in a few days."

I know. My brother Sam has classes starting for the end of his sophomore year. I've hardly seen him, and he's leaving.

Dad's arm encircles my shoulders, hugging me to him. He loves his daughter, Kayla. I rest my head on his chest. He's solid and smells so clean. Closing my eyes, I breathe in, seizing my momentary sanity. Perhaps that's the one and only perk of being a girl: He hasn't hugged Sam since ninth grade.

Rising, he pats my shoulder reassuringly. "Ten minutes."

I smile until he closes the door behind him. Then swear to myself.

Tights are ridiculous. I do not understand why women wear these things. And the dress, it leaves me completely vulnerable from below. I pull at the sleeves to make them sit at my elbows, but the elastic rolls back, leaving the fabric perky and prim at the top of my arms. When I pull down again, I hear a thread pop. Mom will have a fit.

I glance at my enemy, the full-sized mirror on my closet door. In this outfit, I'm six years old. How can I do this to myself? I'm a hypocrite. A fake.

I scowl at the pink wall.

Grabbing my phone, I read over my unsent message to Libby. Never mind. I don't need to tell her all of this. She'll want to talk, and then I'll have to relive it. Once I've deleted, it dings. It's a reply from Libby. Wait, I didn't send that message, did I?

No. It's not there. And Libby's text is about the stupid prom. *I'm creating a list of songs we should learn for prom.*

I don't even want to know.

Some prom favorites like "Livin' on a Prayer" and "Single Ladies."

I am not reading the rest of this list. This is not my music.

I text her back: *I don't think Bekkah's dad will be impressed with pop music.*

Three dots. *Lots of great indie groups do cool spins on lame tunes.* Then she starts listing.

I can't deal with who Libby wants me to be and what my mom thinks I am at the same time, so I don't reply.

I pat down the front of the dress. No pockets. Where do they think I'll put my phone? Screw this. I throw open the door, phone in hand, and nearly run into Sam in the hall. He's in a suit and tie and looks like a damn adult. Eyeing me up and down, his brows rise. "What am I looking at here, Kay?"

"Don't ask."

"Mom's idea?"

I snort. "She wants to have *nice pictures.*" I make my mom voice for the last part.

He starts to argue, then simply nods. He knows what Mom's like.

By the back door, my mother and father wait. Except for the scowl on her face, Mom looks gorgeous. Dad looks cool. He's got some great ties. This one has chevrons in blue and green. I picked it out for his last birthday. Dad fist bumps my brother, then smooths down Sam's blazer with an approving nod. "Very respectable, son."

Sam pulls at the bottom of his shirt to straighten it.

As she clicks toward me in her heels, Mom's nostrils flare, her scrutinizing eyes examining my clothes. Before she can demean me, Sam steps forward like he wants a private word with her, but I can hear him; he's not trying to be quiet. "Why don't you let her wear something else?"

Mom takes a physical step backward. "What?"

"Let her wear something she'd actually wear. The picture'll be so fake if she's in a dress."

Mom's face goes blank. Confusion, maybe?

Out of the corner of my eye, I see my dad nodding.

Sam says, "Jeans and a flannel?"

Mom shakes her head, taking the last few steps over to me. "Did you even comb this rat's nest?" She picks at my messy—very stylish—hair, finger combing my bangs to the side. They weren't cut to hang anywhere but down into my eyes. With a grunt, she ushers me into the bathroom where she tries to make my short hair look feminine. "If we had time, I could at least curl the ends . . ." She trails off as she realizes there aren't any ends to curl. Frowning at me in the mirror, she says, "I wish you hadn't done this to yourself," as if I've cut off my nose instead of my hair.

Like a clamp, she holds my chin, reaching for her mascara tube. "Hold still."

"Stop." I push the tiny brush away, but her vice grip clenches my chin unwaveringly. I grit my teeth. She's kinder to my eyes than I expected, though they still come away dark black and not me. Please no lipstick. She reaches for the brightest, pinkest one she has, but stops. "You'll lick all of this away by the time we get there anyway." She steps behind me, assessing my girl-ified appearance. "Well, it's a little better."

Returning to the door, I hope my brother will say I look ridiculous. He doesn't.

I slip my feet into my Vans.

"Kayla!" Mom is horrified, glaring at my feet.

"My shoes aren't going to be in the picture."

"You are not walking around with us at the mall wearing tennis shoes with a dress." Her arms are crossed now, like she's barring the door.

I dig my nails into my skin to keep from kicking my shoes off in her direction, in her face, even, and go back to my room for the *right* shoes.

"Come on, Mom. I only have three days before I'm due back. She could've worn those." Sam argues for me while I'm upstairs, slipping my feet into some cutesy black pumps Mom bought me a month ago when we got the damn dress, but he doesn't make any progress by the time I return to them.

When I reach for my jacket, Mom pulls my hand away. "You'll wrinkle your dress."

"It's cold outside." My tone is as harsh as I wanted it.

She shakes her head. "No one's wearing a jacket. Let's go."

Now that my shoes meet Mom's approval and my exposed skin will cause hypothermia, we're allowed to get into the car. I finally have time to be truly horrified. Lakeside Mall. With its movie theater and food court, it's the hang out place for most of my school. I can't stand it. Libby and I generally go to Emerald Isle Pizza on the other side of town or Caribou just down the street when we want to chill. Libby knows what it's like to be picked on, too, so we both like that not many people from Lakeside go to Emerald Isle or Caribou. At the mall, though, we're bound to run into someone.

Kindly, the lot has fewer cars than I expected. Still, as I pass Dad holding the entrance door for me, I clutch my phone tightly. Anyone could be inside, even JT because I know he hangs out here. He cannot see me like this. Not ever again.

The route to the portrait studio—the only remaining portrait studio in town—passes by the food court, which, based on the noise level, is teeming with teens. Possibly the whole high school is here. It's a freaking school night, people. Go home and study. My whole body flushes.

Please not Christine. Anyone else. Everyone else. Not Christine.

Mom's staccato heel clicks complement Dad's clomps. My brother strides beside them like the priceless gem they think he is. Keeping pace, I crouch behind Sam, grasping the edge of his suit jacket and then changing my mind.

The food court swarms with high school girls. Most are on their phones, slurping Icees or Diet Cokes. Sam waves at the nearest table we pass. Three juniors. I don't know them, but at the next table I see Tiyana and her basketball friends. My old friends from middle school. No eye contact, thank God.

I pick up my pace to catch Dad who's far out in front of us.

Near the clumps of girls are pods of boys with trays piled high. Tacos, burgers, shakes, fries, pizza. From the crowd, a gruff voice yells out my brother's name. Sam stops when he sees who it is, a smile spreading across his face. He vigorously shakes the guy's hand. "Son of a bitch. You got huge!"

"Been putting up a lot of weight, man." Oh, no. I know that voice. JT Swanson. They used to wrestle together. He waggles his eyebrows at me, then takes a more serious look. His gaze invades areas of my body that I would never invite him into.

For some reason, instead of keeping my pace with Dad, I've stopped with my brother. *Go*, I tell myself, but I don't.

JT gives Sam a shove. "How's college treating you?"

"You know, too much studying."

JT inspects my dress, my body. "And this, of course, is your little sister." He acts like we hardly know each other. Like we don't have this grating, unpleasant relationship. Inching closer, he whispers to me, "You look so good as a girl." His fingers caress the inside of my arm near my chest.

Disgust shudders down my back, inch by inch. I'm about to put my fist up his nose when Sam steps in, shoving JT away. "What the hell?" He steps into JT's space.

I don't know whether to be insulted or relieved.

JT, to my surprise, doesn't laugh it off. Instead, he holds his hands up.

I need to get away from here. Catch up to Dad. I cannot let anyone else see me. Backing up a few steps, I nearly trip over the chair behind me. JT catches my arm, so I don't fall, which only makes me pull away. Hard. So now when I hit the chair again, it moves, despite the person sitting in it. Everything stands still when I meet her stunned hazel eyes. Christine.

Her friends' mouths drop open. The tall one says, "Oh, my God." She laughs so hard she spits out Diet Coke before she can cover her mouth. "Are you wearing mascara?"

Christine says, "Stop it. That's really mean," but she's not unamused.

The pointy-eared friend glowers at me. "Is that what you really look like?"

My fancy shoes slip as I flounder away. I catch myself on Christine's chair to keep from wiping out. And now I'm off center. I can't run. Can't hurry. These stupid shoes. I can't fall in front of all of them. Not farther than I already have.

I break away, the guffaws behind me fading into ambient noise. I'm shaking. JT's breath in my ear, his skin on my skin, the look on Christine's face. I can never make her unsee this.

Mom and Dad reach the studio, and I rush in with Sam following. Squeezing myself down a row of tripods, I hunch down. I'm going to vomit. My head spins, but I can find nothing to steady myself. Then someone has my arm. Sam.

"You want me to punch him in the face?"

What? I breathe in. Out.

"He's always been such an asshat."

He thinks I'm upset about JT. Though it's tempting to have Sam give JT a bloody nose, I shake my head to tell him it's not a big deal, though it's a huge deal. My stupid past with JT is such a mess. Why can't he leave me alone?

Sam's hand on my shoulder allows me to close my eyes. I imagine I can tell him about Christine, that he'll understand, that he has my back.

Softly, he says, "Say the word and he's dead."

"It's not him." My voice sounds so angry.

Confusion covers his face as he tries to piece it together. Then it hits him. "That girl."

I close my eyes, clenching my fists hard.

Dad appears beside us. "Come on, guys. It's time."

Sam squeezes my shoulder. Is that it?

I nod sullenly, averting my gaze.

He cringes. It's as bad as I thought. I know it. Sam knows it. Christine knows it.

Gently, Dad pulls Sam away from me, and while I'm thinking my dad is clueless, he takes hold of my hand and guides me to our studio room. Though he doesn't say anything, his ample fingers around mine make me feel safe. Momentarily.

Crossed arms and a pouty face broadcast that my mother is anything but patient right now. So the photographer talks backdrops with her and double, triple checks his camera. Then he wastes no more time in continuing my embarrassment. He places us all in front of the blue-gray backdrop, my parents beside each other, gently shifted to exactly where he wants them. He arranges my brother beside my mother, so she's sandwiched between her big, strong men. Me? I get the submissive chair in the front beneath them all. "Sit right there, miss," he says. And he says it a few more times since I don't sit right away. "Miss?"

Fine. I am the youngest. I'll pretend that's why I have to sit.

The photographer then tells my dad and brother to rest a hand on my shoulder. "Perfect." He admires his patriarchal work, motioning us to stay as if we're his trained Labradoodles. Flash, flash, flash. "Smile everyone." Flash, flash. "Young lady, smile pretty." Picture after picture.

"Now one with just the kids." He presses Sam and me together like we're married instead of siblings. "Tilt your head toward your brother, sweetheart."

To my brother: "Straight and tall, young man. Keep those shoulders broad."

Excruciating. Flash, flash, flash.

After, we wander around the photo shop while we wait for the results. The glass front of the store lets me see out into the mall toward the food court. I direct my wanderings to the back among the tripods again so no one can see me. Still, I stay behind some shelves, keeping an eye out.

Once the photographer has taken a substantial amount of time loading the pictures onto the computer and choosing the ones to present to us, he calls us over for a slideshow. I recoil from the girl in the photos. The mascara on her face makes her look so feminine, and her hands crossed in her lap. Gross.

"This one turned out the best." Deliberately, he points to the trace of a grin on my face. There really only is one where I don't look disgusted with myself.

Mom glares at me. Surely, I've ruined this, and we need to do it all over again. She leans in toward the screen to determine if my grin is happy enough, but before she pro-tests, Dad says, "I agree. That one's great."

At the photo shop counter, Mom orders a huge version of the thing for our living room. Then to Dad, she says, "What about a New Year's card?"

No. No, no, no. I do not want everyone we know getting this picture. "It's already January." I shove in between Mom and Dad.

Mom angry speaks at me, "We couldn't get this done any earlier," as if it's my fault. Falsely smiling at the photogra-pher, she orders a hundred copies to be printed on a disgusting silver card with exploding gold fireworks.

I'm going to throw up.

Chapter 8

EVERYONE SAW. NOT JUST CHRISTINE. Everyone.

And that picture will go out to whoever wasn't there.

In my room I rip the dress from my body, seams tearing, fabric splitting. I can't believe I let my mother control me like this. I didn't have to wear that. I didn't have to put on mascara. I didn't have to pretend for her. Why did I let her do this to me? I can never face Christine again.

And a bra? I can't forgive her for making me think I had to wear a bra to make her happy.

Once the clothes are off, I shroud my hideous body under a baggy sweatshirt. I throw my head back onto my pillow, my chest heaving from crying. If I were in a nineteenth-century novel, I could wait for a storm, wander pensively on the moors, and die from heartbreak and melancholy. If I were in *The Great Gatsby*, I could drink myself to death at one of his parties. But I'm not. And I can't.

Life should work that way. When a person sincerely wants to die, their body should shut down. Deliver them from their misery.

Covering myself with my comforter, I let myself sob. Ugly, messy tears. I stifle the sound in my pillow. Even though

Mom and Dad are downstairs watching the news and Sam is gaming in his bedroom down the hall, I don't want any of them to know. I wish Sasha was here with me so I could tell her what happened, and she could lick away my stupid tears. I could cover us both in this blanket and bury my face in her fur. She could make me feel less of this. But she isn't here.

I writhe around, trying to be comfortable, but as soon as I settle, the moment comes back. Surprise in Christine's hazel eyes. Surprise and a sort of delight.

Tossing off the comforter, I shuffle to the bathroom. From down the hall, repeated gunfire from *Call of Duty* blends with the weatherman on the TV downstairs. The whole week is going to be below zero. *Call of Duty* shouts, "Man down!"

Darkness has shrouded me for so long that the light over the bathroom sink stings my eyes. I keep them lowered, not wanting to see my girlish face. I kick the door closed. Sticky mascara clings to my lashes. The more I try to wash it off, the more soap stings my eyes. Why does the pain feel so deserved?

The medicine cabinet yields no actual medicine. No expired oxycodone or muscle relaxants. There's aspirin. How many aspirin do you have to take? I set them on the counter. Accidentally, I make eye contact with myself. Repulsive. My eyes rimmed pink from crying with clumps of mascara goo clinging to my lashes, I spit at the mirror. "I hate you."

I slam the medicine cabinet. Instead of the mirror shattering like it should, the door bounces back stubbornly. I pour some aspirin into my hand and down it with a paper-cup-full of water. More aspirin. More water.

Call of Duty says, "Cover me. I'm reloading."

A clunk outside the door. Sam? I stay stock still, waiting.

Aspirin isn't incriminating. Neither is water. At most I'm explaining that I'm a little sad.

I wait longer than I should, as if I want him to knock.

When I hear nothing more, I fill ten paper cups with water and transport them to my room in stages. Close the door. Dump the aspirin out on my nightstand. I cover my ears with headphones and play the songs Libby and I recorded together. Letting the tears run down my face, I take little handfuls of three or four pills. Over and over. After about five gulps, I cough and gag. Bitter chalkiness coats my tongue. I throw down more water, then try to breathe.

I'm such a mess. I can't even kill myself right. I smoosh the empty cups together into a ball, hurling it away from me toward the pink wall. It separates and falls into four mangled piles.

There are other ways. Manlier ways. A few years ago, a boy from school used his belt in his closet. I throw open my closet door, peer inside. How does that work? If only Dad had a gun.

Grandpa's rifles are in the basement storage room in a glass case.

My door squeaks as I open it. Mom and Dad are still downstairs. I can't get all the way to the basement looking a mess like I do without them asking questions and getting in my way.

Something else. Something else.

I've got it. I inch into the hall, past Sam's closed door, and into Mom and Dad's room. The master bath is home to some amazingly sharp things. Like Grandpa's razor, which has become Dad's razor. The one he'll hand down to Sam.

Creeping around their bed in the dark, I stub my toe. Keep going. A pale nightlight outlines the sink basin, toothbrushes, shaving cream. The razor. My fingers close around the ivory handle, then I fold back the blade. Perfectly sharp.

Closing the door, I run warm water in the basin, pushing up my sleeves, then submerging both wrists. This is how a man goes out. Brave enough to cut himself; brave enough to die for his beliefs. Shaking. Cold to my core.

I can do this. Leaving one wrist under water, I take up the razor, but fumble it into the sink. Shit. I recover it and place the top edge against my skin. Do it. Press down.

I take the razor out of the water.

Focus. You can't live this way. You can't be this person.

With new vigor, I force the razor against my wrist again, this time breaking the skin, but only just. A small red bead surfaces with a small red sting.

I can't.

I put the razor back, drain the water. Put the aspirin bottle back and the unused cups. I deserve to be cursed. I was born to suffer.

Back in my bedroom, I can barely make it to the bed. I pull back the blanket with heavy arms. The pink wall looms over me.

In a whisper I say, "Why did you have to do this to me?" But who am I asking? I don't believe in God anymore. What kind of god would let me feel like this?

But there's no one else right now. So, I go through the promises. I promise to be nicer to my mother. I promise not to swear at Sam. I promise not to tell anyone they're stupid. I promise not to judge other people. I'll be as good as I can possibly be. Just let me wake up a boy.

I go through the list:

1. My parents have to believe they have two sons.

2. My brother never had a sister, only a brother.

3. My room needs to be painted a color besides pink.

4. My clothes need to be all boys' clothes—the shirts, the jeans, the underwear, the socks, the T-shirts. There can be no trace of girl-wear.

5. My softball and basketball team pictures have to be boys' teams.

6. My drawing awards have to be made out to my boy-name.

7. My teachers' memories

8. My two years in the Scouts

9. My swimming classes

10. My summer camps

11. My years in band on the trombone

12. My photo albums

13. My friends need to be boys.

14. My name can no longer be Kayla Anne Kinkade. From now on it will be Kurt Alexander Kinkade. (Kurt? Are you sure?) Yep, Kurt.

15. Most importantly, make Christine forget everything she saw today. Make her love me.

Anything I forgot, fill it in. No one can remember Kayla. They can only know Kurt.

The morning finds me in my bed wearing my oversized sweatshirt with pink-painted walls around me, stupid dresses in my closet, girls' softball pictures on the wall. Did I forget to list something? I'm still Kayla. And what's worse, everyone knows it.

Chapter 9

NOT LONG AFTER MY ALARM goes off, my mother knocks on the door to remind me it's the second day of the semester so I shouldn't be late. I pull my blanket up to my chin.

Mom returns ten minutes later, knocking again. "Come on, Kayla."

Rolling onto my side, I yank the blanket over my head.

Ten more minutes, Mom opens the door. Footsteps approach my bed. I imagine her arms crossed, her forehead wrinkled. "Why are you still in bed?" Her tone is not entirely accusatory, leaving room for me to have a legitimate reason.

Folding down the blanket, I peer through squinted eyes.

The back of her hand touches my forehead. "You're a little warm."

I let my eyelids droop; I'm too lethargic to be in the world right now.

Hesitation. "I can call you in sick . . ."

I roll over away from her, drawing the blanket over my head again.

My list of things isn't the problem. Maybe not choosing a name is the problem. I wasn't convincing when I chose Kurt. I just don't like the K options. Any other letter than K would be much, much better.

Keeping the blanket over my head, I shine my phone's light on the tattered paperback. *Best Names for Baby*. Something I'll never use for its intended purpose as I will never be pregnant nor get a girl pregnant. Something I resigned myself to years ago—no kids.

I flip to the most-worn section, the K's, and skim. Kayden. Kai. Kevin. Kyle. Beside each are pencil-written star ratings. Kayden had some popularity in sixth grade, but the third and fourth stars were erased in seventh when I met Cayden Miller. Asshole.

Kane has to be out, doesn't it? Self-fulfilling prophecy and all that. Keegan, Kellen, Killian. We're not Irish enough for those. Keenan, Kenneth, Kendall. Can't be Kendall; that's a name commandeered by girls. Karl, Kase, Kole. Kurt, Kent, Kirk. Koby, Keith, Kolton.

Maybe sticking with my initials is something I'll have to abandon. Kent, Kody, Konnor, Kurt. I give each of them another star. Konnor is up to number three now. Tied with Kael. Still, I'm not any closer to a final choice. This is probably why most people have their parents name them.

Once Mom has left for work, I watch the time pass on my phone. Whenever the numbers mark a class start time, I imagine the classroom, the teacher, the students. I think of who would be talking about what happened at the mall last night. JT must be having the best day of his life today. When he's old and gray, he'll look back and smile, thinking of me in that horrid dress and, strangely, think I look fantastic.

Art class is the worst. From 9:00 until 9:50, I keep tossing around on my bed, throwing off my blanket, covering my head with a pillow. The moment I'm still, I remember Christine's shocked expression and her friends' comments. *Is that what you really look like?* The laughter. Christine believing that was my true self.

I pull my knees toward my chest. This can't be real.

Not long after, I get a text. It's an unknown number, so I don't open it. Instead, I roll over away from my phone at the side of the bed. Wait. Vibration as another text arrives. Shit. This can't be good. Then a third one.

Fine. I scoop up my phone. One is Mom with a clear "Mom Work" ID, just checking on me. Likely checking to be sure I'm still home and haven't wandered off to do evil transgender hijinks. The other two numbers are unknown. One of them must be JT. There's no way he could resist tormenting me after yesterday. He had a front row seat, after all.

Stupidly, I think I should open the text in a different room, as if they'll be able to see my stupid wall is still painted pink from when I was little. The last thing I need is more *proof* that I'm female still, that my coming out was incomplete.

Through half-closed eyes, I click open the second text.

It's a picture from too far away of me in my fabulous dress, hunched over, seemingly just after I've gotten my balance, and gazing ferociously into Christine's face. There's no message. No name. I delete it.

This picture is out there. It could be online everywhere.

I open the next one. Again no name but a different picture. God, I wonder how many there are. This one is much closer, but my face is a blur since I'm moving. I recognize the dress, but the photo's cropping makes it impossible to tell it is a dress and not just a weird shirt of some sort. With this one are the words: "After all this time, Kayla is actually a girl!"

My face is blurry enough that I could have been incognito. Why did they have to label it?

Whatever. That's my nightmare. Glad you could rub it in.

Let this be the worst of them. Please.

By lunchtime, I have some of my sanity back. A peanut butter sandwich and a bit of guitar playing has helped. I start scrawling down some verses to the girl who's breaking my heart, defaulting to A-minor when I determine the melody line. I play it through a few times on my acoustic guitar once it's complete, judging different inflections, different rises and falls. Then for the first time in nearly twenty-four hours, I smile.

> *I could count all the words you've said to me*
> *With just my fingers on this hand*
> *I could list the million times that things went*
> *Other than I'd planned*
> *And I could sing a song about love to you*
> *To make you understand*
> *But I can never put these words down.*

Libby texts, and when I look, I see it's her third. Just checking on me. I send a hasty reply that I'm sick. I wait for her to divulge that she knows about the mall last night, that she's heard stories all day, that she's seen pictures, that Christine is disgusted. But her reply—Stomach? Period? (with horror-filled face emojis)—shows me she might know nothing, but then again, she might want to spare my embarrassment. Can I type "My heart is broken" and have it truly mean that?

A half hour later, another text comes from an unknown number. Christine telling me I looked better in a dress? JT reminiscing about our touching moment together?

But it's neither of them. It's that new, weird girl Madi:

I told Libby I hope he won't mind if I have his number. So, sorry if this is weird. I wanted to be sure we're going to Twelfth Night *this Saturday so I can tell Ms. Sands.*

Turning my back to the pink-painted wall, I text *Yes, we are.* And then I take a minute, rereading her words. She called me *he.* No one has told her about the mall.

Late afternoon before my parents come home from work, I consider taking a shower to clean off the nasty film that covers my body. Instead, I sit on my bed, scrolling through online ads for puppies that are ready for homes. Labradors. Golden Retrievers. Australian Cattle Dogs. Then in the middle of all of them, I find something interesting: Wallin Animal Rescue: Where Unwanted Animals Find Their New Forever Homes. Several clickable photos of mixed breed dogs and multi-colored cats take me to their website where it's page after page of awesomeness. Dog after dog, looking for a home. I click on a wolfy-looking husky named Dakota. Black, gray, and white. Pleading cool-blue eyes. According to this, she was found outside with no collar or chip or anything.

She could be a perfect dog for me. Goodbye loneliness; hello, sweet, fluffy buddy who will lick my face when I cry.

She could be a perfect dog for our family. Wait till Dad sees her. A rescue dog? He won't be able to resist. I should go over there, check her out. Maybe I can have Dad meet me there after he gets home from work. That's what I'll do. I'll text him when he's on his way home.

Chapter 10

MY TIRES THUMP AND DIVE over icy ridges; tire tracks solidified on top of the asphalt. It would be easier just to slide into the tracks, let them guide me to a parking spot, but that's not how I want to go. Instead, I drive my own way. Once I've parked, I can clearly see cheerful blue letters over the door of the Wallin Animal Rescue with a stylized dog lying atop them. I cut the engine and sit, waiting to feel calmer. The car cools until I can see my breath. Go in already. This is as calm as you get.

So, I do. The lobby smells of bleach and emptiness. Running a hand down my leather jacket to ensure it's flat, I scope out the area behind the reception desk. All that's there is another friendly, blue sign with the lounging dog above a desk topped not only with the usual desk crap, but also a handful of dog food, a small red collar, and a stack of canned cat food.

No one seems to be here. I stroll around the waiting room and supply store. No one. Maybe this was a bad idea.

A door opens behind the reception desk and an older woman wearing a Labrador sweatshirt emerges. She spots me immediately. "Why didn't you come back when you got here?"

My mouth drops open, but I have no response.

"We've been waiting for you." She motions me over. Her short hair is dyed a close-to-natural shade of red.

I do her bidding, though I have no idea how she could have been expecting me. Did I click something on the website? Was there some make-an-appointment link?

I maneuver around the desk and follow her through the door into a hallway. "If you're going to work here, Nathan, you're going to have to be on time. Dr. Wallin does not like tardiness."

Nathan?

She stops and touches my arm. "Is it Nate or Nathan?"

My eyes widen, focusing on slight wrinkles at her mouth. "Uh . . . either."

She pulls me with her. "Okay. Here is where you punch in." She hands me a long index card with a name label at the top: Nathan Ashur. Gliding it into an antique metal clock, she says, "Stick it in here when you arrive." Then something in the clock strikes the card. "And when you leave." She slides the card into a clear pocket on the wall beside a few other cards.

Then I'm following her again, this time into a large room filled with panting and barking and everything wonderful. A brown-and-white dog lumbers toward me, rubbing his head against my leg. His fur is soft, his wet nose chilling my hand. A moment later, a guy about my age strolls over. "Sorry about that. Bandit loves people." He ambles over, seeming completely carefree. Dressed in a V-neck T-shirt and jeans, he reminds me of a clean-shaven Shaggy from *Scooby Doo*.

Bandit licks my hand. A Golden Retriever and a Boxer come over to inspect me too. A giddy spark zips through me until I'm laughing, hovering over all of them in an attempt to pet all three at once.

The receptionist pinches my shoulder to straighten me up and present me to the guy. "This is the new hire your dad interviewed last month. Nathan."

The guy raises an eyebrow, suddenly adopting a care of some sort. For too long he scrutinizes my face, then my clothes. He's on to me.

He glances to the woman. "Jeanie, I thought that—" He stops himself, then extends a hand to me. "Hey, Nathan. I'm Troy." His grip is firm, but not like those guys who drill their thumb into your flesh to see if you'll say anything about it.

Jeanie heads back to the reception area, throwing words over her shoulder as she goes. "You better hustle. Nathan was half an hour late."

When the door closes, I'm alone with Troy and the dogs. He holds a leash in his hand that he turns over and over as he watches me. As if providing me with a choice, he says, "What would you like me to call you?"

Tell him. Right now. Before this goes too far.

But I shrug and say, "Nathan's fine," trying to lower my voice as much as I can.

Troy whacks my shoulder. "Let's get to work." His long legs take him away faster than I can follow. I scamper after him, Bandit and the other dogs at my side.

We spend some time cleaning out the dog runs in the other room, though only a few of them are occupied right now. Change the water bowls. Fill the food bowls.

On our way back to the big room with the dogs, Troy gets me a copy of Nathan Ashur's schedule for the week.

Apparently, Nathan agreed to work one day on the weekend and two nights a week. Not sure how my parents will feel about that. "You'll be a great help around here, Nathan." He says *Nathan* like it's a foreign word he's trying out.

He knows I'm not Nathan. But does he think I should be Natalie?

He's too polite to say.

I wonder when his dad will come by and out me as an imposter.

Leading me back into the large dog room, Troy shows me where the water bowls can be filled, where the dog beds are, and warns me not to feed any of the dogs. "Some have special diets." This room is the big dogs' social room, the playroom. They try to keep as many of the dogs here as possible. Keep them acclimated to other living creatures. "We figure out pretty fast who needs their own space."

Along one of the walls is a short series of doghouses, room for a single dog in each. "Some of the antisocial ones are fine if they have a habitat to themselves." He gestures to the end doghouse where I can see two furry gray feet beneath a lounging gray and white head. Eyes closed, looking peaceful.

"Is that Dakota?" My surprised voice is annoyingly high and girly, so I clear my throat.

Troy meets my gaze. "You know Dakota?"

"I saw her on the website." Wait. Crap. "I mean, I wanted to see the dogs I'd be working with."

He sighs. "She's been hard to get to know. We don't even have her real name. She came in without a collar, but it really seems like she belongs to someone."

When I start for the doghouse, Troy stops me. "Slow." After I take only two steps, Dakota's eyes open, shockingly blue. Another two steps get me a quivering left lip that becomes a quiet snarl in another step. I'm only about three more steps away, but she clearly is satisfied that I have progressed far enough, and I have no desire to see more of her teeth.

Troy is at my side. He crosses his arms. "She came in a few weeks ago. Someone found her outside, wandering around when it was below zero. Remember that blizzard we had on the weekend? Dakota was out in it."

The night of the talent show. That was a really messed up storm. The wind was fierce, and the flakes kept piling up. Would've been a nice night to spend snuggling with a dog.

"The guy who brought her in said she was curled up in a ball to keep warm, but her paws were frozen to the snow." He exhales. "For a while we thought we'd have to amputate most of her back toes."

Oh, no. I squint to see her feet better.

"Ended up having to take two. Poor thing."

I step forward, longing to pet her and tell her everything will be all right. She slinks back, exposing teeth in a snarl.

Troy's hand comes down on my shoulder. "It's nothing personal. She hasn't let anyone touch her. Not willingly."

Her stark eyes gaze out at me, so I don't let my stare falter. I understand you. I don't like people either. She winks an eye at me. Probably a twitch. But it could be a sign.

I'll be the one to coax her out. I'll be the one to help her.

When Troy isn't paying attention, I do a search on my phone for Nathan Ashur. Google wants to correct my spelling, but I resist. After Twitter and Instagram links, I find one for

Caring Bridge. I skirt around the sign-in page, but I'm not able to access the information. Luckily, there's a short article about him that I can access.

His parents are asking for support—spiritually and financially—for Nathan's hospital bills. Doesn't say what he's got, but the picture of him with an IV and monitors hooked up everywhere makes me think he's there for a while.

Which means he won't be coming around here any time soon.

Chapter 11

I HAVE TO GO BACK TO school. I can't skip every day until the end of the year.

All eyes must be on me the next morning as I trudge across the parking lot, into the school, and down the long hall to the locker room. I've seen a few more postings from my marvelous moves at the mall the other night. So far, it's had similar views. But someone must have something worse. Why aren't they posting it?

Anyway, there's nothing worse Christine could see since she had a front row seat to my humiliation. But Madi is another thing.

Inside the locker room, a few sophomore girls are arranging their clothes to change. I avert my eyes, but not before they all glare at me. One whispers, "Just wait until she's gone. Don't change now."

Fine with me.

I disrobe in an adjacent bathroom stall, straighten my binder—taking a moment to press down some of the welt-like bumps that sting when I pull the fabric away—and pull on my gym clothes. I need to get a binder that fits. On my way past the sophomore girls again, one of them is holding up her phone to show another. They both peer over it to me. "No way," one says.

"My sister says that's her. She was there Monday night."

The first one grabs the phone and thrusts it in my face. "Is this you?"

As a reflex, I shove her arm away.

"God, you don't have to be such a freak about it."

Her friend calls after me, "Are you a girl, or aren't you?"

I spin around, ready to scream at her that I'm not, but I catch myself. How is that going to go over? I don't want to be in here with them and they don't want me here, but to say I'm not a girl makes me a boy in the girls' locker room. Which I am, but I'm not.

I charge out the door. I should've looked at the stupid picture. What if it's a new one? What if it's one where my face is completely clear, where my eyes bug out, where I'm falling in front of the girl I love?

As hateful images swirl in my head, I find myself already inside the weight room. Most of the class is here, and each of them stops what they're doing as I come in. The whole world is on hold for a count of two, three, four, five, then everyone returns to their tasks.

Thank God. Maybe that's the worst of it. Coach isn't here, yet. I wonder if he knows.

I stroll to the loser free-weights across the room, grab the twenties, and lie back for presses, my knees coming up instinctively as usual. Over the clinking of metal, I hear gruff, obnoxious voices. They're all a jumble until an abrupt stop, snickering, and some encouraging, "Go, go, go."

This can't be good.

I keep lifting the twenties, though I'm sure whatever is about to happen is about to happen to me. Breathe. Focus on the weights.

Before I complete five reps, I hear them return. They whisper inaudible things to each other, interspersed with laughter. They grow louder and louder, until I realize my time to be prepared is lost. I sit up with the weights and see Hunter, Dirk, and JT, all of them with clown-like makeup, exaggerated blush in too-round circles, messy lipstick that spreads into their chins and cheeks, and worse, each of them wears a makeshift dress—robes or towels, far too short. Their legs are like those of apes, furry and well-muscled and absurd.

They line up before me. JT reaches between his legs, under his dress, exaggerating scratching his balls. "I can see why you like this. So much easier." He puts his head back as if he's found a particularly satisfying place. "Oh, yeah."

Repulsive.

My fingers tighten on the dumbbells. I could shove one of these right where he's scratching. That would shut him up.

Dirk flips the skirt of his dress back and forth. "Don't you want to play dress up with us?"

I stand, raising the dumbbells in front of me like I'm willing to box with them. "I'll leave that to you guys. It's more your style than mine."

JT's smirk disappears. "But it looks so good on you, princess."

Behind them, not ten feet away, Tiyana works a rowing machine. Her gaze is firmly on the three dirtbags. Do I want her to step in? Would she?

Dirk runs his fingers over his cheeks, smearing red lines through his Amish-style beard. "We could do our makeup together."

Hunter snickers.

JT's eyes drift to my chest. "Why're you hiding your tits? Huh? They looked so nice the other night."

My forearms shake with the burden of the twenties. I will myself to hit him with one, but I hold back. "Shut up."

Hunter grabs Dirk's towel-dress. "Dude, let's go change before Coach sees us."

Dirk and Hunter skip off to the boys' locker room. JT doesn't notice or doesn't care.

I do a quick scan of the room. Still no Coach. No adults at all. But everyone is paying attention. Tiyana has stopped rowing, but she's silent. Most of the class looks away while I look around, some before I even reach them.

"Leave him alone." Danny is behind me, facing off with JT.

I don't need—wait, did he call me "him"?

JT's eyebrows rise. Specks of whatever he's painted on them fleck off onto his cheeks. He tries to speak out of his lip-sticked mouth, but only chuckles.

I take a few steps back, so Danny and I are shoulder to shoulder.

Danny clenches his fists. "Why do you always have to be such an asshole?"

JT shakes his head. "Kayla needs to—"

Coach blows his whistle as he comes in the room, blabbing about setting goals and other nonsense I can't focus on.

JT crouches down to put his face in Danny's face. "Mind your own fucking business."

Danny's cheek ripples as he clenches his teeth.

So Coach won't see his outfit, JT ducks behind some of the equipment and manages to sneak out of the room.

When JT is gone, I let go of the weights, my arms like deflating balloons. Danny and I stand side by side, just breathing.

Then he says, "Spot me?"

I follow him to the bench where he loads a barbell with twenty-five pounds on each side. Twenty-five plus twenty-five plus the barbell at forty-five. "I think you can do more than ninety-five," I say.

Danny meets my eyes. "I don't."

"All right. Just do a set with this. You'll see how easy it is for you." If Danny wants to be a tough guy, he'd better bulk up.

Danny squirms under the bar and circles his hands around it. How long has he had his nails painted black? Why didn't I notice that before?

He fights bringing the barbell down, wobbles bringing it back up, but he seems to have it. I place my hands near the bar as it moves, just to give him peace of mind. After eight reps, he lays the bar back on the rack and sits up, rubbing his pecs. With his black-nail-polished hands.

"See what I mean?"

He shakes his head. "No. I think that was plenty."

I'm about to insist we add about forty more pounds, but then I look at his face. "That's cool."

He gets up, still rubbing his chest. "Your turn."

I nearly laugh and say we need to add more weight, but then I stop. I'll just do ninety-five like he did. I don't need to make him feel bad. I wiggle under the barbell, bringing up my knees.

"All right," he says, "I can add the rest of the weight if you want."

"No, I——" I don't correct him. I want more weight.

He moves plates on and off until he's secured a total of a hundred and thirty-five pounds for me. While I'm doing my set, he encourages me. Then he says, "You know it's okay with me that you can lift more."

Luckily, I'm pushing the barbell up and can't talk.

"You're a different kind of guy than I am."

I clunk the weights back on the rack and scramble out from under them. "What's that supposed to mean?"

He doesn't see the fury in my eyes. "I don't know. You're more athletic. It's not really my thing." He smiles. "I'm just in here because of my dad."

"Your dad?"

He pokes at the weights on the bar, trying to get them to spin. "He was hoping for a wrestler, and he got me."

Should I feel bad for him? At least he was born a boy. But that's not what I want to say, and I do feel bad about being more athletic than him. "Well, if it helps at all, I know a thing or two about not living up to parents' expectations."

He laughs. "But you're so . . . talented. You're good at basketball and you write music, and you sing."

A hundred things come into my head all at once. Answers for why my parents would be disappointed in me. But I can't say them. I can't put them out in the world. So Danny's words just sit in the air between us.

Once I'm back in my regular clothes and on my way to Art, I pull the front of my flannel closed. I've always left these shirts unbuttoned over my tees so they could billow out, create uncertainty about my chest. But if JT knows, does everyone know? I don't want them to think I'm binding my chest, but I don't want to think I'm not binding my chest. They shouldn't be thinking about my chest at all.

Readjusting my shirt all the way to Art, I try to find the perfect way for it to lie. Throughout the hall and at the lockers, there is judgment in the faces of everyone I pass. Based on the multitude of ways I'm lacking, I can't imagine what I'm being judged on.

A few steps from the art room, I stop and wait for my bravado to kick in. Perhaps it's back in the weight room with my self-respect. Wherever it is, I need it to be able to face Christine. A hand presses down on my shoulder and I shudder.

"Hey." It's Libby. "Feeling better today?"

I try to grin.

"You don't look so good." She tugs both sides of my shirt collar, delving into my eyes. Does she want me to cry right here in front of the whole school? As if she hears my thoughts, she wraps an arm around my shoulders and steers me toward the art room. "Let's do this class thing. Whatever's bothering you won't look so bad once you've got a pencil in your hand."

Maybe she's right. Since this semester started, Libby's been working on something top secret. No idea what it is, but I know she likes to use art to process her feelings. I'm not like her, though; I can't lose myself in my drawing when I can't suppress all the feelings I had that night. My fancy, beautiful self. And there she is, at her desk and so lovely. I don't want her to know I'm here. She's covering the paper in a light coating of charcoal, and I imagine her chalky fingers covering my face with smudges of gray—

Dirk's ugly face invades my daydream, Dirk with his lashing tongue and smeared red blush in his Amish beard.

"What is it?" Libby scowls.

"Bad thought. It's nothing." I let Libby go into the room first, screening myself behind her though we're the same height.

When she stops abruptly, I nearly slam into her, which makes her laugh. "Here." She hands me a piece of paper folded into a tiny rectangle. "Our playlist for the prom," she says to my questioning look.

She misses my disgust as she goes to take her seat.

Christine hasn't noticed I'm here yet, which is just fine with me. Maybe I could just sit in someone else's spot.

I check around for an open stool, but there aren't any. If I'd just sat next to Libby before . . .

"Kinkade." My name from across the room. It's Ms. Horvath at her desk.

I report to her summons. "It should've come up excused. My absence yesterday."

The loose skin under her chin waggles as she turns her head sharply to me. "That's not what this is about." She lays down my art portfolio that I usually leave in the classroom. From inside she pulls a few of my sketches from last semester. Sasha lying in the sunlight. Sasha running in the grass. "I recorded everyone's goal for the semester yesterday. So I'd like to discuss yours."

This is so false. My goal in this class is to draw, to let my mind focus on something that isn't dark, hopeless, and infinite.

"What will your portfolio be based on?"

I trace Sasha's face with my eye. I make her mouth turn up ever so slightly so she looks like she's grinning in all my drawings.

"Kayla?"

I clench my teeth. "I thought I'd work on the illusion of depth."

She cocks an eyebrow. "But your subject matter. It isn't going to be this dog again, is it?"

This dog? "I haven't decided." I try to see around her to the rest of the class. Is Christine watching me? "I've been feeling a little under the weather."

Horvath clears her throat. "I'll need to know by the end of this week."

"Right." Slinking away, I still don't see any options for where I can sit other than next to Christine. So, I slide in next to her without a sound, no clanking of the stool, no clambering on the desktop. I lay out some paper and my HB pencils.

She stays as she was, sprawled over her charcoal. I think it's how I like her best. Intent on her art. Wait a minute. That's not charcoal; those are pastels. What is she doing using pastels? This entire school year I haven't seen her use anything but charcoal. Now, all this color.

Trying not to stare at her sandy blond hair caressing the curve of her neck or the oddity of colors on her fingertips, I grasp my favorite pencil, but I stop before I mark the page. What do I draw if I don't draw Sasha?

Christine sits up straight, inspecting her work. I can feel her watching me out of the corner of her eye. Just get it over with. Just have a good laugh or tell me it was nice running into me at the mall. Do it already.

"Don't know what to draw?" Christine says.

The calmness in her voice rattles me. "Uh . . ."

"You usually draw your dog."

"I do, but . . ."

"You want to try something else," she concludes for me.

"Yeah."

The strangest smile appears on her face. "I was wondering how to bring this up." She leans closer to me. "I've been thinking about the other day."

Oh, God, she means the day. At the mall.

"I thought we had a moment there." Her full attention is on me.

My stomach churns but I can't tell if it's love or nerves or the return of my humiliation. "You did?"

"Yeah. I felt like you were reaching out to me."

My stomach settles. "Was I?"

She rolls her eyes. "I mean, after that misunderstanding at the talent show." She laughs. "You can't even imagine how relieved I am."

Relieved?

Absently wiping blue pastel residue on her jeans, she pulls out her phone. "I was thinking about you yesterday."

Whoa. I nearly tell her I was thinking of her, too, but luckily, I'm too stunned to speak.

"I think I can help." Scrolling through her phone, scrolling, scrolling.

If by "help" she means go out with me . . .

She finds what she was looking for, "Here," and lays the phone in front of me. YouTube video. A short-haired girl on the screen applies eyeliner and mascara.

"What is . . ."

Careful not to touch the screen, she points. "Doesn't she look pretty?"

I scroll down and read the title: 10 Marvelous Makeup Tips for Tomboys. I slip on my stool. "Why would I—"

"It's okay," she says. She pats my arm, takes the phone, finds another makeupped boyish girl. "Look at how she did her eyebrows, nice and subtle."

Instead of looking at the girl on the screen, I look at the girl I love. "I don't get it."

She gives me the side-eye. "We all make mistakes. I mean, this hair." She flips the inch of hair that has fallen over my ear. "But you've come to the right person." She nearly wiggles with glee.

This is what she was thinking of when she was thinking about me? It will be impossible to dislodge this dagger from my heart.

Can anyone else see this? Or hear her saying this? Over a row, Libby glances at me, seeming unable to hear, questioning if she should step in. I give her a nonchalant head shake. Madi's right next to her, oblivious, or could she be hearing every word?

"You could come over after school. I'll show you how to do . . ." She shoves the phone in my face. " . . . this."

I look from the screen to her and back to the screen. "Come over after school?"

She nods. "We can pick up Caribou on the way. You could probably stay for dinner."

Can Libby hear this? Christine inviting me over to her house? No, Libby is too far away. Next to her, Madi talks about something I can't hear, but Libby pays more attention to me. When you've spent years being treated like shit, you keep an eye out for trouble. Libby's been teased for her hair and her taste in music, but mostly for being Black.

Is anyone else listening? Ms. Horvath is consulting with a student. Everyone, actually, seems to be doing something that has nothing to do with me.

Christine's eyes are hopeful. "So, want to come over?"

Chapter 12

HER HOUSE. HER ROOM. NEAR her bed covered in a pure ivory blanket. Immersed in the smell of fresh laundry. Her fingers near my face. Her soft voice . . .

Explaining how to apply eyeliner.

No. No way.

Make pouty lips so I can apply bright pink lipstick on you.

I don't think so.

Sitting back on my stool, I let the atmosphere morph back into scratching pencils, conversations, and the combined odors of ashy charcoal and earthy clay. And now the new aroma of pastels. "No thanks."

She lays her phone on my empty paper. "But you made real progress the other day. It's only a matter of making a choice to shade things a little differently." She waves a blue pastel at me like she's made such a perfect metaphor.

I can't even give her a perfunctory smile.

Slipping her phone back into her pocket, she rubs blue on her page. "Think about it."

In front of me, my empty paper accentuates my delicate fingers and slim wrists, which Christine can see perfectly.

Thankfully, she's not looking my way. She's adding green

now, only I cannot tell for the life of me what she's creating. No form. No shape. It's the most nondescript thing I've seen her make. Madi passes by, and my face must register my massive confusion; when Madi meets my gaze with her dazzling blue eyes, she looks pointedly at Christine's paper, then back at me with a comical sneer, mouthing, *What the hell?*

I shrug, then wonder for too long if I should have responded at all. Guys shrug, I decide.

A few minutes later, while Libby talks with Horvath over by the kiln, I look up to find Madi motioning me over to her table. Obediently, I wander over. Madi has pastels strewn around her art desk atop her tropical forest picture with varying shades of greens and blues. Semi-abstract and captivating. The colors so rich I can't help but get lost in their depth. Her fingers are a mess of blue and green with new bits of yellow waiting to be worked in.

For too long she says nothing. Then, "She doesn't see it."

She means Christine. Does she mean what I think she means? A mix of ice and fire spreads through my stomach. Christine doesn't see me?

Madi lays her delicate fingers down on a bluer part of her forest, blending the color. The hidden yellow on her fingertips merges perfectly into the blue, birthing an absolutely gorgeous new color.

"Out of blue comes green." Her voice is low, alluring, like we're alone in the room. "She's using the pastels like crayons. She's not making them live on the paper." The hue of Madi's new green morphs through different shades as her fingers glide across the page.

At first, I think I've heard her wrong, but she continues,

"Blue can't truly live without a bit of yellow." When her gaze meets mine, she sends a shiver through me like I've never felt before.

Instead of saying anything, I swallow hard.

When she tucks her deep brown hair behind her ear, she leaves traces of green. She gives me a smile, but then is distracted.

Libby is back. "Taking lessons?" she asks me. "I've never seen you work with color."

"I don't." Though I'm thinking about it now.

Libby worms into the space between me and Madi, raising her eyebrows at me. "Don't you have some work to do?" She angles her nod toward Horvath, who's glaring at me from across the room.

On Libby's side of the table, I see an assortment of black pens and cardstock paper. One piece of cardstock has varying patterns of black and white, some curving lines, some straight. I guess her tree phase is over.

She sees me studying her art. "It's going to be a box." She holds up the cardstock, gently folding it in a few places to simulate a cube. "See?" Each side has a different optical illusion.

"Cool." There are a few discarded cardstocks. One has clubs and spades in different arrangements, not nearly as well ordered as her current work.

She shakes her head. "Yeah, that didn't work the way I wanted."

"I think it looks pretty great. Oh, I get it. You're making that for Doug?" He loves to play cribbage, taught Libby years ago, but regrets it because now she wins most of the time.

When she tucks her head against her chest, I regret saying anything. She hates that I think Doug is her new dad because she already has a dad. Only she hasn't heard from him in more than a year, so is he really? Anyway, we don't often do big emotions, Libby and me. So I keep quiet.

For the rest of the class period, I'm back at my seat beside Christine, accomplishing nothing, not even picking up my pencil. A few more times, Christine shows me a video on her phone of a tomboy getting a makeover. One moment I freeze from head to toe, the next, I break into a sweat. How can she be this confused about who I am?

When the bell rings, I make no attempt to say goodbye to Christine, an opportunity I usually never miss. Then Libby is beside me, evil-eyeing Christine's departure. "What was that crap earlier with Christine?"

"Never mind." I busy myself replacing my unused supplies in their spots.

"Did she really invite you over to her house and you said no?"

"Forget it."

"Kay, tell me what's going on."

I jerk my backpack onto my back. "You're getting too far in my business, that's what's going on."

She steps out of my way before I can shove past her. A second later when I'm in the hallway, a glob of people appears to be waiting for me. They stare as if each step I take is an air horn blast in a silent cathedral during mass. A couple of freshman boys hover over a cell phone, giggling, eyeing me. One of them passes the phone to the girl beside him, who ushers her friends over to look. They keel over, they're laughing so hard.

Someone says, "You have to click Play."

Oh, my God. It's a video.

By the time I'm able to straighten out my steps, Libby emerges from the art room, flanking my side. She guides me in the other direction, spinning with a double-bird-flip to the guffawing crowd. Once we're around the corner and down a flight of stairs, she gives me a bit of a shove. "You can fuck off too."

Difficult to say whether the day gets better or not. The video of me in the food court nearly landing on my ass in my lovely dress has made the rounds, totally viral all through Lakeview High School and likely the greater Twin Cities area. It's been sent to my phone so many times from harassers, do-gooders, and questioners that I've turned my phone off.

The not-so-bad part is that people in my classes are mostly not assholes. After glancing at me a few times, they leave it alone. Not even a smirk or a giggle.

I suppose my expression doesn't encourage them. Libby always says that my resting face is I-want-to-kick-your-ass. Good. I do.

At lunch time, I hunker down in the library where the librarian won't bother me. The library is open during lunch for anyone who wants to study or get help from her. I don't want either. I immerse myself in *Wuthering Heights* for AP Lit. We've just started it, and we're supposed to be finished in another five days so we can write an essay arguing whether Heathcliff truly loves Cathy or only wants revenge.

I put headphones on to block out the people who have access to the internet and my new-found fame. So, everyone. I power my cell phone on and scroll through my hundreds of texts with video attachments as well as laughing face emojis and vomiting emojis. No Libby.

I reach into my pocket and come up with her tiny, folded setlist for prom. She's planned out the songs, the order, made suggestions about whose version I should watch online to get a sense of how to make it gel with my style. So much work went into this. Libby being Libby, and I blew her off.

The time speeds by until I need to slink out and down the hall to AP Lit.

Madi's in this class too, not just Art and last hour Drama. Here, though, she sits on the other side of the room. Which is good. I don't know what to say to her after her lesson in using pastels. I love what you showed me? I think you're right about green? I think you sent some sort of spark through me?

Maybe she still has traces of green pastel in her hair.

By now, she must have found out from someone that I'm not—technically—a boy. It had to happen sooner or later; I just thought I had more time.

Drama class. I'm already in my out-of-the-way spot when Madi arrives. If she sits next to me, she doesn't know about the mall. I cross my fingers without thinking.

It occurs to me our theater date is probably over. No more *Twelfth Night*. I'll have to figure something else out. I wonder if Libby would go with me.

Madi stops by the grand piano, where Ms. Sands is organizing a few stacks of paper, and starts up a conversation.

Come on. I need to know what she's going to do. Ignore me? Shun me? Tolerate me?

I shake her off. I'll ignore her and work on my art—shit. I left my portfolio in the art room. I opt for a notebook and sketch hexagons and octagons, but I can't get past the lines on the notebook paper; they block me. So I make a treble clef with a few notations to match the melody I wrote just yesterday for Christine.

I don't want to think about Christine.

When I look up again, Madi's finally done. She looks around at the class like she's trying to find somewhere to sit. Like she knows another soul besides me. Then she heads straight for me. Thank God.

Or not thank God.

Dropping her bag, she gives me a smile, tucking a dark hair behind her ear. No green pastel lingers in her hair, unfortunately. She has a new button on her bag: Green is the new black. It takes me a second before I realize it's about recycling, not art.

She crosses her legs, her knee dangerously close to mine. "Hey. I asked Ms. Sands if I could tell you what we did yesterday."

Weird girl. Like you need permission for that.

"We're supposed to do a scene for the class where we memorize lines and do actions and have props and everything. We all partnered up yesterday."

Great. Of course I'd miss a stupid partner thing. I'll get stuck with some loser no one else would choose. I almost laugh out loud. Some loser no one would choose, like me.

"I told her yesterday that I'd be partners with you. I hope you don't mind." Her leg brushes against me.

Deep breath. "I don't mind." I find myself smiling at her, my whole body growing warm. Not cool. Cool guys don't smile. I scoot a little away from her; her other knee is in my space now, as is most of the left side of her body. "So what scene are we doing?"

She laughs. "I didn't decide everything without you. We'll have to choose together. We can do whatever we want. I mean, it can't be anything with sex or swearing. Well, it can have some swearing if we get it approved." She goes on for a while about requirements for the scene, but all I notice is how pink her cheeks have been since she said "sex."

And now that I'm thinking about a scene that has sex in it, I'm sure my cheeks are red too. I wish Sands had just assigned us a scene.

"I was thinking we could do something by Tennessee Williams." She flips through a worn paperback.

I don't know any of his plays except *Cat on a Hot Tin Roof* that we read sophomore year. I'm not a fan, but I'll go along. "Sure. Whatever."

Laughing a little, she says, "We could do *Streetcar*, and I could be Stella." She presses a hand to my shoulder and gently shoves me as she says, "You'd be Stanley."

I try to suppress my grin. I'd never considered I might get to act a male role in this class. Wait. She gave me a male role. That really means she doesn't know about the mall. "Stanley?" I pretend to be clueless.

"Yeah, he's Stella's husband. They have this really hot relationship." She reddens again. "He gets drunk and beats her—"

"Wait. I don't want to—"

"And then he tries to apologize."

Okay, I want to play a guy, but I don't want to play a wife beater.

"We could do that scene when Stanley wants to apologize. It's that part in the movie where Marlon Brando rips off his shirt and screams, 'Stella!'" She whisper-screams, seeming amused with herself.

"Where he what?" I shudder. Rip off my shirt?

Her cheeks darken. "It's just one idea. There are a bunch of good scenes. Or we could do *Glass Menagerie*. I'd be a ridiculous Amanda while you're the tragic Tom, longing to sever himself from the burden of his mother and sister." She continues to give me example after example of who we could be in what play, and in each one, I'm a male character. I mean, of course, I'm a male character because she thinks that I'm male, she accepts that I'm male, but each time I'm anxious and excited while moths flutter in my stomach.

And I have to wonder: Has she been asleep all day? Everyone has that video of me at the mall. Everyone knows how ridiculous I look in a dress. Some of them must know what I felt when I was in front of Christine. How could Madi possibly have missed all of that?

She's looking at me as if I'm supposed to give her an answer. "Which one is most interesting to you?"

"Were you at lunch today?"

Her eyebrows lower as she considers this as an obscure Tennessee Williams title. "Oh, yeah. But you weren't."

"What did you and Libby talk about?"

She thumbs through her book some more. "Like this scene." She hands it to me.

Not accepting the book, I repeat, "What did you and Libby talk about?"

"Not a lot. She seemed angry about something." She shoves the book into my hands. "This one."

I skim a bit of it. *The Glass Menagerie.* Tom tells his sister about the magician who escapes from a coffin without removing any nails. Tom clearly equates it to going off on his own to live his life, leaving his mother and sister without harming them. Yeah, 'cause that's possible. Do what you want while not harming your family. Those two things can never exist together.

"Did Libby say anything about me?" I don't want anyone else to hear me, but I fear even Madi didn't hear me.

She's quiet for too long, but finally says, "Have you felt like everyone's been distracted today? I mean, like, everyone?"

So, she's not totally blind. I only raise my eyebrows in response.

"It's like they all know something big is going to happen, but no one told me." She laughs too loudly and too suddenly. "What should I expect, being new? Who's going to tell me anything?"

Well not me. I have no intention of telling you what's going on.

Flipping a few pages in her book, she settles on another definite scene we could do together and hands me the book. This time I have no intention of reading it, so I simply say, "Let's do someone other than Tennessee Williams."

My phone vibrates. It's Libby. *After school,* she texts.

I only reply, *OK,* but I close my eyes for a few moments to digest this piece of mercy I've received.

When the bell rings, Madi gets out ahead of me, slowing me down so she can talk to me about our unchosen scene. I'd planned to ditch Madi right away to find Libby, but I can't get around her just yet.

"—that we could definitely find—"

"Yeah, yeah. That'll work," I say. I've almost gotten past her when she stops to pick up a discarded water bottle. She hangs onto it until we've reached a recycling bin and tosses it in. All the while she's talking about scenes she thinks we could find.

"That sounds great, Madi. Gotta go." I give her a bit of a wave and speed walk to my locker.

Libby's there, arms crossed, leaning. She still looks pissed. Usually, after a few hours, we aren't mad at each other anymore. This time, I stepped over the line.

I wait until we're side by side before I say, "I didn't mean to blow up at you."

Her mouth is clamped shut, her stare severing every ounce of my self-respect.

"Everyone has it out for me today." My shoulders tense. "It's that stupid thing at the mall the other night."

"That stupid thing you never told me about?" Steam would be coming out of her ears if it were possible.

I lower my gaze. "It was so embarrassing." I hope she hasn't heard me, but I know she has. "Everyone saw me. Everyone. And Christine was an inch away from me."

"Why didn't you text me?"

"I couldn't. I didn't want to relive it all."

A few girls in letter jackets pass by, one whispering to another something I don't catch other than " . . . wearing a dress . . ."

I close my eyes.

Libby punches me in the shoulder. Hard. "That video is not flattering."

Of course, she's seen it. Why wouldn't she have seen it? It shouldn't embarrass me that Libby has seen it. It shouldn't. She knows me better than anyone.

"And then Christine wants to give you a makeover." She shakes her head.

I laugh because I can't do anything else. "She's right. I need one."

Libby keeps herself from laughing. "Just because your life is shit doesn't mean you can take it out on me."

"I know that." I don't know what she wants me to say. "I'm sorry." I feel like I need to tell her the whole truth. "Yesterday, when I didn't come to school . . ."

She waits.

"I wanted to kill myself."

"What? Why? Because of a dress and some makeup?"

"No, because . . . she saw me in that dress and makeup."

"Christine?"

I nod because I'm tearing up and I don't want to cry. "I can never erase that from her memory. She's always going to think of me that way. Even when I'm a boy."

Libby softens. "You are a boy." She leans against the wall beside me and pulls my arm down until we're sitting with our backs against the lockers. Her arm moves around my shoulder. "You don't have to prove anything to her or anybody else."

"It's not just her. It's not just anybody. It's everybody. Everybody is going to see me in this way I've been fighting not to be seen. Everybody is always going to think of me as female no matter what I do. I can't have them thinking I'm a fucking girl."

Libby eases away from me. "And what do you mean by that? Do you think being a girl is the worst thing a person can be?"

"That's not what I meant."

She scowls at me. "I think it is. You know, you're going to have to make up your mind. Are you trying to be something or are you trying *not* to be something?"

There's no response to that. I'm trying not to be a girl. Is she saying I'm failing at trying to be a boy? No. Libby wouldn't say that. "All right," I say.

That should be it. We should be all better, but the vibe between us isn't right. Should I apologize again?

"You got time to come over and jam?" She means hanging out in her basement, laying down some tracks on her uncle's old recording equipment.

For a moment I'm completely psyched, but then I remember her ulterior motive. Prom. I think through the list of songs she gave me earlier. So many revolting options. Songs I can't believe she'd ever want to play. Popular music neither one of us would ever listen to. Artists I haven't heard of. "I'm not doing Miley Cyrus."

Once we're in the unfinished basement where the winter cold still radiates through the cement floor and my shoes freeze my feet, I'm actually impressed by the work Libby has done to persuade me. She has the chords and even tablature for five songs, ones she's found at different prom song websites. She says this like it's something I'll be able to relate to, like we're both searching prom music in our spare time.

Thankfully, these five are ones I've heard, which I assume is why Libby chose them.

Footsteps clomp down the stairs. Gene. He gives me a little wave, then to Libby he says, "Was I going to get an invite to this jam session?"

Libby's response is to thump each drum in succession, then strike a repeating beat on one cymbal.

He straps on his bass across his Prince t-shirt, but I yell, "Don't do it. She wants us to play prom music."

"Oh, hell, no," he says, immediately removing his instrument from his shoulder.

"Save yourself! It's too late for me." I lay my arm across my forehead, poor me.

Libby stops the cymbal. "All right. All right." Puffs of smoke seem to encircle her head. "Just play a few of these, and tell me what you think."

Gene plucks up his bass again and thrums a series of notes.

I page through "I Don't Want to Miss a Thing" by Aerosmith. D, A, B minor, G, D, E minor. I can do this. Nothing too extreme. F-sharp major is a bit weird but not difficult. I hand the page to Gene so he can at least see the chords. Libby didn't download anything for him. But, of course, she didn't; Gene can easily pick up on any song with his bass. He sees the notes in his head or his long fingers have their own intuition.

"Okay. Let's do it," I say.

My amp crackles instead of picking up my notes. I chuck my guitar pick at it, which naturally does nothing to the amp, and causes me to have to get up to retrieve it. "I need to fix this stupid amp." I crouch over it, lay it down, and look over the back panel for screws I could undo.

Gene freaks out. "You don't want to do that."

"Why not?" I barely glance at him before I ask Libby for a Phillip's head.

"What do you know about electricity?" Gene crosses his arms over Prince on his Purple Rain motorcycle.

Nothing. Not one single thing. "I know enough."

Gene grins. "Okay, then you know it's not safe to go poking around in there."

I sit on the cold cement floor.

"The voltage going through that thing is intense. Besides, there's nothing wrong with your amp."

I laugh at him. Has he not been paying attention? "Right. The crackling is supposed to be there."

"Well, on an amp that small, there's not much more you can expect." He scratches his chin where five black hairs are attempting to form a tiny beard. "You want to fix your amp problem, you got to get yourself a better amp."

Libby groans. "Can we just play? No one cares when your amp crackles, Kay. We're used to it."

"Fine, fine. Let's do this one. The Aerosmith one."

Libby starts us up, but I ruin the end of the first verse, so we play it again. Gene's got the rhythm down, doesn't miss a note. We play it through a few more times, then move on to the next song.

"Kay, you gotta be able to play the melody line, not just the rhythm."

Fine, fine, fine. "I don't want to miss a thing," I joke.

Neither of them laughs.

"It's important. This could be our big break."

I swear in my head instead of out loud. Libby really wants

to hold on to this dream that Bekkah Ingram will talk to her dad about our band. Assuming we even get the gig. Assuming Bekkah even goes to prom. Assuming she'd be impressed by us or even notice we were anything but a cover band.

"Again," Libby instructs. "Let's play it again."

Once I play it through to satisfy the enforcer, she insists on playing the other four before she'll even consider playing anything that's not for prom. But I notice that she's tweaked each of the popular songs in significant ways to suit our style. Blue-ified, she calls it.

We take a hit song from the radio and speed it up, aggressive percussion robbing it of its sweetness, giving it a punk rock flavor. Then the three of us growl the lyrics in the chorus so they're all but unrecognizable. It's a tune everyone wants to hear at a dance but with a cool spin. All of this Libby records in her notebook.

All in all, we're cranking out some great sounds for more than a few hours before I can get her to try the new song I wrote. With Gene there, I don't want to say the song is for Christine, but I'm pretty sure Libby knows. The final notes of our last tune ring in my ears, though the basement is completely silent while Libby acclimates to my new song.

Libby's poised to say something—my relationship with Christine is a dead end—but instead she watches Gene's long fingers pluck out an alternate bass line for the song we just played. It doesn't matter; there's not much Libby could say that I haven't already considered, but she doesn't get it. Once Christine understands who I am, she'll think about me completely differently. She'll stop trying to give me a makeover and accept me as a real guy.

When Libby finally speaks, she doesn't mention my love interest. "What kind of a beat were you thinking of?"

I've laid out my lyrics and chords on the rusted music stand in front of me. Skimming through the first verse, I have a hard time imagining a drumbeat with it. I make the rhythm with the lyrics.

She taps out a few patterns for me, Gene accompanying with notes from my usual key signature.

"Maybe the last one," I say.

So, we try it. But it's not right. I can barely focus on singing. I stop before we've even gotten to the chorus. "No, it's got to be different."

Libby taps out something new. Again, though, it's not right. I stop strumming. "That's not it." I can feel pressure tightening like knots behind my eyes.

Gene sits his small frame with impossibly long limbs down on top of his amp, scratching the few hairs on his chin again.

"Look," Libby says, "let's just go through the whole thing once so I know where it's going."

My temples throb. "Okay."

"I'll try some different things." She twirls a drum stick, a trick she only perfected a few months ago.

Neither of us bothers to check in with Gene; he dutifully follows our lead. He's only a freshman, after all. He has no rights here.

I strum the intro again while she beats out a slurry of steady notes. My amplifier crackles and I want to stop playing, but I force myself through the song; nothing Libby's playing is melding with what I'm playing. Gene's bass line follows Libby's rhythm and my melody, but strangely can't seem to bridge us two together. I skip one of the verses to get to the end, to stop my misery.

"That last part felt really good," she says, crashing the cymbals again.

I stare at the lyrics on the page in front of me. They felt so right the other day. Now, today, something about them is really off. The whole thing just isn't coming together.

Chapter 13

D R. BEHMANN'S FLESH-COLORED MOLE ON his cheek stays perfectly still as he raises his eyebrows at me. "I'm glad you decided to come back."

I'd cross my arms if I didn't know he would interpret it as a sign of my stubbornness. "My mother decided I should come back."

He only stares.

"I know," I say. I hate when he does this.

"What is it you know?"

I want my voice to be normal, not aggravated, but he pisses me off so much. "I shouldn't let her make my decision for me." I laugh ironically. "But if I didn't, I wouldn't be here." Not in this office, maybe not on this Earth.

"Kay, you need to figure out where you're supposed to be. Maybe it isn't here."

My nostrils flare. He's said this before like he wants me to stop seeing him. I want to storm out. He's such a contradiction.

"I will say, though, I'm happy to see that you've made up your mind." He gestures to my clothing.

I double check what I'm wearing. Jeans, T-shirt, leather jacket, and I'm definitely bound. "What?"

"This is what your mother doesn't want."

"Yeah." Absently, I flatten the front of my jacket.

He nearly smiles, making a note on his yellow legal pad. "Tell me about the jacket."

It's been so long since I had a session with Dr. Behmann that he doesn't know about the talent show or any of that. Which, of course, means he doesn't know about Christine. So I tell him all of it. About reinventing myself. About Christine not recognizing me. About JT harassing me. About my argument with my mother.

"That bothers you," he says.

"Which part?"

"Your mother."

All of my muscles tense. "That she wants me to wear what she wants, act how she wants?"

"You tell me."

"I told you. I explained it to her years ago." I shake my head without wanting to. "I don't want to talk about her."

"We need to talk about her."

"We don't." I don't have to say anything. He can't make me. If he were any good at his job, he'd be able to get me to talk about what happened at the mall with Christine and why I tried to swallow all the aspirin in the house.

"Remind me how old you're going to be this year."

I glare at him until he finally gives himself away with a smirk.

"The point is, you're about to be an adult. Should you allow your mother to have this kind of power over you?"

He doesn't get it. He doesn't understand how hard it is to let my mother down. The way she manipulates, the expectations.

I could sit in this chair for the next ten years and not get him to see her the way I do. I won't answer that question.

He doesn't mind the quiet. He's made silence his bitch. And here we sit in it where he descends into a pleasant Zen-like state, while I writhe uncontrollably as if in a vat of acid.

"All right," he gives in. "You need to think about this. It's good to see that you've accepted yourself, and you're willing to show that to everyone else."

A shiver goes through me. I don't want to show anything to anyone else. It's none of their business.

He's smiling. "I thought you had made this decision at your last appointment."

"You mean, when you said I hadn't spent enough time being a girl yet?"

He's confused. "That's not how I phrased it, and I certainly didn't want that to be your understanding."

"You said I might want to take more time before I transition."

His nod is slow as he processes how I took those words and mangled them into something he thinks is vastly different. "I wanted you to evaluate whether you're ready."

"I'm ready." I want to hold out my arms in a melodramatic gesture that makes him see how different I am, but I stop myself.

"You also need to consider that all of the things you struggle with now while you're viewed as a girl by everyone will not necessarily change once you're viewed as a boy. Your mother will still be difficult to deal with. Your brother will still be away at college."

I roll my eyes. "I know, I know, I know. I understand

transitioning doesn't solve all my problems." But he doesn't understand all the problems it does solve.

He purses his lips, staring intently at me. "I hope you mean that." He grabs his laptop, opening the calendar. "We should get back together in a couple weeks."

"Fine. I'm free—oh." It occurs to me that I might not be. I have a job. "I might—" Shit. I can't tell him about the job, or I'd have to tell him about Nathan Ashur, and he's got a real thing about lying to people when you don't need to.

"Might what?"

"Nothing."

We set a date and time. Before I can get out the door, he says, "Next time we'll talk about taking control of your life away from your mother."

Mom slouches over the kitchen table, painting her left pinkie nail a bright pink. She squints a bit in the setting sun. "Can you get the light?"

I'm leaning against the counter, reading, despite Mom's intrusion. I despise the smell of nail polish because it's always accompanied by an offer. I flip the switch for her.

She blows gently on her nails, one finger at a time. Without losing her focus, she says, "You know, Kayla, I can show you how to do this anytime you want."

I pivot around the counter with my book so she can't accost my color-free nails. I swear Mom needs an audience for everything she does. She really should get going. Mom and Dad are going to a party tonight, which is why I get to snack and read *Wuthering Heights* without her giving me weird looks for being home on a Friday night. And reading a book.

She pops open her makeup mirror, selects a vial, and applies thick black liner above her wrinkled eyes. "Liner can really make your eyes pop."

I hold back a snort. "Why do you have to do that out here?"

"Your father is making the bathroom into a sauna. I am not going to put on my face only to have it melt." She's peppy. Her college friends from back in the day are holding the party. They always make her feel like she hasn't made the worst life choices since two of them are divorced and the other never married. On top of that, one of the divorcees is a cocaine addict. The nineties were a strange time.

I read the first sentence of chapter nine again.

"Besides," she says, "this gives us a chance to talk."

I read the first sentence again.

"This blush makes me feel so much younger."

Feminine propaganda again. I keep my glare to myself and read the first sentence again.

As she brushes deep pink on her cheeks, her eyes close as if she's powdering on a layer of ecstasy. Embarrassing. "Kayla." She pulls out the chair beside her. "Come over here and we'll do your cheeks."

Don't scream at her. Don't.

She flexes her fake smile muscles. "Come on."

My stomach fills with stinging nettles. "We've talked about this." My teeth press hard together.

"Just a little color."

Why can't she stop this? "No. Thanks."

She pats the chair. "We'll see how it looks."

"Are you serious?" I whack my book against the counter.

"I was thinking that—"

"No, Mom, you weren't thinking. If you were thinking, you'd remember that I don't wear makeup, that I have never worn makeup, that I have no interest in makeup."

"We could change that. I could find some colors that look good with your complexion."

"I don't want colors that look good with my complexion. I don't want to wear a dress to have my picture taken. I don't want these useless things growing out of my chest. And I don't want to be a fucking girl."

"Kayla! Language!"

I fumble with the book, unable to pick it up at first. Once I have it, I fly from the kitchen in a haze of red. Reaching my room, I slam the door, dropping the book to the floor. I can't calm down. My breath comes so hard, I crouch over to try to control myself.

I hear Dad's voice in the hall, calling to Mom. "What's going on?"

Why can't they just leave already?

I don't hear Mom's reply, but I know what's next: Dad will try to fix everything. It can't be fixed. I brace myself at one end of the dresser and then push until it slides in front of the door. Good luck getting in, Dad.

I should have left. I should've gotten in my car. Driven far from here.

He's knocking now. "Kayla? Can we talk?"

Without thinking, I yell back, "Not if you insist on calling me that name!" Then my stomach roils. It just came out.

Reflex. But I haven't told him yet. I haven't wanted to disappoint him.

He's not knocking or talking now.

Shit.

"I don't know what you mean by that."

"Forget it, forget it. Just leave me alone." All I see is the pink wall across the room.

"Kay—sweetheart, let's talk first. Tell me what you mean."

I drop onto my bed. "Ask Mom." I'm startled by a thud as the door smacks into my dresser. I sit up.

"What's going on? What did you do here?" He's more panicked than he should be.

"I just need to be alone."

He thwaps into the dresser a few times to make a point. He can't possibly think he can move a piece of furniture with that flimsy door.

"Everything's all right. Really, Dad."

He's quiet. Or has he left? Then I hear: "Your mother and I will only be gone a little while." It's some kind of a warning.

"That's fine." I close my eyes tight. I didn't want to worry him. "I'm fine."

"I love you, Kay—" He clears his throat. "I love you."

A muffled discussion comes from the kitchen. Dad's voice is agitated, but it doesn't take too long for his tone to change. Clearly, Mom has convinced him nothing is going on. Has he asked her about my name? What that means? Maybe. She won't tell him, though. She'd never admit she knew about it any more than she'd admit it's the truth.

When I hear the garage door lower and know my parents are clearly gone, I slide the dresser back; then I grab some crackers from the kitchen and settle in to the best part of the couch in the living room. I place the throw pillows just so, opening *Wuthering Heights* to chapter nine.

Peace. Quiet. Book. No interruptions. Just me, Heathcliff, and Cathy.

I've nearly finished the chapter when a flash of tomorrow night comes into my head. Madi and me at the college auditorium, surrounded by college students only a year or so older, but more educated, more independent. People who all have their lives on track. There I am, dressed like my true self, acting like my true self, but everyone around us sees Kayla.

Scowls. Raised eyebrows. Strange looks.

And then Madi starts to look at me differently too. She's the only one who has ever seen me as I truly am. She, and Christine for those two minutes in the parking lot. Tomorrow night could change that.

Tomorrow night could be a good night to read *Wuthering Heights* too. Maybe I'll be too sick to go to the play. I'll call Madi. No, no, I'll text Madi. Can't make it. Maybe another time. But I'll have to wait until tomorrow or she'll think I could recover.

Now that it's decided, I return to reading chapter nine. Cathy is going to marry Edgar Linton even though she shouldn't. She loves Heathcliff because "he's more myself than I am. Whatever our souls are made of, his and mine are the same."

There will never be anyone like that for me.

Saturday morning, I awaken with Heathcliff in my head, chasing Cathy over the moors, wanting her to choose him over Linton, but going about it all wrong. I'm Heathcliff, awkwardly pursuing a phantom-like girl across the windy plain, yelling unintelligible things to her. When she turns back and screams for me to stop following her, her face is cloudy, but the voice is unmistakenly familiar. I can't place it.

I sit in bed, breathing hard, tired from running.

Madi. Cathy's voice was Madi's.

I shake it off.

I have a shift today at the Wallin Animal Rescue. Troy said Saturdays can be unpredictable. Sometimes wildly busy, sometimes completely dead. "We try not to use the d-word around here, though. Gets some of the older dogs riled up."

After I shower, I put on boxers and bind my chest, then search my closet for my most Nathan-esque clothing. Everything feels like it has a hint of girl in it. Jeans. T-shirt. Flannel. None of them look right, so I choose clothes at random, put them on, and slip out of the house before Mom or Dad realizes.

As I enter the animal rescue, light flakes float down from the winter sky. Inside, down the cement-floored corridor is the door labeled "Large Dog Playroom." I enter the giant space with a few raised beds, single doghouses, and most importantly, dogs.

Troy mingles among them, instigating play for some, separating others. Every little furry face watches him closely, waiting for him to look their way for just a moment. He sees me and waves. "Nate," he calls out. "You made it."

Nate. All right. Perhaps Nathan Ashur would go by Nate. I wave, too, not sure if I can call across the room in a low enough voice over all the barking.

I need to keep my eyes open for Troy's dad. He's the only one who'd know what Nathan looks like. The second he sees me, this whole façade is over.

Troy scoops up a water bowl and delivers it to me. "Go around and put fresh water in all of these, okay?" He points at the bowls around the room and then the sink.

No small talk. That's fine with me, though I would like to know what school he goes to. If he goes to Lakeview, I would at least know to look out for him. Of course, I don't know if seeing him would be good or bad. Hallway? Possibly good. Strength Training class? Mostly bad. Any class? Bad. *Is that your real name? Are you a boy or a girl?*

It's possible he graduated. I try to size him up more as I move around the room, filling bowls. He's hard to read. He could be my age, but he could be older.

Each time I bend over for a bowl, I get a wagging tail in my face or an unprompted lick from someone now at my level. I don't mind at all. When I'm finished, Troy is no longer around. No problem. I have about twenty dogs to hang with.

I stroll among them, hands dangling to intercept soft fur and random wet noses or tongues. I end up alongside the doghouses, wondering if Dakota is still here. Sure enough, she is in the same house as before, about a foot or so inside the opening. Her eyes follow me as I get closer. Making sure she can still see me, I shrink down beside the opening, far enough away that I'm not threatening, and I'm not blocking her in.

Her claws scrape the floor of the house as she stretches, but she doesn't let me out of her sight. Not even to blink. Still, she isn't snarling or growling. I cross my legs and sit there on the floor, letting her see I'm up to nothing suspicious. A number of the other dogs become overly excited that I'm now perfectly at their level, taking the opportunity to lick my face or put a paw on me as if I'll play. I stay calm to encourage them to leave.

I'll get back to them in a minute. Right now, I want to see how close I can get to Dakota. After most of the others have given up on me, I hear Dakota take a bunch of short breaths. Is she trying to smell me?

"I thought we could be friends," I tell her. I stare at her for a moment, then look away before she sees it as a challenge. "Maybe you could come home with me some day."

She sniffs the air, then lays her head on her front paws. She hasn't stopped watching me, but she allows herself to blink. Then she closes her eyes for a bit. They burst open a moment later, reminding me of when I'm fighting sleep. "It's all right," I tell her. "You're safe."

Before I get overzealous and get closer or startle her in some other way, I force myself to get up. "See you, Dakota."

Chapter 14

MADI TEXTS A NUMBER OF times while I'm at the animal rescue. *I'm so excited about tonight.* And: *This play should be really good.* I type in the response that I'm sorry, but I can't make it but delete the words. I can't do it. Doesn't matter that I don't want to go, I just can't disappoint her.

I text Sam, hoping I can get some older brother advice about girls, but I start with *What's going on with you?* and I don't get much more serious than that.

Is something wrong? Is it Mom?

I want to tell him that Mom doesn't understand me, but he knows that. After too long of a pause, I send: *Nothing's wrong. Mom's being Mom.*

So, I'm waiting for Madi without Sam's advice at Emerald Isle Pizza where we agreed to meet for dinner. It's a place Libby and I go sometimes because not too many people from our school come here. Emerald Isle makes a mean slice. I'm not a fan of their house special—cheese pizza with orange peppers and a basil leaf, a play on the Italian classic with an Irish color scheme—but their pepperoni is pretty great.

Words keep repeating in my head. She thinks it's a date. She thinks I'm a guy. And this whole thing was her idea.

Is she interested in me? Does she like me? She thinks it's a date.

The bells above the door jingle as chill air flows in and swirls around my feet. A couple of letter jacket jocks from my school. Not Madi. I sip my Coke, but all I get is a rude noise since it's empty.

The jocks take a table too close to mine. While it's clear they don't notice me when they sit down, it takes them only a few minutes to realize that at the next table is the girl who dresses like a boy and seems to have somehow lost her boobs in the last month. After a few minutes of snickering at my life trauma, though, they lose interest and talk about their wrestling match and other equally trivial nonsense.

When the bells sound again, Madi ducks inside, wind following like a gust from a frozen sea. Her mittened hand holds her scarf closed against her throat. "It's just bitter out there tonight." She slides the scarf from her neck and her coat flops open. The top two buttons are missing. I scan her coat to find her liberal agenda, but realize I've only ever seen her pins on her backpack, not her clothes.

"Sorry I'm late." Her cheeks are pink, but I'm not sure if it's the icy wind or embarrassment. "We're still getting to know the area."

I must look confused because she adds, "Oh, we moved here about three weeks ago." She tucks a strand of dark hair behind her ear, giving me the sweetest smile.

"So that's why you just started at Lakeview?" I poke at ice cubes on the bottom of my glass.

She removes her mittens, tucking them in her pockets. "Yep."

"That must suck."

"Which part? Starting a school when I'm four months from graduation, or moving here?"

I smile. Lakeview has a reputation for being judgmental and elitist. "Starting a new school as a senior."

"It's not ideal. At least all my credits transferred. It'd be worse if I had to do summer school." She flags down the server and orders a Diet Coke.

I make another rude noise with my straw, hoping the server will get the message since she didn't stop long enough for me to ask politely. "So is it true then? Your family declared bankruptcy?"

Now her cheeks definitely redden. "I forgot I told you that."

I apologize before I remember that guys don't apologize. To distract her, I add, "We don't have to talk about it if you don't want to."

The server appears with two drinks then whisks away again.

"It's not a very good story."

"All right." I drink about half of my Coke. "I'll try not to expect much."

"My dad got laid off. His boss said the company is 'right sizing' itself." She stops there, waving a hand at me.

"No, no, keep going."

She wants to talk about this, I can tell.

"So we're left with just my mom's job." She laughs awkwardly. "Doesn't pay the bills."

The server comes back and asks for our order. We look blankly at each other.

"Medium pizza," I say. "What do you want on it?" I ask Madi.

"Oh, no, none for me. Just get what you want."

I grin. "Pepperoni."

The server writes it down. "Anything else?"

"That's it." When she's gone, I ask, "What were you saying about your mom?"

She thinks before answering. "She loves what she does, but she's a teacher. They don't make any money. It wasn't enough for us to keep up with our house payments, anyway."

"Where did you live, Wayzata?" Wealthy Wayzata.

Madi laughs wryly. "Funny." She picks up her glass as if she'll take a drink but starts speaking again before she does. "We lived in Minneapolis, just outside of Uptown. Our house isn't big or fancy, but it's ours. I mean, it was." She has to pause to calm herself down. "My dad blames himself."

"He could just get another job."

"No one's hiring machinists." She rolls her eyes. "They're not going to be any time soon either." She busies herself adjusting her coat. Then adds, "He was up again last night. I was going to go sit with him—he was in the dark in the living room, alone. Then he started crying."

I shift a little.

"I just couldn't."

"Why not?"

She wipes her eyes that are now rimmed red. "I didn't want to embarrass him."

Exactly. What guy wants people to know he's crying?

"He has this ancient belief system. Men shouldn't cry. That it's a weakness or something."

"Well, yeah. Don't you think it is?"

She laughs like I'm kidding. "You can't be serious."

Warmth rises through me. That look on her face. "The guys I know don't show their feelings. They've learned to keep them in check."

"Kay, that's absurd." She stops herself there, taking a drink from the edge of her cup to retrieve an ice cube. While she crunches it, she shakes her head.

I consider naming off the guys I mean. My brother Sam? No, he seems to run the gamut of emotions, so not him. My dad? He cried when Sasha died. He cried when Sam came home from college too. Not him. What about Danny? Not enough evidence yet. I finally come to a guy I know who controls his emotions. JT. But I can't think of anyone else. I mumble, "It's not absurd."

"I suppose it depends on what kind of man you are."

Wait, is she asking me? I think about it for a second. What kind of man am I?

With a sigh, she breaks the silence. "Tell me about your family."

"How much time you got?"

Madi laughs. "They can't be that bad."

"They're all right. My dad's a good guy. My mom is another story." Maybe I shouldn't have said that.

She raises her eyebrows and waits.

"She wants to make me into who she thinks I should be." I pray Madi doesn't ask follow-up questions. I should have kept things simpler. Something about Madi, though, makes me want to tell her everything. Anything. But maybe not that my mom wishes I was someone else.

"Why wouldn't she . . . ?" She stutters at the end. "You're smart and funny and good at art . . ." She trails off, seeming embarrassed.

When was the last time anyone made a list of my positive traits? For too long, neither of us speaks. Something in her smile, the way she takes in a breath, invites me to move closer.

No. I hold myself back. The pull, the need to be closer to her is unreal.

To save me from overanalyzing this moment, the server comes with the pizza and sets an empty plate in front of each of us. I grab a slice—hot, hot. Madi's captivated by the line of cheese that connects my piece back to the whole, but she doesn't reach for any.

"You know, everyone thinks their mom doesn't love them sometimes."

"It's more than sometimes." I take a second piece of pizza and notice her plate is still empty. "You should have some pizza. I can't eat it all."

"That's okay. I had a sandwich at home."

I laugh. "But you knew we were going out—" It finally clicks. Bankruptcy. She doesn't have money for more than her drink. Her family's poor. "I hate leaving leftovers." She doesn't move. "It's going to sit in a box in the car while we see the play. Just have one?"

She debates with herself, then submits. As she takes a bite, it's clear the sandwich she had earlier was made mostly of conjecture. Her eyes close as if she's eating the first satisfying food in months.

Maybe I could keep her in pizza, and she could keep me in compliments. Relationships have been built on less.

Madi takes a second piece. "Are you sure—"

"Please."

Before she takes a bite, she says, "Why do you think your mother wants to change you?"

Luckily, the list is long enough that I don't have to bring out the big guns yet. "She thinks my future plans are ridiculous."

When Madi doesn't immediately respond, I consider that this may be the perfect time to tell her the truth. The absolute truth about me. Stop acting like she doesn't have a right to know what everyone else knows. If there was ever a more perfect moment . . .

"Well, she has a point. Somewhat." Madi meets my gaze.

Oh, God. She does know. Someone told her about the mall. Someone texted her a picture or a video. She's seen female-me and she knows.

"You can't blame her for wanting you to have a less painful life."

My breath comes faster. Instead of saying anything against this, I take a drink of Coke to drown my words.

Madi suggests, "Maybe she doesn't understand how talented you are."

Talented at "pretending" to be a boy?

"Did she hear the song you played at the talent show?" Madi smiles. "Everyone says it was amazing. If she heard your music, she would know you have a chance. I mean, it's not easy to make it in music, especially when so many people know each other in the business, and you're just an unconnected teenager. But she has to see how great you are."

My breath stops. Music business. What a relief. Maybe this isn't the perfect time to come out to her.

Chapter 15

THE COLLEGE SITS JUST OFF the freeway, an odd oasis of brick buildings, athletic fields, and walking paths amidst city buildings. Outside of winter, it's a beautiful campus with well-trimmed shrubbery and finely tended flowers, but now, the best that can be said for it is that pure white snow covers everything but the carefully shoveled sidewalks.

Cars are parked along every street for local residents, which makes finding a parking spot time-consuming. "Hope you don't mind walking a bit in the dark," I say.

In response, Madi gets out of the car, securing her mittens. She exhales a cloud of smoky breath, smiling. "This is going to be a great play." She holds the top of her coat closed.

I meet up with her on the sidewalk and consider taking her hand as we walk along, but I stop myself. It seems like the natural thing to do, but does she want me to?

After only a few paces we're approached by someone in a dirty down jacket and winter hat who shuffles toward us, saying, "'Scuse me, 'scuse me," clearly wanting to talk to us. People always mistake me for sympathetic.

I make a move to go around him, but Madi stops. "Let's go," I say. No telling what he has hidden under that jacket.

"Miss," he says.

"What?" I say, but he isn't talking to me. He's talking to Madi.

To no one's surprise, he asks for money.

Madi pats his outstretched hand. "I only have two dollars, but you're welcome to them." She digs two bills out of her pocket.

What is she doing? She doesn't have money to give away.

We get walking again as he thanks her. Once we're out of earshot, she says, "I probably should've given that money to you for the pizza, but . . ." She glances over her shoulder at the man in the dirty jacket walking away. "You ate tonight, and he might not have."

Good point. I stare after him, wondering if he has somewhere to go.

On the college campus, everyone seems so much older and bigger than we are. Madi pays no attention to any of them as she tells me about one of the bands her dad likes from when he was in high school. I don't tell her that I am familiar with The Cure; don't stop her flow. I need her to fill the space around us with words and ward off the older people's glares that we're too young to belong. And the telltale stares attempting to assess whatever is off about me.

In line for tickets, she's reciting lyrics from one of The Cure songs she likes while I nod along. It's cool that she has decent taste in music and a little eerie that she chose one of my favorite songs. "I love that song!" I tell her, and we sing the chorus together, quietly.

When we step up for tickets, her face pales. I should pay for her. I don't want to insult her, but guys still do that, right?

I hand over enough money for both of us—it's only ten dollars a ticket—and slowly the color returns to her face. Touching my arm, she thanks me. Then we mill in with the college students moving to the theater.

As we walk, a couple guys beside us talk about the last play here. I slow to let them pass us. They don't look much older than we are, but the differences between me and them are ridiculous. One, facial hair. Even though their faces are cleanly shaved, it's clear that they shave. Me, not so much. My smooth, feminine cheeks quite obviously say that I do not and never have had facial hair. Two, build. No matter what I do with weights or any other training, my pants will never sit on my body like that. Stupid hips. Three, clothes. One of them wears a T-shirt that emphasizes his enormous pecs and biceps. Tight clothes. What a joke. I can't wear anything that hugs my body like that. Probably never will.

I glance at Madi, loping along with a dopey grin on her face. No interest in these college guys. A smile comes to my lips.

An usher hands each of us a program, then Madi thumps my shoulder. "This is going to be tremendous."

She must really like plays. Personally, I could come down on either side, so I might as well come down on the guy side. Only, that's tricky. While it's true that some of the greatest playwrights of all time have been male—William Shakespeare, Oscar Wilde, Tennessee Williams—I don't think that I'm supposed to know any playwrights, nor do I think that I'm supposed to acknowledge any interest in plays.

I think about the guys I know, especially my brother Sam. He's never talked to me about a play that he's liked. Movies, sure, but those have all sorts of masculine elements in them. Do plays? I would guess that even though Shakespeare's *Twelfth Night* begins with a shipwreck, we won't get to see any actual ship or catastrophe. Would Sam like that even though we don't see it? *Cool, it has a shipwreck in it.* Probably not.

But there are lots of guys here. Maybe they're here for a class too.

Madi and I find our row. As she takes her seat beside me, her arm rests against mine on the shared armrest. A pleasant shiver runs down my body. I'm supposed to make conversation, only I tell myself that's a social pressure only girls need to observe. Whatever. It will take my mind off of thinking about whether I'm interested in Madi or not.

"Do you know everything we need to write about for the assignment?"

Her eyes spark as she rattles off the details. Her dream assignment, it seems. Then she adds, "We should discuss it after. You know, so we have commonalities. But not too many."

My lips sputter as I surprise myself with a laugh. She's funny. Maybe not on purpose. For a moment I examine her cheekbones and her neck but force my eyes away as they wander farther down. Knock it off.

Paging through the program, Madi reads a few paragraphs to me. The plot. "It promises to be hilarious."

I snort. "I'll be the judge of that." I discover my gaze perusing her face again. Long eyelashes that don't look like chunky mascara. Soft cheeks. Lovely neck.

"Listen to this: 'The lovesick Orsino pines for Olivia who in turn is in love with the person she thinks is the young man Cesario who is really Viola,'" she reads.

M. E. Corey

"What?" Did she just say that there's a guy who is actually a woman in this play?

She continues, "'Viola is actually disguised as her twin brother Sebastian, whom she thinks is lost at sea. Viola, however, is secretly in love with Orsino, but she is supposed to help him seduce Olivia.'" She laughs.

"Holy shit. Wait. Viola is Sebastian? Or Viola is Ces-ar something?" I'm half thinking about the gender switching and half thinking about how confusing that sounds.

"Cesario. Viola goes by Cesario, but I guess because they're twins, Viola looks like Sebastian."

I shake my head. Shakespeare always has twists like this. Even though I've only read a few of his plays, I've been paying attention.

She holds her program out. "Look. They made this chart to help us keep it straight." She finds this hilarious.

I take the program from her instead of opening my own. Yeah, the chart helps. It's not that confusing at all, really. Viola and Cesario are the same person. That makes total sense.

"Don't you think that's kind of sad?" She takes her program back.

"What?"

"That Viola is in love with Orsino, but Orsino loves someone else *and* wants Viola to help him win her over. And on top of that, he thinks she's a man."

"Sad?"

"Yeah. Can you imagine the person you love thinking that you're someone you're not?"

Is she making fun of me? Or is she totally serious? "That would really suck."

132

She squishes up her lips as she contemplates the situation, then, checking her phone for the time, she pops up. "Only fifteen minutes until it starts."

"Where are you going?"

"Bathroom." She shimmies past me to the aisle.

I stand. "I should go too." The Coke I drank at dinner has gone straight through me.

Once we're in the lobby, I can see the bathroom line has grown out the door. Typical. Madi takes a place behind the last woman, and I stand beside her. "Do you think it has to be more than a page?"

Madi startles. With a laugh she says, "The assignment? I was thinking page and a half."

I nod. Her gaze makes me feel like I'm suddenly clothes-free.

"You know . . ." She leans closer to me. "It's really nice of you, but you don't have to wait here with me."

Shit. I am waiting in line with her for the women's restroom. Shit.

She points briefly to where the men's room is.

Recover. I have to recover from this stupid mistake. Faking a grin, I say, "Have it your way," and saunter away. I keep myself rigid as I go, not wanting attention drawn to my body. Is she watching me leave?

The men's room.

Everything tells me to stop, to at least think this through.

It's not that I've never been in a men's room before. It's just something I haven't done often. Okay, I've only been in one once. Generally speaking, I avoid public restrooms entirely. Avoid any looks, any questions. No matter which one I use, someone's always there to make it awkward. I should just go back to our seats. But Madi can see me here, and ever since she mentioned the bathroom, my bladder has been pressing crazily on me.

Keeping my head up, I step inside. There's a line here, too, which I hadn't anticipated. But it's not the same. This line ends at the urinals. I am talented in a lot of ways, but this is not one of them. I ensure I'm a decent enough space behind the sweatshirted guy in front of me and wait. What if they need the stall? What do they do?

Unclear.

Most of the guys going in the stalls are peeing. It's the luck of the draw. When you're next, you get whatever's available. Shit.

What if I sort of straddle the urinal? Not likely. What if I hang out until all these guys are done? Could be all night.

I cinch my legs together, my bladder pressing.

Wait. That's an open stall. Sweatshirt in front of me doesn't see it. Be calm. Be calm. He's next in line. Urinal for him. But stall for me if he doesn't see it.

He doesn't, so I press the door open to find my relief, and instead find a broad-shouldered guy urinating. When the door nearly hits him, I slink back. Disgusting. Why didn't he latch the door?

I can't move away. Should I? What do you do when this happens? Do I just wait? I don't want to get back in line. If I get back in line, I could get stuck at the urinal.

Wait and the stall will be yours.

He finishes, shakes, zips, does not flush, and runs into me.

"Sorry, sorry," I say. So girly.

He hits a shoulder into me, knocking me off balance, but continues to the door.

Wash your hands, dude. He's not going to wash his hands?

Whatever. I slip into the stall, placing my body carefully so I can get the door closed and latched. Finally.

Unbutton, unzip, but before I can settle in, I stop. The entire seat is splattered with drops of varying sizes. Seriously? Graffiti behind the toilet reads: Be like Dad, not like sis, lift the seat before you piss. Guess nobody reads that.

I spool out a wad of paper and wipe down the seat, flush his liquid gift away. And now I'll be like sis, but at least I'll get to piss.

Now what. Do I stay here a while longer, so people don't know I sat down to pee? So they think instead that I . . . I should pretend everything's normal.

My shoe squeaks as I open the stall door. I try not to think about what's all over the floor. Avert my eyes. Wash my hands. Avoid the mirror, avoid the mirror, avoid the mirror.

Too late. There I am. Pathetic little me acting like I belong here. I scowl at myself. I hate you.

And I'm out.

Back in the theater, Madi's settled in her seat like I've been gone an hour, her arm planted on the armrest with her program propped up. She doesn't notice me. Sitting down beside her, I open my program, my arm slapping against hers a little harder than I intended as I try to claim the armrest. Pulling her arm to herself, she rubs it a little. "You could've asked me to move." She laughs.

Shit. Instead of apologizing, I let her have the armrest. Then up and over a few rows, I see the guy from the bathroom.

God, I hope he doesn't see me. I slouch a little more. He'll catch me watching him and kick my ass. And figure out I'm only a girl. And broadcast it to everyone here. And Madi will start treating me differently, just like Christine did when she found out. No more smiles in the hall.

When the house lights go down, Madi hops in her seat and pats my leg. "It's starting." Giddy like a little kid.

Once it's dark enough, I smile at her enthusiasm. Then I notice her hand is lingering on my leg. A spark shoots through my body. Her soft, cream-colored fingers are the last thing I see when the theater finally darkens, but I can still sense them against my leg. For a moment. Until she takes them back.

After the opening scene, I adjust to the language enough to follow the story. Madi seems to understand it well. She hangs on every word. The best part isn't in the play, though; the best part is that Madi and I laugh at all the same lines.

The character Viola doesn't dress up like a man for a while. Disappointing. When she does, she doesn't really look like a man; her figure is still so obviously womanly. Is that on purpose because we need to remember she *is* a woman? Or does she look that way because that's how all women look when they try to dress like men?

And she doesn't sound anything like a man either. It's embarrassing. I glance at Madi. Is she thinking what I'm thinking? That my voice sounds like that? Too high, forcing a masculine tone?

A short time into the play, Viola dressed as male Cesario nearly swoons when talking with Orsino on stage. Madi laughs with the rest of the audience, leaning over to me, whispering, "I'm not fooled."

My toes curl. They're freezing all of a sudden. The play. She's talking about the play.

She checks in with me like I was supposed to respond, her eyebrows lowering.

I give her a little smile, though my toes feel like ice.

At intermission, Madi leaves for the bathroom, and though I have to go again, I don't think I can summon enough courage to play Russian roulette with the urinals again. Think of something else. Writing my drama essay. Singing a prom song.

When she returns, her face brightens. "Don't you just love being at a play?" She gestures to the stage.

A list of smart-ass comments comes to mind, but instead I answer honestly. "Yeah. It's interesting. The guy playing Orsino is good."

"Right?" She takes in a deep breath. "And that smell. It's like a mix of stage makeup and sweat and dreams." She inhales again.

I laugh.

She shakes her head to tell me she's not embarrassed and takes her seat beside me. Patting my arm, she presses closer. "My mom took me to this play once."

"Yeah?" I lean in, thinking she's going to whisper.

She deflates. It happens so suddenly that I question whether she was just smiling. The quiet between us makes her grin. "That was a long time ago."

Say something. Ask her why. Tell her a funny part from the play.

But I wait too long, the lights dim, curtain opens, and there's Viola's supposedly dead twin brother Sebastian, alive and well, thinking Viola instead is the one who is deceased.

At the end of the scene, Madi covers her face. Sebastian agrees to marry Olivia, which makes her overjoyed because Olivia thinks he's Cesario/Viola.

I grab hold of her hand, her chilled fingers closing around mine. She laughs, knowing she shouldn't be tense. It's a comedy after all. For the rest of Act Four, she clutches my hand against her thigh, squeezing from time to time. Stage lights illuminate her lips, her cheeks. Beautiful.

She releases her grip at the top of Act Five, giving me the sweetest smile. Everything is about to explode in the storyline. All the misunderstandings and doppelgängers will be revealed. As the confusion is unraveling, Viola, still dressed as a man, confesses that she loves Orsino "more than I love these eyes, more than my life."

Orsino, of course, doesn't understand. My chest tightens. Viola's words are heartbreaking. To love someone who doesn't understand who you truly are is heartbreaking.

Madi lets out a tiny gasp. A tear slides down her cheek. Do I dare take her hand again?

I do.

This time she covers my fingers with her other hand as well. She's sad for Viola.

Gradually things on stage work out. Sebastian and Olivia, Orsino and Viola all live happily ever after. It's all fine; it all ties together. My English teacher this year said that fiction makes sense out of life. In fiction things have to fall in line, events cause other events. Of course, Viola can dress up like a man and still end up with the man she loves at the end. It's fiction.

When the actors come on stage for their bows, Madi lets go of my hand to clap. Pausing for a moment to wipe away a few tears, Madi gives me a nervous laugh, then cheers some more.

Once the applause dies down and the mandatory Minnesota standing ovation is over, I shake my head. "Wow."

"I know."

Not sure what she knows, what she thinks my "wow" was about, but I don't know how to ask her. Instead, I say, "I can't believe Shakespeare got all of that to work out in only a few hours."

Laughing, Madi covers her mouth, but only a moment later, her laughter changes to sobs.

"What is it?" I put a hand on her shoulder without questioning whether I should.

She waves a hand at me. "Nothing, nothing."

"You can talk to me." My other hand goes to her other shoulder.

Sharp intake of breath, her eyes meet mine. "Not here."

Chapter 16

WITH EVERYTHING THAT'S HAPPENED IN the past few hours—from dinner to the play to the men's room to Madi holding my hand—I can hardly remember where I parked. But since the weather is kind this evening, I don't mind walking around a little. It's cold, sure, but it's above zero at least, and no wind.

When the crowd from the play has separated off into little bunches and couples, Madi and I are mostly alone. She occasionally wipes her eyes but doesn't speak.

I should say something. Let her know I'm still here. After making several false starts, I finally say, "I'm glad we went to this."

A smile. That's all.

"I mean, I forgot how much I like plays."

She pulls on mismatched mittens and watches the ground where she steps.

Keep it going. She'll say something if you keep it going. "The story was a little confusing . . ." I trail off.

She kicks limp snow with her next step. Still quiet.

Until we're in the car and the heat is on, the conversation is paused. But her tears come again, and I'm thankful only because I want to know what hurts her so much. "What is it?"

"I feel so stupid, crying like this." Fingers wipe her eyes once the mittens are off. A stray bit of yarn dangles from one.

"You shouldn't."

She snorts through her tears. "I've known you for like two days, and we're supposed to be having a good time."

"I'll have you know that we've known each other for an entire week now."

Madi snorts again. She evaluates me, sizing up my trustworthiness. "Uh . . . take the next right."

Not what I was expecting, but okay. I wait for her to say something more.

She gives me more directions to her house.

As I follow her suggested turns, the neighborhood grows dirtier, more crowded, houses get smaller, more rundown. While the houses degrade, Madi's tone grows cynical. "Pull over here. Don't pull in the driveway."

The "driveway" is only gravel leading to a box-like house. I must be staring at the copious imperfections for too long because she finally says, "It's not much."

I force my gaze away from the house and onto her, which is much more pleasing anyway. The streetlight shows me the red around her eyes. She's not done crying. But I don't know if she wants me to ask her questions or just listen or wait for her to be ready or walk her to the door or simply say goodbye.

"I can't believe we're living here." She fiddles with the string of yarn on her mitten. She winds the stray yarn around her finger, pulling another inch free. "The play just reminded me—" The tautness of the yarn turns her finger red. "My brother and I used to be so close. He kept everything sane with us. With all of us." She wipes her cheek.

I think about my brother Sam. I wouldn't say he kept my family sane, but he certainly would make a difference if he was around all the time. "What happened with your brother?"

"He graduated and moved out. Now it's just me."

In spite of her seriousness, I smile. That's exactly how it is. With Sam gone, there's only me. To reason with my parents. To try to keep them rational. To state a younger point of view. I'm outnumbered now. "I know what you mean. My brother left for college two years ago."

Her shoulders relax. "So you get it." She unwinds and rewinds the yarn around her finger. "Without Charlie around, it's like my parents don't have anything to talk about anymore. And my dad feels so ashamed about his job." She winds the yarn more quickly.

"That's—" Something I haven't had to think about. Guess I'm lucky in that way. "That must be difficult."

"Yeah. My mom tries. After she gets home, she tries to talk to him about her day." The hole in her mitten has grown. "He thinks she's rubbing it in, saying he's worthless because he doesn't work."

"Why would he think that?"

She's quiet, enlarging the mitten's hole even more. "He buys into all that men-have-to-be-the-breadwinners crap from the fifties or the eighties or whatever. He thinks Mom shouldn't have to work."

My mom would never let that thought enter Dad's mind.

"Stupid patriarchal bullshit." Realizing she's nearly ruined her mitten, she winds up the strand of yarn and shoves it inside the hole.

"Yeah."

"I can't think of anyone I know other than my dad who thinks like that. Like men have to be a certain way. And women a certain other way. Instead of being who we are."

But I am a certain way. Does that mean I shouldn't tell her I'm trans? That she'd think it was stupid that I care about which gender I am?

She can't mean that.

She sighs deeply and sits up straighter in her seat. "I'm all right. I'm better now." She reaches for my hand like it's the most natural thing for her to do, and though her fingers are cold, I don't mind even a little.

"Talk to me," she says. "Tell me more about what you meant before about your mom."

What do I say? She doesn't accept me as male? I came out to her two years ago, and she still won't recognize the real me?

"She won't let me be myself." It's not enough, so I keep going. "She's always trying to change what I do, what I wear."

"What's wrong with what you wear?" This, unfortunately, makes her look over my body more closely to see if she's missed something incriminating.

Clearly, I can't say my clothes aren't feminine enough, but nothing besides the truth comes to me. "She doesn't like anything about me. Not my grades or my friends. She even got ticked off when I stopped playing basketball." I shouldn't have said that. I'm not telling her why I stopped playing. I'm not.

"That's your choice, though."

"That's what I thought." For a moment she's only a few inches from me, and her eyes are a brilliant blue, and her lips are a little wet, and I imagine that it would be all right for me to kiss her, for me to take the next step.

But I can't do that. I don't know how she'd feel that I'm not technically a boy. I don't know what she'd do.

"She's just so stuck in—"

"In what?"

"Expectations, you know. Being like everyone else."

She seems to be checking out my clothes again, then my face, my body. I shift so my jacket falls differently across my chest, though I doubt she can see anything in this light or with my binder so tight. I smile. "Maybe she wants me to be more like Sam." In every way but being male, that is.

I gaze past her at the little, rundown house. It's hard to believe that her parents are both inside, likely asleep. It doesn't seem like a place where real people live. Once I've thought that, though, I feel like an ass. Madi lives there. She's real.

Then I wonder if her parents are both inside, not sleeping but waiting up for her. I make a point of staring at the time on the dashboard. She has to have a curfew, right? "Oh, man, I didn't realize it was 1 a.m."

She's uninterested in the time, but after a moment she says, "I suppose I should go."

I feel like she's waiting for me to protest, and I want to, but I also don't. If we keep talking so honestly, I'm likely to say more than I should, tell her I'm trans, and I'm not sure she's ready to hear that. I was prepared to tell her earlier tonight, but now, I don't really want to anymore.

She's watching me as if she thinks I'm going to kiss her goodnight, like this was a real date. I stay still. Inching toward me, Madi puts a hand on my hand. When she tilts her head,

I turn away. But that doesn't stop her from kissing my cheek and pretending that's what she'd intended all along. "I had a really nice time," she says.

My cheek pulsates with the sensation of her soft, wet lips. I keep my body turned away from her, so I don't take this further. "Maybe we could do the community theater play together too."

Her smile is answer enough.

Chapter 17

I'M STILL THINKING OF HER smile at school. With my cleanly laundered gym clothes in my hands, I stand outside the girls' locker room, not wanting to go in. I've been avoiding the girls' gym class changes by coming super early in the morning, but today, I'm not as early as I want to be. Likely I'll be partially clad, and the group of girls will arrive.

Even if I'm in the adjacent bathroom stall, I'll still have to pass them on my way out. They'll still get the opportunity to harass me.

Down the hall a door opens. Though I flinch, I don't know which way to turn. Do I go into the locker room or turn around like I'm not going in?

Coach Wendell emerges from the open door.

Go in the locker room, I tell myself. But my feet don't move.

"Good morning," Coach says as he approaches.

I echo his greeting.

He slows and stops beside me, looking at the locker room door in front of me. Why can't I just go inside?

"Do you have a second?" he says. He gestures for me to follow him back to his office. He opens the door, staying in the hallway. "I wanted to ask you something."

This can't be good. Whatever a football coach has to say to me is not going to be good.

"If you feel like it. It's completely up to you. I wanted to tell you that there's no one in my office before weightlifting. It's completely empty."

I check his mouth for a smirk. I check his eyes for mischief. Is he asking if I want to use his office to change for class?

He rubs the back of his neck. "My brother's kid has been having a hard time. He's in middle school, and you know how kids can be."

I nearly smile, but I don't really follow.

"She," he says too loudly. "Sorry. I talk with her a bunch, and I'm not used to switching my pronouns yet."

Every nerve on my body awakens. He has a transgender niece? Is that what he's telling me?

He smiles. "She's always been my favorite. Great kid. Athletic. Really good at tennis."

I swallow.

Awkwardly, he steps just inside the office and pulls on the inside of the door. "There's this little hook here. It'll hold the door closed so no one will bother you."

"Are you sure?"

His smile grows. "I can't imagine you like changing in there with the girls."

Something in my throat silences my *Thank you.*

He reaches in his pocket, pulling out a lanyard with a key. "I'm not supposed to let students—" He places the key in my hand and puts a single finger to his lips. He steps by me but pauses. "You ought to hold on to that for the rest of the year."

Briefly he touches my shoulder. Then he's gone.

I step inside, close the door, and secure the hook. Before I remove a single piece of clothing, I check out the room. Simple. Harmless. Normal seeming. There's a desk and a file cabinet, a variety of athletic equipment, a chair. I fold my shirt and jeans and leave them on the chair. Slip on my gym clothes and lock the door behind me.

Back in the hall, JT nearly runs into me, coming around a corner, and instead of sneering or swearing or insulting, he stares. If it was weeks ago at the talent show, I'd get it. The surprise in his eyes seeing me as a boy for the first time would make sense. But the way he looks at me now, it's like he doesn't recognize me. When I know he does.

Even though I'm as taken aback as he is, I don't linger. If he wants to make up for this missed harassment opportunity, he has the whole class hour. I don't have to give him time now.

But he's still confused, even among the barbells and weights. I station myself at the losers' free weights, curling twenty-five-pound dumbbells one arm at a time. While I don't keep a constant eye on him, I sneakily check on his location from time to time. Each time he's watching. Something's brewing in his little brain.

Danny watches him too. "Is he up to something?"

"Don't know."

Danny chuckles to himself. "Looks like he wants to come up with a plan, but the thoughts just aren't there."

I laugh too.

When Danny changes exercises, he tells me about a band. "They play industrial and some harder stuff, but also a bit of low-core punk. They're called The B Batteries."

I nod along as he describes them. Dumb name. But then I consider how there are A batteries, C batteries, D batteries. There aren't any B batteries. Maybe it's a clever name.

"They're playing at my uncle's pub. I thought we could check them out on Friday."

Danny and I seem to like some of the same music, and he's so easy to be around. Not to mention the most important thing: he accepts me. When I haven't responded for a while, Danny says, "They go on about eight. Probably play a two-hour set."

"Sure, yeah. Let's go."

I relax into my workout, ruminating over what kind of people name themselves The B Batteries. It's now when I've let down my guard that JT appears at my bench, uncomfortably behind me as I'm bent over to keep my form. I sense him there before I can spot him with a careful glance. I'm torn between finishing my set and whirling around to clock him in the head with the dumbbell.

"What are you going for, Kinkade?" he says. He slinks onto the bench. Too close. The hairs on my arm just touch the hairs on his.

Not sure what he means, and even if I was, I don't think I'd answer.

"If you want bulk, you need to increase your weight. Fewer reps, heavier lift." He scrubs his hand against his blond flattop, then lays his palm against Danny's chest. "Got that? If you want to bulk up—"

Danny steps back so JT's hand drops.

I'm coming up on fifteen reps with this weight mostly because if I stop, I have to change sides, and that would mean facing JT for my next set. With the sixteenth lift, I let out an accidental grunt.

He laughs. "If you want definition, by all means keep doing what you're doing. I just don't know what you're working on defining. I mean . . ." He trails off like we all can tell I have no muscles to speak of.

"Screw you," Danny says.

I straighten up, bringing the weight close to my body. He's so tall that even when he's seated and I'm standing, he's nearly as tall as I am. I stand a little straighter.

Without warning, he seizes the dumbbell from my hand and trades it in for one that's ten pounds heavier. "Try this one."

I accept it from him, though I worry it's somehow laced with smallpox.

"Go on," he says.

Moving down the bench, I position myself for a tricep extension, but I keep him in my sights. Thirty-five pounds is more than I've done on triceps. As I draw the dumbbell up, fire spreads from my elbow through my whole arm. One. I force myself to lower it slowly. Then back up. Two.

"That one's too light." He launches up from the bench and when I bring my arm back, he switches a forty pounder for my thirty-five pounder.

My arm falls back down, unable to compensate for the difference. I let the weight drop.

"Oops," he laughs. "Found your limit already."

Danny steps up, saying, "You're such an ass——"

But I don't hear the rest. I throw myself at JT, both hands out to force him off the bench, but he barely moves. He grabs my wrists, pulls me toward him until my ear is by his mouth.

"Going out with a girl doesn't make you a man. It makes you a lesbian."

I seize my wrists back, stumbling but finding my footing. I'm not a les—

Winking, he saunters to the other side of the weight room where his jock buddies wait.

How does he know I went out with Madi?

No one knew we were going to the play together but Madi and me, and she wouldn't have said anything. Who else knew we were going out?

"Forget him," Danny says. "Guys like him don't get it."

I stand stock still, staring down JT, who gives me a little wave and blows me a kiss. Through gritted teeth I ask, "Don't get what?"

"What it's like to have a personality or perspective or empathy. To, like, have an interest in other people and what really matters. All they care about is getting ripped and playing sports."

Danny walks around me to encourage me to walk away from where I can see JT. "He's going to remember these days as the best years of his life. Would you want that short of a lifespan?"

I smile because I know he wants me to cheer up, but a hollowness opens inside me. Maybe these will be the best years of my life. Maybe after high school, all I'll have is judgment from everyone else in the world, being told I'm a mistake, being assessed as not a real man.

"Kay, what's going on with you?" Danny has taken me to the far end of the weight room.

My jaw tightens. "He's a narcissistic, homophobic,

misogynistic, transphobic idiot who'd rather control people than be kind to them."

Danny smiles at my assessment. "All true."

"Everyone accepts him for what he is. No questions. He's fine. But me . . ." I trail off. I don't want to say what I am.

"Dude, it's not like that."

"It is." I meet his eyes. "Girls want to go out with him, guys want to be like him, but they all think something's wrong with me."

He leaves those words alone. Then he discreetly points across the room at Tiyana. "You think that girl wants to go out with him?" The permanent sneer on her face intensifies while she does preacher's curls.

At any other moment, that would have made me laugh. "Of course not."

He points out several other girls in the room who would absolutely never go out with JT.

"You know that wasn't what I meant."

Danny says, "And as for guys who want to be like him, I think there's only Dirk."

"Hunter?"

Danny shakes his head. "Hunter's nobody's hero, but he doesn't idolize JT."

I let out a long sigh, but my tension over JT keeps my whole body rigid.

"I certainly don't want to be like him," Danny says. "Neither do you."

My shoulders relax a little. I don't want to be like him. But if he's a man, and I want to be a man, doesn't that mean I have to be like him? A little?

When I see Libby across the row in art class, I consider venting to her, too, about JT, but I don't feel so mad anymore. Besides, she's heard me bitch about him too many times. Instead, I collect my pencils and sit down.

Beside me, Christine shades the edges of tall blades of grass. She has returned to charcoal, which truly shows her skill. Pastels, though, not so much.

Christine is clueless about my life. She still wants me to come over for my makeup lesson.

Madi appears, leaning on my desk. "I had a really good time Saturday night."

Peripherally, I see Christine glance over, then increase her shading speed.

"Yeah. The play was great." My words are flat. I don't want Christine to think that Madi and I had a date, but at the same time, if she did, maybe she'd be jealous. But I don't want Madi to think I didn't have a good time. I had a great time.

This is getting complicated.

"I was looking at some of the community theaters around here." Madi lays her phone down in front of me, scrolling through a Google search of results with theater and play names. "We could really go to any of these."

I read a few, check Christine's response—nothing—read a few more. "Which one do you like?"

She answers, I'm sure she answers, but Christine has moved on from shading the blades of grass to articulating the ground below. She's not paying any attention to our conversation. How do I make it more obvious that this is a second date?

"Yeah, all right," I say when Madi is silent.

"Which one?"

My gaze darts up. She gave me an option? Whichever. It doesn't matter. "The first one?"

She takes her phone, pointing at me knowingly. "I thought you'd say that."

Later in the day when I know I'll see Madi at lunch, I hope she'll tell me which play I've agreed to see. Before I can join Libby at our usual table, I come across Madi in the lunch line. Don't know if I've ever seen her buy food here. Does she have money? For some reason, I remember her giving her two dollars to that homeless guy.

When I join the back of the line, she leaves her spot and comes over beside me. "I'm glad you're here," she says.

My stomach does a little flip. "Really?"

"I was thinking about writing my review about the play, and I thought maybe we ought to talk about it. Like whether we should include parts from the play."

"Like when Olivia marries Sebastian thinking he's Cesario?" I laugh without wanting to. Very unmanly. I grab a lunch tray and check my choices.

She touches my arm. "That was a funny part." Then she recites a line from the play, stressing the wrong syllables just like the actor had.

I can't stop laughing. "That was perfect."

"Thank you, thank you." She takes a tiny bow.

I hear swearing and overconfidence approaching, which I try to ignore. Hunter, Dirk, and JT clatter into line, dislodging more trays than they need to and shoving freshmen and sophomores out of the way.

Madi glances at the sound, but then returns to talking to me. She delivers another perfect line from the play, and I want to laugh. I do. But I feel JT getting closer. The hair on my neck stands up. Madi lowers her voice. "Do you know them?"

"Only since first grade." My voice is so quiet that I don't think she hears me.

Dirk skips ahead of the next person in line, then the next. He's only a few people away from us now, and the lunch ladies aren't paying enough attention to send him back. The other students just let him push them around; they're not the least bit startled; they just step aside. It won't be that easy for me.

Dirk shoves in line beside me. Then he checks out Madi, scratching his Amish beard. "Your girlfriend is hot."

My throat tightens. "She's not—"

He shoves past so he's between us, leaning close to Madi to loudly whisper, "Dyke," before moving past her, too, and asking the lunch lady for three pieces of pizza.

JT's face appears over my shoulder; my arms cover in goosebumps. He's blocked me so I can't elbow him in the gut. I try to meet Madi's eyes. Does she see how powerless he makes me?

Slowly he inhales right by my neck, then exhales sticky sweet mango with a side of vanilla. With his exhale, he whispers, "You still smell like a girl."

When my elbow finally shoots back, it strikes only air. JT is gone. Dirk finds this incredibly funny. My whole body gets warm. I leave Madi and my empty tray, smacking into Hunter's shoulder as I leave without a lunch. I nearly say I'm sorry before I growl at him.

I stomp through the cafeteria until I can drop myself into a chair across from Libby, arms crossed in front of me.

"Where's your lunch?"

I give her an evil look. "JT's up there."

"So what? That means you can't have lunch?"

"I don't want him to—" Give me away to Madi. I glare over at the food line. I can't see any of them from here, not even Madi. Why did I leave her by herself?

Then I see her coming toward us. She has her lunch tray; she didn't abandon hers like a coward.

Fries. That's all that's on the tray she lays down. "Where'd you go?" she asks me.

"I just changed my mind about lunch." I pull myself up so I don't look like a moping idiot. "Did that guy bother you?" A little too little, a little too late, Kinkade.

"Which guy?—oh, no, not really. He has me confused with someone else."

Right.

Without a thought, Libby takes a fry from Madi's tray. I nearly tell her off, but I catch myself before I air Madi's dirty laundry. Libby probably doesn't know how poor she is.

"Tell me about this play you two saw," Libby says.

I snort. "Really?"

"You both seem to have liked it. You should've told me you were going."

Madi speed-chews her fries so she can say, "One of the best plays ever. Sincerely. I don't think I've ever understood *Twelfth Night* so well." She does her impersonation of Olivia realizing Sebastian isn't Cesario again.

I crack up.

Libby forces a grin. "I haven't read that one. What was it about?"

Madi rattles off the convoluted plot faster than I can remember the first act. She ends with, "But you really had to be there. It sounds confusing, but it really wasn't."

"I wasn't invited," Libby says with a glare at me.

"I figured you were going to GameStop to meet Aniyah and Everett."

Her glare does not change. "That doesn't mean I don't want to be invited."

Madi doesn't seem to hear any of our exchange and instead reminds me about the scene where Viola confesses her love for Orsino. For a moment I feel like I'm in the college auditorium with Madi holding my hand. I wish we were back there.

"You wouldn't have liked it," I say to Libby. And anyway, she would have been a third wheel. It was a date, after all. Mostly.

If Libby had been there, I doubt Madi would have been so excited when the play began that she bounced up and down in her seat. Or that she would have told me that she loved the smell of the theater.

Or that she would have held my hand. I smile quietly to myself. She held my hand.

Chapter 18

DR. BEHMANN'S OFFICE IS SO dull that I find myself staring at his skin-colored mole again. I think through sentences to explain my date with Madi but can't come up with a good one.

"You seem more chipper than usual."

Chipper? Here's where one of those sentences would work. I went on a date with a girl and we held hands and she kissed my cheek. "I guess." Or a non-answer.

"Good week? Good day?"

Though I want to keep my smile to myself, hold on to my happiness about Madi, I can't stop it. "Good weekend. I had a date."

He perks up. As much as he ever perks up, which is to say a tiny spark alights one of his eyes.

I recount my weariness before attending the play, then reveal the absolute wonder of the evening. Madi holding my hand. Trusting me with her family secrets. Wanting to see another play together.

"And all this time she continues to believe you're male." His tone exposes a bit of disapproval. Or perhaps, disbelief.

"What's wrong with that? I am male." My breath comes faster.

Cursory nod, then silence just long enough to bring on my

discomfort. "Do you like Madi?"

How does he always do this? My gaze traces his shoe.

He crosses his feet under his chair. "Does she deserve to know the truth?"

I want to yell at him that no one deserves the truth, but I don't.

He grins. "No one said this would be easy."

I scowl at his cliché, but he redeems himself a moment later when he places a business card in my hand. At first, I assume it's his, and I already have several of those, but the logo is different. It's the University of Minnesota. The Institute for Sexual and Gender Health. There's a short list of names and a phone number.

"It's time for you to take the next step."

I turn the card over like the secret to my future is written on the back. It's not. "You think my mom'll pay for this?" I wave the card at him; it's meaningless.

"You don't have to worry about that. Their insurance will cover it."

Oh. "But what about when she finds out what it's for?"

He gives me a Dr. Behmann look. "You'll talk with her."

I suck in a breath to tell him off, but he's right; I'll have to talk to her.

"You can do this, Kay."

"Sure." I'm not convincing in the least.

"Not everyone has access to these resources. When you're ready, I hope you'll make the most of it."

"What resources?"

"It hasn't been that long that insurance has covered trans-gender-related therapy."

Fine, I was born in the wrong body but in the right time period. I only glare at him.

He continues, "And, of course, not every transgender patient has medical insurance. Some insurance will cover surgery as well."

I didn't realize, but I decide not to give him the satisfaction of knowing this is news to me. But I tell him, "I suppose I'm lucky then."

I feel lucky to be meeting Danny at O'Sullivan's too. The B Batteries have gotten some strong local reviews. Maybe I can learn some stage-presence techniques from their singer.

O'Sullivan's has brass door handles and a clover-shaped sign with their name in dark gold letters. Inside at first it looks like a restaurant but the other side is clearly a bar. The restaurant part has booths with little lamps centered on the tables and red-leather chairs and upholstered benches. Nice place.

At the far end is a simple stage a few feet off the ground. A bass guitar, a drum kit, synthesizer, and a few other guitars are set up, but no band yet.

While I'm gazing around at the framed pictures of Irish actors and musicians, Danny arrives. We take a table as close to the stage as we can get and order a couple of Cokes. Across the table from me, I notice that with his dark bangs and semi-sarcastic smile, Danny is also wearing eyeliner.

"It's not a huge venue, but he manages to get some good live music in here," Danny says. The eyeliner makes his eyes stand out.

Stupidly, I stare at his eyeliner. Is it because it looks good on him or because I haven't seen him wear anything but nail polish? *Snap out of it.*

Behind the stage is a Guinness placard and a photo of an Irish castle. Everything all around announces a love of Ireland. Even the painting of sheep on a green landscape.

"This place is cool," I tell Danny. I try to look away from the makeup on his face.

He's about to agree with my comment about O'Sullivan's, but instead he says, "You've never seen me outside of school."

"Uh . . ."

"Not a lot of boys at our school wear makeup."

"No." It fits for him. Two weeks ago I would've thought it was out-and-out stupid, but why? I think I like it on him. "I didn't mean to stare at you."

He shrugs. "I've just always liked it. My mom used to get so mad when I would get into her stuff, but she's pretty used to it now."

"Huh." I don't know what to say.

"You know I do makeup for theater, don't you?"

I shake my head.

"It's so satisfying to make someone look flawless."

"I suppose it's a little like painting," I offer.

"Yeah. I don't personally wear eyeshadow, but the shading and blending you can do is pretty remarkable. And foundation and bronzers."

Huh.

He meets my eyes intently. "I don't usually tell people how much I like makeup. They make a lot of assumptions about me, then." He gives me a brief smile. "But you're different."

Say something kind. But I can't think of the words. And before I can, the band members clamber onto the stage and switch on the hum of their amplifiers.

They start with "London Calling" by The Clash, and Danny nearly loses his shit.

I laugh at him, but I'm swept up in the music too. He yells to me that this is his favorite song, but that was obvious.

The whole set is great. The songs are all punk and indie ones I know, a few Blue has played. For most of the songs, the lead guitarist and bassist share a mic for backing vocals, and the whole time their elation for being on stage fills the entire pub.

That's what I want. Music and happiness.

By the end of The B Batteries' set, Danny can barely speak, hoarse from yelling with the songs. But he's pleased with it all. He's had four Cokes to my three, and his uncle has sent over two baskets of wings, some mozzarella sticks, and a plate of onion rings. Each time, the server wants to know if we need anything else.

Frankly, I'm stuffed and exhausted.

As the band packs up their instruments, a pale, dark-haired man comes to our table. He wears a green apron with a gold "O'Sullivan's" across the chest. Danny stands when he sees him, shakes his hand, and allows himself to be pulled into an embrace. "How you doing, boyo?"

Danny pats his uncle on the back. "This is my friend, Kay."

I stand up and shake his hand like I've seen other guys do. "Nice to meet you."

"Likewise." Even in a single word, his accent is noticeable.

Danny elaborates about the quality of the band as I assess Uncle Brian. Seems a decent guy. No lingering, questioning stares. A definite plus.

I listen to Danny and Brian talk about the band, then some family matters, then nothing in particular. Abruptly, Brian says, "I should get back to it. Nice meeting you," and he returns to the bar.

Danny sits back down, slurps up the remainder of Coke in his glass, and says, "What'd you think?"

"They were really great. Or do you mean your uncle?"

Danny laughs. "I know my uncle's great. I meant the place, the experience."

I nod at him. "One of the best things I've done in a long time."

A few days later, I have a shift at the Wallin Animal Rescue, so I head straight there after school, prepared to be Nathan. Something's going on, I can feel it. Someone inside knows something about me. Maybe it's the head Wallin, back from whatever sabbatical he's been on. As I'm walking across the icy parking lot, I imagine Dakota, how she cowers in the doghouse and growls. I might relate to her a little too much.

Waving to front desk lady Jeanie, I breeze into the back room. She calls after me, "How was school, Nathan? Hold on a minute," she calls to me.

A chill spreads over my body. The real Nathan Ashur came in. Jeanie only called me Nathan to give me false confidence, to prove I'm stealing his identity. And now undercover cops will emerge and arrest me for being an imposter.

"We still have some paperwork you need to finish." She

rushes up to me with a clipboard and a pen.

It's an employee sheet asking for specifics about my name, address, employment history, and "Driver's license number? Why would you need that?"

"Actually, we need to keep a copy of it on file. You know, just as proof of identity for your paychecks."

Shit. Paychecks. Why didn't I think of that?

"Hand it over. I can do that right now." She motions with her fingers.

This isn't happening. Not already. I don't want them to have my real name. I don't want to give her my license with the giant F for Female.

She holds her hand out, eyebrows raised.

"Oh, you know what?" I laugh to ease her tension and hopefully my own. "I don't have it with me today."

Her look becomes suspicious.

"Yeah, my dad needed it f—for our car insurance."

Her suspicion doesn't fade. "All right. But bring it next shift or we can't get you your paycheck."

Next shift. Right. Why didn't I tell her I don't have my license yet? That would have been more believable.

When the phone rings and she's distracted, I abandon the clipboard and slink out.

I find the Caring Bridge site on my phone while searching for Nathan Ashur. He must be recovering or—dare I say— dying by now. But this time, there's no article to read; there's only his page that I can't sign into without a code.

Fingers crossed he's still on the mend.

Back in the playroom, the dogs cluster around me, some of them nosing my hand, some of them wagging so hard, their butts wiggle. I trail my fingers through their fur, distracted by the doghouse across the room. Dakota sticks her nose out. I'd like to get closer. But I wait, mixing in with the other dogs.

Once Dakota lays her head on her paws again, I take a few steps in her direction. Then mingle, step. Mingle, step. Soon enough I'm across the room by her little house. I back up until I'm against the side of it, then I slide down to the floor.

I hear her rustling a bit, but I know she doesn't want to be challenged. So I wait, listen. When the rustling stops, I give her a few more minutes, then sneak a peek at her. Slowly. Her eyebrows move as she looks at me. Her mouth is still. I keep my focus there, waiting.

The other dogs stay back, seeming well aware that Dakota wants no one near. I even out my breathing, lay both of my hands to the floor, one just in front of Dakota's doorway.

The longer I sit here, the more I relax. I let myself close my eyes. Something presses down on my hand; my eyes pop open. Hard yet soft at the same time, and a little wet.

Don't move.

Dakota rests her head on me. Her fur is as warm as her mouth is slobbery. But I do nothing. She's never been this close to me.

After a while, my hand prickles as it falls asleep. Still, I can't move it or Dakota will recede into her little home, and I'll have lost her. I lean my head against the hard plastic of the doghouse. Gently, I inch toward her so I can pet her with my unstuck hand. I take my time resting my fingers down on her fur, then slowly stroke the gray, black, and white strands. So soft.

A noise across the room startles me into grasping Dakota's fur momentarily. Surprisingly, she doesn't pull away; she merely opens her rich blue eyes. The door opens and I can hear more than one pair of footsteps.

"Nate, are you in here? I wanted to introduce you to Dr. Wallin."

Oh, no. Not his dad. Not the one who hired Nate Ashur. They're coming toward me. I should get up and get out of here. But Dakota still has my hand trapped.

"There you are," Troy calls when they've come around the corner.

He's with someone in a lab coat and to my immense relief, that person is a woman.

"This is Doctor Julia Wallin." He smiles too much. "My sister. She's a vet here." No surprise she's his sister; they have the same brow, the same chin.

I give her a quiet hello.

"I wanted to talk to you," she says. Her tone is confident, yet her expression is confused. After a considerable pause, she says, "Nate, is it?"

Oh. The confusion is about me. Is that what she wants to talk about?

"How long have you and Dakota been close?" She smiles.

"Just a few days." I keep my voice soothing, quiet.

Nodding, she says, "I need to do a check-up with Dakota. I thought you could help and hold on to her for me."

The numbness in my hand prickles. "Uh . . ." I'm barely keeping this position here without getting my face bitten off.

Troy takes a partial step toward me. "I've been able to get her vitals, but I'd like to have more time to look at how her paws are healing."

I study their faces with their earnest looks, then Dakota's

twitching brows, the way her eyebrow whiskers move minutely up and down. "All right."

Dr. Wallin gives me a handful of dried liver snacks. "Lure her with these."

Dr. Wallin backs out of the room slowly, motioning me to follow. Dakota unpins my hand from the floor, so I pet her shoulder. I expect her to nip at me or move away, but after an initial glance, she sniffs at the treats.

I lay a liver treat on the floor beside her nose. She's not even the least bit suspicious; she inhales it. With a laugh I say, "I guess we can work with that."

My laugh makes her ears fold back for a second, then she sniffs me to reassure herself, tail wagging. Slowly, I get to my feet, offering her another treat. Again, she doesn't hesitate. She trusts me. Inch by inch, liver treat by liver treat, I get Dakota to come out of the doghouse and follow me across the room. When I reach for the door handle to take us into the hallway, she shies back. Another treat changes her mind, and she follows me to exam room one.

Dr. Wallin crouches, opening her hands for Dakota to smell. Dakota stays at my side, though, sniffing, until Dr. Wallin holds out a liver treat, then she wanders over. She doesn't take the treat at first, just sniffs at it.

Dr. Wallin is gentle, takes her time, lets Dakota become accustomed to her before she starts her exam and waves me over. While she sticks a scope in the dog's ear, I pat Dakota's side, gently stroke her fur.

Dr. Wallin checks the other ear, whispering, "Keep doing that."

The rest of the exam moves along easily. Dakota has

relaxed. The doctor comments more than once how much of a difference I'm making, how calm Dakota is with me. As she runs her hands over the dog's shoulders, back, and haunches, continuing over her chest and stomach, she stops, scowls, and presses under the dog's armpit. Dakota cries out like she's been kicked. My arm goes around her body, but I stop before I try to pull her away from the doctor.

"Sorry about that, sweetheart," the doctor says, but she doesn't move her hand. "We're going to have to get a sample of that." She seems to think I know how to respond.

When I don't get the thing she needs for whatever sample she wants, she says, "Can you get—" She points up to the cabinets and talks me to the tool she needs. While she takes whatever sample she needs, she says, "Keep reassuring her."

Dakota whimpers a bit but doesn't growl and doesn't try to bite either of us.

"What are you doing?" I ask.

To answer my question, Dr. Wallin holds up a thin tube with a sharp end as if I'll know what it is. Dr. Wallin scratches Dakota behind the ears. "That wasn't so bad, now, was it?" Then, getting to her feet, she looks me up and down, smiling. "She's a totally different dog with you."

Dakota lies down beside me now that the doctor's leaving her alone.

"I don't think we would have been able to help her if it wasn't for you."

"What's wrong with her?" I nod to the sample in her hand.

"Don't know yet. Best case scenario it's a lipoma and completely harmless. Worst case, it's a tumor."

Chapter 19

WORST CASE IT'S A TUMOR. I can't stop thinking about those words. During weight lifting. During Art. A tumor.

On the blank sheet in front of me, I sketch the back legs of a dog, twirling clumps of fur like Dakota's. Black, gray, and white. Bushy tail. It feels like Christine is watching me.

A tumor doesn't mean certain death. Dogs get tumors all the time. That doesn't mean dogs die all the time.

Christine leans a little closer to me. "That's not Sasha."

The name hits me like a stab in the chest. I didn't think she knew Sasha's name. "It's the dog I want."

"Looks like a wolf." She smiles.

"She's a husky. At the rescue."

She places her hand on my desk, moving even closer to me. "This is really good."

My legs quiver.

She moves the paper closer to her, dipping her head. I can smell the citrusy wonder of her hair. When she lifts her fingers, charcoal prints are left behind.

I can't believe she did that.

"Kayla, I'm so sorry."

I wince. "Just Kay."

She scrunches up her face like leaving her finger prints is a crime I can never forgive.

"It's fine," I say. I try erasing it, but it doesn't fully disappear.

A whispered "sorry" slips past her pursed lips. She tries to work again with her charcoal but glances over to me too frequently.

"What happened to the pastels?" If she had them out today, I'd consider showing her how to use them better, but that feels like betrayal.

She shakes her head. "I wanted to see if Ms. Horvath would tell me I couldn't switch my medium this late in the year."

I laugh. "Like she said to me."

"Exactly. She has a double standard when it comes to girls like you."

Her words sting as they enter my mind. How can she keep saying things like that to me?

"Oh, Kayla, I didn't mean anything by it. You can be whatever kind of girl you want." She lays her hand on my arm, but I pull away.

Whatever she saw that night of the talent show has faded from her memory. Like he was someone she met for a flash, then turned to mist and was gone.

At lunch time, I call to see if I can talk to Troy or his sister. Check on Dakota. Stupid. I've never gotten Troy's cell number, so all I can do is call the rescue's main line.

Jeanie says everyone's busy. Someone'll call me back, but before I can give her my number, she hangs up. Which means now they'll call Nathan Ashur's number and give the update to him. What happens when Nathan doesn't know what they're talking about?

I dial back but it rings and rings. Everyone's busy.

Throughout my next class, I keep imagining how Nathan Ashur will respond to their call. Hard to imagine, though, since I don't know anything about him but his name. Will he be dismissive? Will he be confused? Doesn't really matter as long as he doesn't ask too many questions. Don't ask questions, Nathan.

When passing time comes, I rush to the hall, dialing the rescue. It rings, once. Twice. Three times. The fourth time, Jeanie answers, and gets Troy.

"She didn't tell me, or I would've called you. We don't have the biopsy results yet," Troy says. "I can text you when—oh, here's your number—"

"No. Don't use that number." I rattle off my cell number for him.

"All right." He laughs.

"Will you give me yours?"

He texts: *I'll text when I know something*, and then says it out loud too. "I'll text when I know something."

Maybe I don't want to know. Maybe it's best if I think she's okay.

"Nate? Hang in there. It could be nothing."

Since I took Madi home after the last play, she doesn't mind me picking her up this Friday night. I've already seen the house she's embarrassed by. As I grow closer to her street, my fingers tighten on the steering wheel. Her parents could be home. She warned me. I hate meeting parents, their too-long gazes while they pretend to be happy to meet me, the what-gender-box-can-I-assign-you question forming in their heads.

My cell phone rings, which only happens when it's some spam call, so I ignore it. Then it beeps that I have a voice message. Crap. I'm almost at Madi's house. When it rings again a few seconds later, I answer. "Yeah?" It's Libby.

"Hey, you doing anything tonight?" She sounds bored.

"Actually, yeah."

"Come over and jam with me. We should work on some songs."

"I can't. I'm already doing something." I'm turning onto Madi's block now. Her parents are probably standing at the window waiting to see who this "boy" is that Madi's going out with. This has never happened to me before. I've never gone to pick up a girl at her house and met her parents. My knuckles are white on the wheel.

"Kay? Tell me what's more important than music."

"I'm going to a play with Madi." I think that was a little too loud.

"You just went to a play with Madi."

I say nothing.

"You said next time we could all go."

"I already got the tickets." I lie. I need to hang up. I'm at the driveway.

"You didn't even ask me if I wanted to come. Can't I buy a ticket there?"

"No, you can't buy a ticket there. You can't come. It's a date, Lib."

Now she's quiet.

"I have to go. I'm picking her up."

Not sure if I should pull into the driveway. Is that rude or is it rude not to? I pull into the driveway. I shouldn't honk. Even though it would lessen my anxiety a thousand times over to stay outside until she comes out, I know *that* would be rude. I have to go to the door.

I kill the engine, take a quick breath, and get out of the car before I lose my nerve.

Let Madi be the one to open the door. Let Madi be the one to open the door.

I knock, but it's not Madi in the doorway. It's a woman my mom's age with Madi's dark brown hair and Madi's delicate smile.

Her gaze travels down my body and back up; to her credit, her smile doesn't falter. "You're . . . Kay?" I hear, *You're a boy?*

"It's nice to meet you, Mrs. Sayer." Extend my hand?

Madi's mother stands aside so I can come in. "Nice to meet you too."

Stepping in, I don't see Madi, but the scent of old house surrounds me. It has an odd, comforting feel to it. Though the house seems small, the kitchen I'm in is quite spacious, and clean.

Mrs. Sayer pulls out two chairs at the kitchen table and sits in one, so I take the other. "Madi says you're an artist."

That could mean a lot of things. My drawings. My music. My acting, such as it is. All I say is, "Yeah." Which one do I talk about? If I talk about the wrong one, she might read me as pretentious. If I talk about the right one, I might tell her things she's already heard.

"What kind of art do you do?" Her hands lay in front of her on the table, as if reaching out to me.

"Mostly drawing. Just pencil." I have to say something more than that. She's going to think I'm boring. "Uh, Madi showed me how to work with pastels, so I was thinking I'd branch out a little."

"She's always had a gift with color. Since she was a little girl. She was one of the few kids in her kindergarten class who used all of the colors when she painted."

I move a little in my chair. There's a too-familiar uncomfortableness from down below. I adjust again. It can't be. Not tonight. It's not due for another week.

Hurried footsteps approach. "Sorry, sorry. I got side-tracked." Madi's securing an earring as she enters with a scruffy, sandy-colored dog at her heels. When he sees me, he stops short, eyes wide, two shrill barks erupting from him. Madi startles. "Cooper, it's okay."

Cooper eases over to me, sniffing my pants, then my hand, until I scratch behind his ears. Unlike Dakota, Cooper's fur is wiry, but he's super waggy now that he's judged me. It flashes through my mind that I still haven't heard back about Dakota. I need to call again. Not now.

Cooper moves closer, trying to sniff between my legs a little too eagerly.

Stop.

"He's getting old. He didn't even know you came in," Madi says. She swallows noticeably. "I see you've met my mother."

I adjust in the chair. I need to get to the bathroom ASAP.

"We've been having a nice talk," her mother says.

Madi places a warm hand on my shoulder. "We should get going."

"Right." I get up, and the movement makes it abundantly clear that what I have suspected must be true. I have my period. I can't believe I have to ask this. "Uh, can I use your bathroom before we go?" I really can't wait until we get to the play. Too much could accrue between here and there.

I've always been a heavy bleeder.

Madi points the way and cryptically adds, "My dad'll be home soon."

Not until I'm in their closet of a bathroom do I realize that she's warning me to hurry up. She doesn't want me to have to meet her father. I would be insulted but I don't blame her.

This can't happen today.

I stare into the toilet at the tell-tale redness that proves I've not gotten past my curse of being female. How am I supposed to go back out there? I don't have a pad with me.

I check my boxer briefs and sure enough, a massive dark spot covers the center. How could I not have realized this was happening until now? This much blood must mean—yep. Right through the crotch of my jeans too. It must be the size of a quarter. Is it far enough between my legs not to be noticeable?

Outside the bathroom, I hear Madi talking to her mother, but not what she's saying. The good news is that I can't hear her father. I have to hurry. I don't want to meet him, especially like this.

Blood in the toilet. Blood on my pants.

I unroll wads of toilet paper and blot my jeans and underwear, but very little blood comes up. It's solidified into an odorous gossip, attempting to literally air my dirty laundry.

I sit back down. I can tell already it's going to be heavy this time, but when isn't it. Some girls in gym class used to talk about their periods lasting only four days. I'd give my left pinkie for mine to be that short.

There's a vanity under the sink. Surely, with two women here there must be something I can use. Leaning sideways, I manage to pop the door open. The vanity door thuds against the wall. Shit. I don't need them to know that I'm going into their things.

I hear voices again. Her mom. Madi. I'm pretty sure her mom just asked what was taking me so long.

I have to lean too far off the toilet to peer into the vanity. Cleaning products, extra rolls of toilet paper. Ah, here. Tampons. Nope. Not a chance in hell. There must be some pads in here somewhere. I shove the toilet cleaner aside, check behind the tampon box. Nothing else.

A door closes and I pull my pants up as quickly as I can. But the noise has nothing to do with this door, so I let my pants fall down again. Now I can hear Madi and her mom both at the same time, welcoming her dad home. Shit.

A flurry of movie clips sails through my memory—get away through the bathroom window. I glance at the yellow curtains covering what can't be more than a two-foot-wide escape hatch. Stupid. Even if I could fit through there, I couldn't leave like that. What would Madi think?

I do another pointless check of the vanity, then roll out some toilet paper.

Unrolling more paper, I construct a make-shift pad of as many layers as I can. It'll do fine for a few hours. But there's nothing I can do about my pants.

I clean up the seat with wetted toilet paper, flush the toilet twice just in case, wash my hands with a considerable amount of soap, and slink out of the bathroom.

Though it's silent when I step out, all three voices talk at once when I appear in the kitchen. Not to me. To each other. Madi's dad seems to be about a foot taller than I am, somewhat muscular. He shrugs off his winter jacket revealing a red plaid shirt. His eyes narrow as he sees me, yet his newly ungloved hand wants to shake mine. "Nice to meet you, Kay." His grasp catches the tender web of skin between my thumb and forefinger, pinching.

"K, for Kinkade," I say. I make my voice sound gruff like I'm getting a cold in case there's any chance it sounds too feminine and because the pressure on my hand is severe. I hate guys who shake like that. Like they were taught to show dominance by maiming others through the pretense of social convention.

I try to keep my front to them so no one can possibly see the stain on my jeans.

Cooper noses at my hand. I can't tell if he just wants attention or if despite a thorough washing, some evidence still remains.

"Where do you think you're taking my daughter?"

"Our daughter," her mother adds.

"Dad!" Madi grabs hold of my hand.

I squeeze my legs together. The blood feels like a deluge. "Uh . . . a play. At the community college. For school."

"For school?" He crosses his arms to show me his bulging biceps.

"We have to attend some different kinds of plays." I try to think of the three types Ms. Sands requires, but I'm coming up blank. "Community theater and . . ."

Madi stops me. "I told you this when I went to see Shakespeare."

"Right. That teacher wants you to get some culture." Her dad rolls his eyes.

Madi squeezes my fingers to tell me we should go.

"She wants us to compare different performances." I defend Ms. Sands' idea, though I think I know the takeaway without doing the work.

"Are you a big fan of the theater?" her father asks, accentuating *theater* like he's a Shakespearean thespian.

I glance at Madi. What's the right answer? I think I am a fan of theater, but will he think that's not manly? "It's growing on me."

Madi tugs my hand.

"Are you?" I ask.

Immediately, I regret this. From the look of disgust on his face, I guess I was supposed to stereotype him as a working-class buffoon who doesn't take in culture.

Cooper barks.

"Do I look like I'd go to a play?" He steps forward as if it was an insult, but his arms drop to his sides as he laughs. "The only plays I ever went to were the ones my little girl was in." His face brightens unexpectedly.

"He doesn't need to hear about this." Madi pulls my hand again, but I don't move.

"You've been in plays?"

Madi speaks quickly so no one can answer. "Do you guys have money for my ticket?" Then her face pales.

Now that every ounce of sound has drained from the room, my anxiety grows louder. Her dad lowers his head.

"No, Madi, you must've forgotten. I said I had to get the tickets early." I laugh at how ludicrous it is that she doesn't remember this thing I never told her.

Her fingers tighten on my hand in a thank you.

"What is it you're seeing?" Her mother clears her throat.

"*The Importance of Being Earnest.*" Madi's tone is enthusiastic.

Mrs. Sayer clicks her tongue. "I don't care for that one. Everyone pretending to be something they're not."

Mr. Sayer meets my eyes as if I'll have a response.

"I like it," Madi says. "It's funny." She finally pulls my hand so hard I have to follow.

Now that my back is to them, I pray neither of them gets curious about my pants. They aren't going to look. Why would they look? They aren't going to look.

"Nice to meet you both," I throw over my shoulder. When they don't reciprocate, I assume that means I've read them correctly. They're confused by me as parents always are.

"Be home by eleven." Her dad's words accompany us out the door.

Chapter 20

AT THE DOOR TO THE community center, we find the end of the
ticket line. I'm trying to remember how much money I
have left. Really wish I'd been paid by Wallin Animal Rescue,
but who knows what that will look like. A check for Nathan
Ashur. Do I just fake a signature and deposit it in my own
bank account? Why would Nathan Ashur give Kayla Kinkade
any money? Banks must ask these questions.

We're stuck in limbo, half outside and half in, so we get to
enjoy the last moments of the March day that seems so warm
in contrast to last week. A lot of the snow has started to melt,
and a breeze that wants to be warm brushes against flattened
yellowed grass. Fists jammed in her jacket pockets, Madi
stands too close to me though there's plenty of space. Guess
she doesn't think it's as nice outside as I do. But I don't mind.

"Sorry about my parents," she says, and I can hear her eye
roll in her words.

"You already said that. Three times." I put a hand on her
shoulder. "They're parents." I adjust how I'm standing, overly
aware of the toilet paper I've crammed in my pants.

When the line moves, Madi maneuvers into the vestibule
to get out of the so-called cold.

"I'm sorry," I say. "You haven't met my parents. I should apologize in advance."

She playfully hits me in the chest, making me wonder for too long what it felt like to her. How many guys has she hit in the chest? Did they feel more solid? Nothing registers on her face, though, and she's talking about her parents, how embarrassed she was.

Was she embarrassed by me too? I want to ask, but it's a pitiful question.

When the line moves again, we're all the way inside the community center, though the door remains propped open by those behind us. Scores of couples wait to take a program and enter the auditorium, most of them my parents' age or older. Actually, I don't see anyone our age. No one under thirty, even. Great. Like I need to stand out more than I already do.

Pulling up my jeans a little, I hope to readjust my make-shift protection down below, but it's becoming clear that I need to get to a bathroom soon.

The line moves without my noticing, so Madi gives me a little shove. I stumble. Wait a minute. I could swear that couple there—I think I know—that guy in the yellow jacket is one of my dad's friends.

Shit. He's been to our house a bunch of times. I know his name. It's Steve something. Something really ordinary. Larson. That's Mr. and Mrs. Larson. Why would they be here at a community theater play?

Stepping closer to Madi, I try to block the Larsons' view of me. They're almost to the auditorium doorway when Mr. Larson glances back. I turn away, but I'm sure he saw me.

He knows I'm here. He's going to come over and act all happy to run into me and ask who Madi is and what's new and be all chummy like I'm as much his friend as my father. But then what? Will he call my dad? *I just ran into your daughter at the community center. Is there something you want to tell me?*

What if he calls my name?

We're only two people from the ticket booth now. Cut bait. "Madi, we have to go." I stare at her as intently as I can.

She only smiles. "What for?"

"Uh . . . I forgot my wallet." I know she doesn't have any money, so we'll have no choice. "Let's just come back tomorrow night."

"We can't. I have to work." Her eyes dart across my body until they stop abruptly. She purses her lips. "You're wallet's right there." She pats my jeans pocket where it clearly bulges out.

Flinching away from her too late, I silently curse. "Oh, right. Of course."

There still is the possibility that I haven't brought enough money. But I have.

I look for Mr. Larson in his yellow jacket, but he's gone.

Whether I'm ready or not, we're next up to buy tickets. It's fine. We'll just be sure to sit far away from them. It'll be dark. The Larsons can't possibly see me in the dark.

Madi snatches the tickets from me, then laces her fingers with mine. Swinging our arms, she looks like she's about to skip. I am not skipping.

I spot a second door that leads into the auditorium—one the Larsons didn't use—so I steer Madi that way. This will be safer. They'll be on the other side. Nearing the door, I can see most of the seats already occupied.

Others in front of us obscure my full view, but Madi motions me to follow her. "There are two together over here."

Once others have found seats, I see the ones Madi intends for us. Not bad. Only a few seats in from the end. But, wait. That yellow jacket that man is removing is just like—no way. Madi, no way. I scan the auditorium. There are a few scattered seats, none with two together. A-ha, there in the third row, way on the side.

I grab her hand to stop her. "Let's go sit over there." I point.

Her nose curls in a way that clearly says I'm ridiculous. "It's so far over. These are much better. Look at the view we'll have." She continues toward the Larsons.

"No," I say too loudly.

As if she doesn't hear me, she descends down the ramped aisle straight to my dad's friend. Now she's talking to him, and now he and Mrs. Larson are standing so Madi can get by. An hour passes as I watch this happen, an hour of chaos in my stomach, until I will my feet forward and slip past the Larsons in pursuit of Madi. Mrs. Larson is wearing her usual overly flowery perfume while Mr. Larson clears his throat, which he will likely do continuously throughout the play. I tried to warn you Madi.

Madi takes the seat farther from the Larsons so I can simply sit down. I lean close to her ear. "Can we switch?"

She pulls me down so I'm forced to sit beside Mrs. Larson and her perfume. When I curve my body toward Madi to escape recognition, instant discomfort reminds me that I'd wanted to use the bathroom. And I can't get up now. I'm the one who'd have to ask the Larsons to move so I could get out. Surely, Mrs. Larson would recognize me as fast as her husband. I'm trapped.

To make myself less uncomfortable, I modify my position, which brings me closer to Madi. She thinks I'm flirting and puts a hand on my arm. The brilliance of her smile banishes the Larsons and everything else near us. Why have I never noticed how beautiful she is?

The lights begin to dim before I can think what to do or say. At the same moment a cramp tightens sharply in my gut. I shouldn't do or say anything.

Out of the corner of my eye, I can see Mrs. Larson giving me a look. Please let this be my imagination. Please bring the darkness faster.

Before Mrs. Larson speaks, the lights shut off and the actors come on stage. That doesn't stop her from glancing over at me. She needs to knock it off. I can't turn away any more than I have.

Throughout the first act, I keep my eyes on the stage, but peripherally I'm watching the Larsons. At some point she whispered to her husband; he's leaned forward twice now to see if he recognizes me. The last time they were over for dinner was before the talent show. Before I cut my hair so short. Before I started letting myself dress this way. They might not recognize me.

Everyone around me claps and the stage lights go out. It's over already?

As the auditorium lights come up, I check the other way down our row to see if we can get out, but there must be at least a dozen people still in their seats that way. The Larsons, however, are up. They've even moved into the aisle. Thank

God, they're leaving. It's over.

When Madi stands, she starts talking about one of the actresses. I'm listening, walking backwards. I hardly hear her say "Lady Bracknell," before I'm in the aisle right beside the Larsons. They haven't left.

Mrs. Larson puts her hands on my shoulders like she's going in for a hug. We don't hug. "Kayla, how are you? It's been so long." She hugs me. Her perfume is so intense this close up I barely catch myself before I sneeze.

Mr. Larson pats my head like I'm a puppy. "Your hair is so short," he says, to which Mrs. Larson scowls. She's always seemed more aware. Whether she understands why I've cut my hair like this, she at least understands her husband shouldn't draw unneeded attention to it.

Madi moves up beside me. These people must seem more important to me than they are. Did she hear them call me Kayla?

"Hi, I'm Madi."

Shit. They're going to ask who she is. Why she's here. What we're doing. Shit, shit, shit.

Mrs. Larson introduces herself and says, "You must be a friend of—"

I clear my throat loudly as she says my real name.

Madi's expression stays the same, so it must have worked.

The Larsons and Madi make polite conversation as we all move up the aisle to the door. No questions about her or about us. Yet. Only pleasantries about the actors and the set and how no one can hear Algernon's lines. In the entryway, people are drinking cups of lemonade and eating cookies. The play's not over. It's intermission. Shit.

Mr. Larson gets lemonade for everyone, and here we are standing in an awkward circle, sipping beverages, discussing how funny the play is as if we're on a double date in *The Twilight Zone*.

I try to stay in the conversation enough to keep it from turning to me or to how anyone here knows me, but for the most part, I stare dumbly at them in turn. I'm planning a desperate voyage to the bathroom. I can't imagine the mess this body has made by now. But if I leave them alone together, what will they talk about?

Over the intercom comes the theme music to tell us to return. I can't believe my dumb luck: No one has given me away. Not Madi saying I'm her boyfriend. Not the Larsons saying, *We know* her *father*. As I finish my lemonade and Mrs. Larson insists on taking my cup, her husband says, "Well, ladies, we better get back to our seats."

Heat creeps up my face. He just lumped me in with the women. As simple as that. My cheek stings like he's slapped me. Ladies.

But Madi doesn't understand he means all of us, thank God.

When the Larsons move ahead of us toward the auditorium, Madi takes hold of my hand. Her skin feels cool in my sweaty palm, but I let go, faking an itch on the back of my neck that must be scratched. She can't hold my hand right now. Once the Larsons are out of earshot, I lean towards her. "Can we please sit anywhere else?"

Madi laughs, then cocks an eyebrow. "You're serious? What's the matter?"

"We'd be able to hear Algernon better if we moved closer to the front." It's as good a reason as any, and certainly far better than saying the Larsons are going to give away my secret, and then the jig is up. Or even saying I don't like them when they've been nothing but nice to us.

"I don't want to be rude." She grabs my hand and hurries me down the aisle to our row. I'm barely able to get my hand free when we're passing the Larsons to get to our seats.

The discomfort of sitting again conjures up images of vast red stains drenching my pants as if I've been gutted. How huge is the stain now? I need to get to the bathroom.

How long until this is over? I page through the photocopied program.

This can't be right. What play has two intermissions? "Act One. Intermission. Act Two. Intermission. Act Three." They've got to be kidding.

Calm down. Just wait until intermission two. Go then.

Act Two is torture. Between denying Madi's attempts to touch my knee and play with my fingers, and stewing in my expanding humiliation between my legs, intermission two arrives too late. Through the applause and the change in lighting, I'm poised to spring up, but it doesn't matter; I have to wait for the Larsons to move first, and then I have to announce where I'm going to all of them. Otherwise, there will be a chorus of *Do you know where* she *went? No, I don't know where* he *went.* And that will be the end of my charade.

When the four of us reach the entryway again, I make my announcement. The response is nothing I was prepared for. Mrs. Larson says, "Let's all go."

No, no, no. Not the girl trip to the bathroom. I should have slipped away when I had the chance.

Mr. Larson chimes in, "I'm in," which his wife and Madi find hilarious.

All four of us move toward the restrooms, weaving through the other play-goers, all heading the same way. Each step delivers a seeming deluge from between my legs, and each step suggests a new tactic. Use the women's room and come clean with Madi. Use the men's room and hope the Larsons go with it. Say you don't need to go anymore. Abandon Madi and drive home.

By the time I need to decide, I still hesitate. Madi and Mrs. Larson pair off from Mr. Larson, each headed for the corresponding restroom. I have to ditch them all. I don't correspond.

I'm moving against the flow of the other play-goers now, heading I don't know where. Around to the side of the auditorium and down the hall, I find a custodial area. Sometimes there are hidden bathrooms in places like this, in the dregs of a building. After a number of turns, I've gotten turned around, but I find what I was looking for: a room with a single sink and toilet. I lock the door and get down to business.

The anticipated reveal does not disappoint. It is a royal mess. And naturally, there is nothing available to staunch the flow but another wad of toilet paper. The whole ordeal takes me much longer than the allotted intermission time, I'm sure, but being so far away from the auditorium, I don't know if the return-to-your-seat music has played or not.

Once I've gotten rid of all the evidence and washed my hands, I hurry back down the hallways, but again, I get turned around. I only have a general sense of which direction I should go as it is, and now, every hall looks the same.

I begin to jog. I have to get back to them before they talk

about where I am, before someone reveals to someone that I'm not who I say I am. But where is the entryway where we drank our lemonade? Where is the auditorium where I should be sitting between Madi and Mrs. Larson? At least when I was there, I had a tiny degree of control over this mess. Now . . .

I see an illuminated exit sign. Once I've reached the door, I go outside into the much colder air. Even with my leather jacket on, I'm freezing. I get my bearings and circle around to the front door, out of breath.

Moments later, I'm walking through the emptied entryway, straining to control my breathing. The auditorium door releases a miniscule squeak as I open it, but a second later the crowd laughs; my entrance has gone unnoticed. Maybe I should crouch down so I don't block people's view, but I remind myself that a man who's late has a good reason for being late and doesn't need to act apologetic. A teenage girl should be apologetic, but not a man.

Mr. Larson is startled to see me. Both he and Mrs. Larson stand so I can get past. Mrs. Larson whispers, "We were worried about you."

I give her a courtesy smile. Sitting down beside Madi, I quietly tell her, "Sorry."

Her response is a lingering stare.

What? What happened while I was gone?

The audience laughs again. Frankly, I have no clue what this play is about or why anything that's happening is even mildly amusing.

By curtain call, the audience seems to have exhausted themselves with the hilarity in front of them. Everyone but me and Madi. She is clearly unamused, but it has nothing to do with *The Importance of Being Earnest.*

Out in the parking lot, we say goodbye to the Larsons. "Nice to meet you." "So strange to run into you here." Madi, slipping on her mittens, is all smiles and compliments until they walk away. Then I'm left with her silence and the coldness of the night air to accompany me to my car.

I wish she would say something.

She takes off her mittens, sighs to herself, then puts them back on.

We've driven half way to her place before she speaks. "Where did you go?"

I don't want to answer that.

"I was getting worried." She doesn't look at me but fidgets with her mittens.

"I just got lost."

"I texted you like twenty times."

Shit. I silenced my phone for the play.

"Nobody knew what to say. I mean, they don't know me. I don't know them. We didn't know where you were or if you were coming back." She removes the mittens and slaps them down on her thigh.

I laugh. Absurd. Of course, I was coming back. But then, I did consider leaving momentarily. I try to suck the laugh back in, but it's too late.

Madi glares at me. "I don't understand you," she says.

"It's not that big of a deal." I have to stop the car when the light ahead of us turns red.

"Are you kidding me?" Her voice goes up an octave. She stops glaring and starts shifting around, gathering her mittens. A second later her car door opens and she's getting out.

"What are you doing?" I reach over like I'm going to pull her back in the car.

Leaning back into the car, she locks eyes with me. "When we saw *Twelfth Night*, I thought you were this amazing guy who listened to me and liked going to the theater. Then at school you're all standoffish and silent, like you think being an asshole makes you cool." She bites her lip. "And tonight? You disappear without any explanation, leaving me with that couple who clearly don't know you're trans—"

"Wait. What?"

"And what should I do? Out you? Maybe you don't want them to know. And now . . ." She trails off. "You can't even respect me enough to tell me what happened."

She knows? Why didn't she tell me she knows? My skin freezes over inch by inch.

She waits like I'm going to say something, but I only stare. And freeze.

Finally, when it's clear I'm not going to stop her, she shakes her head, slams the door, and storms off.

Chapter 21

BEFORE I KNOW WHERE I'M going, I find myself in the parking lot of the animal rescue. It's after 10:00 on Friday night. I'm not sure what I'm thinking.

I thought I'd fooled Madi into thinking I was male, but I didn't, and I'm probably not fooling anyone else either. Maybe I should be relieved I don't have to explain myself to her, but I thought just once, someone had seen me for the person I am inside.

No one will be at the animal rescue this late. Still, I get out of my car and go to the door. Peering inside, I see a few lights are on. Night staff. They always keep a few people on overnight in case there's an incident. Dog emergency.

I need to see Dakota.

I don't have my work badge with me or I could get in the back door. Wish I knew where it was. My face. Nathan's name. It better turn up before someone like JT finds it.

I knock on the glass of the front door and wait to see if anyone pops their head out. I knock a few more times, but no one comes. Around back, I try the same approach. I knock a few times. Wait. After the fourth time, someone calls out, "Who's there?"

I don't recognize the voice, so they likely won't recognize mine either. "It's Nate Ashur. I work with Troy."

When there's no response, I continue, "I was hoping to stop in to see Dakota." Then I add, "Just for a few minutes."

The door opens. It's a young woman with dark hair. "Troy didn't say you were coming by."

I laugh and then I lie. "That's weird. He said he would."

"Why didn't you just buzz yourself in?"

"Forgot my ID at home." I put my hand on the door, hoping she'll move inside. "I just want a few minutes."

She backs in. "I guess that won't hurt anything."

Once she's out of the way, I head to the playroom and Dakota's doghouse. Her gray and white feet rest sweetly under her chin. All around her, the protective walls of the doghouse secure her from whatever could come at her.

When I'm a few steps in the door, Dakota's head darts up, searching. Then she sees me and puts her head down again. Though I get closer, she doesn't get agitated; she watches me, eyebrows twitching, but doesn't move. Reaching her doghouse, I take a seat outside her doorway. If there was room, I'd go in there with her, escape this torturous human realm, bury my face in her fur.

The woman who let me in has followed me here. She lingers by the door. "You're the kid Dakota likes." She comes a few steps toward me until Dakota raises her head. Then she stops as if the dog is a giant anaconda about to ensnare her. "Stay as long as you want." With a small wave, she leaves us alone.

Dakota lays her head back down.

"You sure have a reputation." I rest my head back, closing my eyes.

Dakota grumbles as if to tell me her reputation has been well earned.

I've only had my eyes closed a few minutes when she wiggles herself out of the doghouse and leans her head and shoulder against my leg. Hard. If she were a person, I'd make her move. But she's not, so I wouldn't dream of it.

Keeping my voice low, I tell her all about the evening. Madi's parents, the play, paying for the tickets, the Larsons. Everything. She doesn't judge, only listens. I even tell her about the bathroom and how uncomfortable I was. When I raise my voice a little, she rubs her head against me, I understand. Her pink tongue goes out and in a few times.

"She acted like she liked me." I set my hand down on Dakota's shoulder, winding my fingers through her fur. "She treated me like me." I pet her over and over. "Why didn't she say she knew?"

Dakota grumbles again.

I sigh. "Forget it." I close my eyes. "It'll never be like that again."

Dakota snuffles in protest. I suppose to a dog, I seem like quite a catch. I make her feel safe and loved. I talk to her. But she doesn't understand what it's like to be a person. Why would Madi say that to me? I think being an asshole is cool?

"I'll be that old guy with the run-down house and too many dogs."

Dakota sits up and licks my face; she knows my pain.

Draping my arm around her, I bury my face in her fur, and for a moment, I only focus on the softness and warmth. Then I hear the door open. And Troy's voice, "Nate, hey."

Shit. That night lady must've called him. Through Dakota's fur, I say, "Hey," back to him.

Once he's beside me, he lets Dakota sniff him and takes a seat on the floor next to me, not next to the dog. He knows better.

As he speaks to me, his voice grows softer. "Did she tell you? I knew I should have called you back, but I got tied up with some things and . . ." He stops. "I didn't want to be the one who had to say it."

It's not until I erase Madi from my thoughts that I understand what he's talking about. He knows what's going to happen to Dakota. "She didn't tell me."

He cringes, swearing under his breath. "I wish it were better news."

I run my hand down Dakota's chest over the lump I know is there. Doesn't feel life-threatening to me. Troy tells me that the tumor is cancerous. Don't let him say that they can't remove it, there's nothing that can be done. I put my face back into her fur and let myself cry.

He speaks. "The tumor's close to her heart and lungs. I don't know if it will help to operate."

"What if I pay for it?" I don't have any idea what a veterinary surgery costs, but I'll come up with it. Dakota doesn't have anyone to help her. It's got to be me.

"It's not the cost." He stretches sore muscles in his neck. "It's about what's best for Dakota."

"What kind of an animal rescue doesn't rescue an animal when it needs them to?"

Dakota's ears perk up.

Troy's eyes say I've just told Dakota his secret. "It's not

about wanting to help her or not help her." Getting to his feet, he grabs my arm and pulls me up. "Come with me."

Dakota's nails click on the floor behind us as we go into one of the exam rooms. She brushes her head under my hand as we go.

Troy turns on all the lights including one on the wall: a light box that's holding two x-rays. "My sister did these earlier today." He traces his finger along a shadow, which I assume is the tumor. "This is the problem. It's so close to Dakota's heart."

"But she has to try." My fist pulls Dakota's fur too tightly.

Troy sighs. "She's going to. The operation will be next week."

Chapter 22

IT FIGURES. DAKOTA HAS A tumor that's threatening her life. The dog that I want, the one I love. Nothing in my life can ever be easy. Why did I let myself get so attached?

I could say the same thing about Madi.

I saw her earlier. Didn't speak to her. Didn't look at her. Not really. Skipped lunch and sat in the library. While I'm pretty sure she skipped too, and Libby had to eat with Everett and Aniyah, I didn't want to take a chance of facing her.

But Drama class could be a whole different thing. I go to my normal seat.

Madi arrives not long after. She joins a junior girl with blue hair and a beanie-wearing boy near the front. This is her new group? She's going to do her scene with them? I watch her tuck her hair behind her ear.

No problem. She can do that. I don't care. I'll find a monologue and blow everyone away. I'll memorize some Shakespeare. Something meaningful and complicated. Something that will make her see how awesome I am.

After class, I try to catch up to her. Not to talk to her. Just to make sure she doesn't have anything to say. I'm mere feet away for the length of the senior hallway and never once does she even look in my direction. Now who's the one that thinks being an asshole is cool?

Madi may not want to talk to me, but Libby sure does. She's texted me all day about a new song she wants to do for prom auditions. Cyndi Lauper. I've said no. Still she wants to meet and talk about it. Since the sun is shining, we meet outside by the tree we like near the student lot.

Libby has her drumsticks with her, her mom's jean jacket with the frayed cuffs. I drop my over-weighted bag beside the tree as she starts in on her idea. The same things she's already told me.

I stop her. "I can't sing Cyndi Lauper. I don't want to sound that . . . feminine."

"No, no. You could sing it in a different key." She taps out what I assume to be the drum part of "Time After Time" against the tree bark.

"We've got plenty of songs already."

She considers that for only a second, still drumming. "So what? Wait till you hear the drums for real!"

I catch myself before I roll my eyes. "If you're looking for more songs, Lib, you can't choose ones that are only good for drums."

She stops tapping and shakes a tight dark curl from her shoulder. "Let's go rehearse. The audition's in one week."

Libby, Gene, and I go to their basement and spend the next bunch of hours playing the songs on the list. That's not quite accurate. There are so many I don't want to play that we only end up covering Cyndi Lauper's "Time After Time"—Libby's right, it's a good one—and Aerosmith's "Don't Wanna Miss a Thing," plus a few others. Libby's done a ton of research about popular prom songs.

Gene speaks up, "If you're looking for more songs, why don't we try something amazing." He holds out the edges of his t-shirt so we can read better. He didn't need to—it's only five letters: QUEEN. I'm about to tell him he's brave to wear something that labels him so obviously, but I don't know if Gene is gay or straight, and I don't want him thinking I'd make fun of that.

Libby considers his suggestion. "I don't know. Most of their songs are fairly eclectic."

"Maybe, but there aren't many I really like," I add.

Gene scoffs. "You have to be kidding."

"No. I think the only one that really works for me is the one with Bowie, and that's probably only because of Bowie."

"You mean 'Under Pressure,'" Libby says. She scats the first couple of lines in an awful impression of Freddie Mercury.

I cut her off, "Yeah, and we can't do that song. We'd need another vocalist."

Gene clears his throat and redoes the opening Libby just botched. He continues into the first verse, beginning to pluck along on the bass.

He's left the Bowie part open for me, so I step in, strumming simple chords I can make out from the melody.

Libby thumps the bass drum then strikes the snare, and she's matching our rhythm by the chorus.

We get through the whole song without missing a lyric, and we end by snapping in sync, just like the original.

For a few moments, we sit in silence looking at each other.

Then Gene says, "See."

And Libby says, "That worked."

And I say, "It's on the set list," as a final decision, all the while feeling elated that I get to sing a Bowie song.

I hear Uncle Doug on the stairs tapping his feet as we play. He yells down, "Let me know when you get to a good tambourine number. I'll come give you a hand."

I'm pretty sure he's kidding. Libby rolls her eyes.

Gene calls back to him, "Not necessary, Dad."

I strum an A-minor chord and my amplifier crackles, distorting the sound. "The rest of these suck."

"Not even a little." She pounds out the drum opening to "Dance, Dance" by Fall Out Boy, and I let her keep playing.

Gene keeps up with Libby beat for beat, effortlessly finding the notes on his bass.

Even though this song is one I like, I'm still thinking I don't want to play different kinds of music. I want to play my music. I wave my arms until she stops drumming.

"I'll make you a deal," I say. "I'll play any of the songs on the list—all of the songs on the list—if we play five of my songs too. At prom."

"One," she says.

I flip her off. "Whose side are you on?"

"Yours, but do you think anyone wants to dance to music they don't know?"

"At one point every song was unknown." I raise my eyebrows like I'm being profound.

"Two," she says. "That's my final offer."

Gene raises his eyebrows at us. "Don't I get a say in this?"

Libby and I both silence him. "No."

"Why not?"

Libby points with her drumstick. "When you can drive, you can have a vote."

I aim for her Achilles' heel. "I don't think Bekkah will tell her dad about us unless she hears something original."

She crosses her arms.

"You can choose which songs of mine we play," I offer.

"Just because you want something doesn't mean you get it," she says.

I fight her for three, but it's clear Libby is not going to give in.

Only, about ten minutes later when I slip up on the lyrics to "Dance, Dance," she doesn't start drumming again right away. "Do you really think Bekkah won't tell her dad . . ." She trails off. I haven't seen her look this sad since she lost her mom's jean jacket. Near devastation, even though we found it an hour later.

"We could do three original songs," I suggest.

She taps on the high hat as she considers. "Naw. I think two is enough."

There's no fighting her. We've agreed. I'll play prom music, and she'll play my music. And no matter who the girl of my dreams has come with, she won't be able to keep herself from falling in love with my voice, my lyrics, my music. I'll meet up with her after prom, and she'll agree to go out with me.

When I gaze at Christine in my daydream and follow the curve of her shoulder to her neck, her hair is no longer long and sandy brown; it's a dark brown bob that she tucks behind her ear. And when she laughs and peers over at me, her hazel eyes turn light blue. Madi. I take her hand and lead her down by the lake where we sit in the sand. I make her smile, hold her hand. And as I stare deeply into her newly blue eyes, she stares back into mine until she finds the real me there.

That night, trying to fall asleep, I alternate between imagining Madi's tender fingers crushing yellow and blue pastels into green and imagining auditioning in front of the Student Council. I didn't get enough details from Libby, but if the whole council is there, what is that, twenty people? Will their faculty advisor be there? Will the principal? I'm able to tie my mind up into a mammoth ball of tension by morning. This will be the audition of my lifetime. I need to do this right.

At school the next day, it occurs to me in every class that I don't know who's on the Student Council. I look over all of the smart, preppy people each hour, scrutinizing them to see how likely it is they're in the group and how likely they'd be to give me and Libby the okay. Sitting beside Christine in art, I realize, for all I know, she's on the Student Council. But no. I went through last year's yearbook to see what activities she does. Only volleyball and track.

As I watch her, Christine's fingers smooth out a tree trunk. She's a genius in black and white, but the lack of color can't hold my attention. Still, I know if she was on Student Council, she'd vote for us for sure.

Over by Libby, a tight-lipped Madi stays tensed over her desk the whole hour. One time, when she sits up straight, I think I'll go over to her. But I don't. I can't believe she said I'm an asshole. Anyway, it's not like I could help how long it took me in the bathroom. So what if things were awkward between her and the Larsons? That's not my fault. I can't possibly tell her why I was gone so long.

She didn't have to leave like that.

Drama at the end of the day is a repeat of yesterday. I don't care. Let her work with those stupid people. I've found a decent monologue to do from *Macbeth*. I'll get a fake dagger and some kind of cloak and do it right. Madi'll wish she'd stuck with me. Instead, she's probably got a super small role in the stupid people's scene and will end up failing. I want to smile at that, but it doesn't make me happy.

Heading to my car, the refreshing air on this April day reminds me that it's only a few months until graduation. No more high school. No more JT.

In my car and backing out, I brake for a couple sophomores staring at their phones. As I watch them getting into an SUV, I see Madi carrying her gray winter coat with the missing buttons and her backpack. My skin prickles.

She's holding hands with Hunter Vetrelec. JT's friend.

What. The. Fuck.

They don't see me. Not even when another car honks at me to get out of the way. They simply walk to Hunter's car together and get in. Madi?

Where is he taking her? Why would she get in his car?

I should follow them. But that's ridiculous. I hate her. And I hate her more now that she's hanging with Hunter.

And I have to get to work. My route to Wallin Animal Rescue is cemented in my brain, which is good because after seeing Madi with the enemy, I can't think straight.

The collar of my shirt suddenly feels too tight. I swallow

over and over.

Suck it up. Don't be a baby.

Inside, Jeanie's on the phone, but she covers the mouthpiece. "Nate, did you remember your license?"

Shit. Shit. Shit. I stutter instead of saying no.

She shakes a finger at me. "We can't get you a paycheck until you do."

"I'll get it. I will." I hurry into the back room, punch my time card.

No one else is back here, so I stand still for a minute. My head is spinning. Jeanie and my license. Madi and Hunter. Libby and prom songs. Dakota and her tumor.

I need to see my dog. I whirl around and slam straight into someone. I hear her breath knocked out as much as my own and a clipboard clatters to the floor.

Dr. Julia Wallin. That's just great. At least it's not her father.

"I'm so sorry. I didn't see you." I pick up her clipboard that has fallen to the floor.

She takes it with a slight recovery grunt. She laughs, then sobers and touches my arm. "Troy said we should talk about Dakota."

Rushing fills my ears. I'm not ready. "Right. Okay."

"Should we . . ." She looks toward the exam rooms. ". . . go somewhere else?"

"This is fine."

"The surgery." Her eyes soften. "It's dangerous. I'm not sure it's worth the risk."

I lose my voice, feeling energy draining from me. Dakota could die. I knew that.

"I know Troy showed you the x-ray. The tumor——" She

stops herself.

I can't keep the tears from filling my eyes.

Dr. Wallin's shoulders sink. "You need to try to come to terms with this. Spend her last few weeks together. Just in case."

"Weeks?"

"It's so close to her heart. You should spend as much time with her as you can."

In the playroom, I sit beside Dakota's doghouse, wanting so much to crawl inside with her. Soon enough, she comes out, circling a few times before lying down with her shoulder against my leg, head in my lap. I slide my fingers through her fur and rub her soft ears. When tears come to my eyes, I let myself sob until I slump over, burying my face in her side. I can't think of how anything will ever be good again.

Chapter 23

WHEN I GET HOME AFTER ten, Mom and Dad have left a few lights on for me. I told them I've been working at Wallin's Animal Rescue. Mom thinks working there will take care of my need to get a dog, but Dad knows better. I can hear them upstairs getting ready for bed. I'm sure they'd like me to do the same. Honestly, sleep is the only thing that could possibly bring me any solace.

At the top of the stairs, I see a light on in my bedroom. That's not right. What have I done that Mom needs to wait up for me? I run through the last few days in my head. I can't think of anything that I might have done that would come up on her radar. Must be something serious or she'd be happily ignoring me.

Better go face it.

Inside my bedroom on the edge of my bed sits my father, not my mother. He's in a T-shirt and pajama pants, staring at his hands.

"Dad?"

His smile says he's sincerely glad to see me.

"Is something wrong?" I slide my arms out of my leather jacket. "Oh, God, is it Sam? Please tell me nothing's wrong with Sam." College is too much pressure. I couldn't handle it if anything happened to him.

"Nothing's wrong with Sam."

I sit down on the bed beside him. "Okay." There must be something. This is not normal behavior for him. Some horrible thing has happened, and he has to break it to me gently?

He moves something from hand to hand. A white card of some type.

No. It can't be.

He holds it still so I can see it clearly. And it is. It's my ID badge from Wallin Animal Rescue. My picture. Nathan Ashur's name.

Dad waves it a little. "I found this in your jeans pocket when I ran a load of laundry."

I close my eyes to close out this conversation. I don't want him to find out this way. I haven't had time to really solidify my coming out speech for him.

He puts the card in my hand.

How do I tell him his little princess is a little prince? How do I tell him I'm not Daddy's girl anymore? It will break his heart.

"Dad, I . . ." The words are on my lips: I can explain. But the problem is, I don't know how well I can explain. How much does he know about being trans? I've never heard him say anything. He's always seemed supportive of gay marriage and equal rights in general. Believe me, I've been paying attention. But specifically about transgender issues? Not a clue.

His arm moves around my shoulder as he pulls me close to him and kisses the top of my head. "I love you, sweetheart."

With a slight pat of his hand, the warmth of his arm disappears, and he leaves me there with the stupid card in my hand and nothing explained.

Why didn't he ask any questions?

In the morning, Dad's in such a rush he can't take a minute for breakfast. He grabs coffee and a banana, and he's gone, though he does make a point of stopping to hug my shoulders and kiss my head again.

What is he doing? Doesn't he want to talk?

Of course, I could be brave enough to talk to him about it, but I'm not. I'm not ready.

Chapter 24

THE WEEK PASSES WITH DAKOTA still in danger and Madi still ignoring me, though I haven't seen her with Hunter again. I leave school every day and go straight to Wallin Animal Rescue to be with Dakota, not knowing how much time she has left.

Saturday, I plan to spend the entire day with her, so I arrive at Wallin Animal Rescue early in the morning. Grabbing a few clean blankets from the shelf in the playroom, I make a cozy nest outside of Dakota's doghouse, settling myself comfortably into the softness. Dakota lifts her head, nose working, then a full body stretch gets her to her feet. Only a second later she has curled up beside me, shoulder pressing against my leg. The sigh she releases fills the room.

For a while, I let my hand lay on her shoulder without moving. Then my fingers weave into her fur. She's so calm beside me.

My jeans' pocket vibrates. Cell phone. The double tone sounds for received text.

Dakota's ears go back, a low growl drifting from her closed mouth.

Who could be texting me? Doesn't matter. They can wait. I'm busy.

I pet her in long strokes, breathing deeply and overly

loudly to calm her. She lets out short bursts of air, settling down but not certain.

Closing my eyes, I keep my breaths even. Breathe. Relax. Long strokes down her side.

My phone vibrates and pings its tone again.

Dakota shuffles her front feet and growls a bit louder.

"I know. Annoying." Whoever is texting me needs to stop. Sliding the phone from my pocket, I click into settings: mute. But I can't help seeing who has texted. Madi. What could she want? I mean, I don't care what she wants.

I shove the phone back in my pocket.

Maybe she wants to say she was wrong. I'm not an asshole. Maybe she wants to say that she's going out with Hunter so we can sabotage JT in some way.

Never mind. I don't care.

The phone vibrates a third time, but no tone. Leave me alone, Madi. Dakota's ears go back, and she delivers another deep growl. She needs to calm down. How will she adjust to my parents if she can't adjust to my cell phone?

Then the phone vibrates a fourth time, but doesn't stop. She's calling me? Dakota's head is up, teeth just visible behind quivering lips.

I drag my phone out and reject the call, but it's too late: Dakota is on all fours and returning to the doghouse.

Caller ID: Madi. Thanks a bunch.

Not even a minute later, the phone vibrates again.

Dakota is so far in the doghouse I can't see one hair on her body. "There's nothing to be afraid of," I tell her. The dog will never find a home with anyone if she can't stand a few phone calls.

What could Madi possibly want from me? I answer. "What?"

"Kay?" She's crying. "I don't know what to do."

"What's wrong?"

"It's Cooper." She sniffs. "We were at the park, and he——" She sobs. "He's hurt. He cut himself on something."

"So take him to the vet." I would hang up right now, only I can't.

Another muffled sob. "I don't have any money."

I knew that. I shouldn't have made her say that. "I don't have money either——" If I'd only brought in my driver's license, maybe I'd have a paycheck. Probing questions, but a paycheck.

"Is there anyone there—at the rescue—who can help him?"

I gaze around the room at a dozen dog faces. None of them are going to be able to handle this kind of emergency.

"Please, Kay, I can't stop the bleeding." Her voice breaks.

Rushing out of the back room, I find Troy up front, talking with Jeanie. He meets my eyes, sees the phone, excuses himself. With a hand on my shoulder, he leads me back to the playroom again.

"My friend's dog is hurt."

Troy doesn't understand what I'm saying, so I explain it all. Maybe I emphasize Madi's lack of money too much, but I don't have a choice. He dials his sister. "I'll get her to come back in. Tell your friend to bring the dog here."

I get back on the line with Madi. "All right. We've got it figured out. Bring Cooper in."

Silence.

"Madi, are you there?"

She clears her throat. "I don't have a car. And the bus doesn't allow dogs."

Seriously? "I'll come get you."

On the drive to Madi's house, I imagine Cooper with a giant gash from his eye, down his side, all the way to his tail. I so hope it's not that bad.

I remember the exact way to her house, pulling into the driveway, which is thankfully empty of cars so her parents aren't here. Standing in a silver puddle of melted snow, Madi cradles the terrier in a towel, spots of blood seeping through where her fingers hold him. I throw open the car door and rush to her, holding out my arms like I'll take the dog from her. I shouldn't.

His injuries are not evident on his face, but the bloody towel and the heartbreaking little sounds he's making clearly broadcast his pain.

Madi's eyes, reddened and wet, assess me as if I'm part predator, part savior. Whatever. I'm here for the dog. Reaching out, I nearly put an arm around her to guide her to the car before I pull back. "Get in."

Once she's seated and Cooper is secure, I close the passenger door on her, dash around, and squeal out of the driveway.

Cooper cries out. "I'm sorry, baby." Madi adjusts how she's holding him.

"What happened?"

She sniffles. "He was chasing a rabbit, and there's a fence in the park . . ." Through tears she describes a chain-link fence in need of repair and a baby rabbit with a death wish, though the only one who was actually hurt was Cooper. She whispers to him again, "I'm so sorry."

"How deep is it?"

She can't stop crying. It's so intense, she can't answer.

"All right. We'll be there in just a few minutes." I grope around in my back seat for the blankets I took from the rescue and hand her one. "Put this around him too."

When she takes the blanket from me, her hand grasps mine accidentally before she can get ahold of it how she wants. I wait for her to cringe. She doesn't.

Once we arrive at the rescue, I park in a non-spot and meet Troy as he's coming out to the car. He has a wheeled gurney we use for accident victims that he takes to Madi. Opening her door, Troy deftly takes the blanket, towel, and dog from her, placing all three on the gurney and putting pressure instinctively on the bloody part of the towel. "My sister's all ready for him." He moves the gurney with care into the building, down the hallway, and into one of the exam rooms.

Madi's right beside him, trying to keep her hands on her dog. Troy's elbow gently suggests she needs to give him space as he removes the blanket, so reddened with Cooper's blood. Cooper whimpers, unsure where he is, who Troy is, how much longer this will hurt.

Only seconds later, Dr. Julia Wallin comes in, stethoscope swaying. She checks Cooper's eyes, caressing his head and ears to calm him. "Hang on, little guy." She lays her hands on the towel still across Cooper's body, bloody splotches distressingly larger than before. Gently, she lifts it, exposing tan fur matted together with blood. So much blood.

As Cooper begins to cry with each breath, Madi weeps, wrapping her arms around her dog's head. Dr. Wallin grabs one of Madi's hands. "You're going to have to back up."

I touch her shoulder, ready to pull her back if I need to, but she folds herself into me, sobbing. Her body is so soft and her hair smells so good.

Snap out of it.

She hugs me tightly, so I reassure her. When Sasha was dying, I would have given anything for someone to tell me they understood how awful it was.

With a hard swallow, I whisper to her, "I'm so sorry this is happening."

Dr. Wallin is telling Troy to get some supplies. "I can't see the wound well enough. We're going to have to get some of this blood out of the way."

Troy gets irrigation bottles and some gauze, but not long after he has begun to clear the blood away, I have to step in to help. There's so much blood.

Dr. Wallin holds several gauze pads against Cooper's side and says, "We're going to have to sedate him."

Madi's eyes go wide. "But I can't . . ."

I shake my head at her.

Troy readies a syringe. "You need to take her out of here."

Though he hasn't looked at me, I know he means me. I herd her out the door, leading her down the hall to the quiet waiting area. I slide a few dollars into the pop machine and get us each a Diet Coke. When I hand one to her, she pulls her sleeve cuffs over her hands to protect herself from the cold. Steering her toward a chair, I take the seat beside her.

There's nothing to say. Nothing makes this easier. After

she's drunk half the bottle of Coke, she lets out a huge sigh. Guess that's good. But her breath comes quickly, panicky. The next twenty minutes pass like the time I first told my mom I was trans: quiet, awkward, uncertain. I don't know what to say to Madi when I've told her I know how awful this is. I hate that it hurts her so much, but then I remember she was holding hands with Hunter.

I'm only doing this for the dog.

The sky is growing darker when Dr. Wallin finally comes back to give us news. Her face is grim. She sits beside Madi, leaning toward her as if they've become friends. "All right, Madi. It's good news. We have him stitched up. We've gotten some blood and fluids into him."

A tear falls down Madi's face.

"Right now he's resting." She pats Madi's hand. "He's going to be fine. We'll need to get more fluids in him and watch him for a while."

Madi smiles, but tears still fall down her cheeks.

"You'll be able to take him home this evening." Dr. Wallin clutches her stethoscope as she stands.

Madi stands with her, grasping the doctor's hand. "Thank you so much."

"You're welcome." Dr. Wallin nods at me. "You should thank Nathan too."

Shit.

Madi's face goes blank, her lips forming the name.

Heat rushes to my cheeks. Don't correct her. Don't correct her.

Miraculously, she says nothing. Not until she and I are alone again in the waiting room.

"Nathan?"

Chapter 25

I CAN HEAR THE FAR-OFF BARKING of one of the dogs in the playroom while Madi chews on my Wallin Animal Rescue name. Her expression is impossible to read. "I didn't know that was your name."

The tension in my tightly gripped shoulders wavers, unsure it should subside. I don't want to tell her I haven't decided on my name yet. And all the K-names have been so unsatisfactory. Might as well make this one mine. "I prefer Nate."

One little nod. She slinks down in the waiting room chair, folding her hands on her stomach, eyes closing. I guess she has the right idea since we have to wait a few hours. I slouch in my seat too. It's not long before she's asking me my impression of our most recent AP Lit book *Great Expectations* and what I think Ms. Horvath's issue is with my art project.

It's been more than forty-five minutes when she pops up suddenly. "You don't have to stay with me."

"I know." Truth is, I forgot I was mad at her. Talking about books and art with her after thinking she'd never even meet my eyes again has stirred up a crazy bit of hope that she might love me the way I love her.

My stomach clenches, like I have to hold something in that's trying to get out. Why did I just think that? No, no, no, no, no. I don't love her. I love Christine. Christine is going to accept my offer someday soon. We'll go out to Emerald Isle Pizza and have pepperoni. Then maybe we could go to a play together.

Christine and a play. What am I thinking?

I pretend I'm not staring at the slope of Madi's neck as it ducks under the collar of her sweater. I don't see the corners of her sweet mouth turning just a little upward when she speaks to me. Unlike Christine, she understands I'm trans, and unlike Christine, she likes me for me.

Stop. You can't love her.

Abruptly, I stand, falling a bit forward with my momentum. "I have to check on the dogs." I should have done this an hour ago. I should have left her before she confused me, before I trusted her again.

Dakota. I will only think of Dakota.

When I get to the playroom, Dakota is sitting in front of her doghouse like she's waiting for me. Her ears perk up. I've been gone for at least two hours now, but here she is as if she's my dog, as if she already knows I'll come for her. While I stroke both of her cheeks and scratch her ears, her eyes close in ecstasy. I talk to her as I sit down beside her, telling her about where I was, about Cooper's status, and about Madi.

Dakota is such a good listener. She waits until I have settled on the cool cement floor, then curls up beside me with her head on my lap.

I bask in her wonderful doggy-ness until I realize some of the water bowls around the room are empty. My job. Once I get into the routine of filling bowls and redirecting dogs, I let Dakota be by herself.

It's more than a few hours before I go to check on Cooper in the kennel room. There are two cats and one dog recovering from surgeries. Cooper is not that dog. His kennel is empty and stripped of the blankets and towels that had been there. They've already cleaned up. How long has he been gone? I rush out to the waiting room to find Madi, but of course, she's not there.

She left. She didn't even say goodbye. Or thank you. Or anything.

Until almost two in the morning, lying in bed, every time I feel my cell phone vibrate, I check to see if it's her. But it isn't. I sleep for a couple hours, but at 5 a.m. when a notification wakes me, I check to see if she's said thank you or that Cooper's doing better. But it's still not her.

Fine, then. She used me to help her dog and now we're going back to the way things were after *Earnest*. Fine. At least Cooper is all right.

I type a text to Sam. It's far too early for him to be awake, but I can't ask anyone else who might understand. I type a few sentences: *There's a girl at school I like, and we're friends, but we had a fight. I don't know how to get past this and go back to being friends.*

Is that really what's going on? My finger hesitates over the SEND button, and instead, I leave it unsent and turn off my phone.

At school, Libby tracks me down before second hour to hand me a list of songs. It's the order she thinks we should play them at prom. I skim the list, looking for where she's put my songs, but they're not there. Did she forget? Or does she sincerely not want to play them?

At any rate, neither Libby nor Madi inspires me to want to meet them in the cafeteria, so I spend lunch in the library again. Libby texts me over and over about what I think about the order of the songs. But zero texts from Madi. Screw her.

At the end of the day when it's time for Drama class, I have no idea what to expect from her. I suppose I should take a hint since she's been silent since I left her in the waiting room Saturday.

Watching Madi sit with other people in the Drama room should be a relief for me. It's not. From time to time, Madi looks up to my row, almost like she's afraid I'll still be here. And stupid me, I want her to look up at me. I want her to change her mind about me. Sit next to me. Do a scene with me.

What scene? We never chose one. I cross my arms and slouch. Should I go talk to her? No. That's a terrible idea. But maybe that would show her that I'm not trying to be a cool asshole at school.

A few minutes pass then Madi stands, gathers her things, and says something to the kid in the beanie and the girl with the blue hair. I check the clock. Not time to go.

Then she's beside me. I hold my head up, feigning masculine confidence when all I actually feel is uncertainty. Maybe I can make that masculine too. Masculine uncertainty. That could be a thing.

"I don't know if I thanked you." She hugs her bag to herself.

My voice splinters. "For what?"

"Helping me with Cooper." She sits beside me, placing her bag under the chair. "I was thinking. If you helped me with Cooper, then the real you isn't the stoic jerk you pretend to be at school."

I'm about to argue, but I think she has a point. I was about to do it again too.

"The real you has to be the guy who likes to talk about books and movies and laughs at my stupid impressions."

I smile at the memory of her reciting lines from *Twelfth Night*. "I am that guy," I say. At least, I want to be that guy.

Her eyes tell me she's not completely convinced. "Anyway, I was hoping you'd still want to do the scene with me."

I lean forward, flexing my muscles, then feel foolish for doing so. "Yeah, I'd like that." Before we lose this moment, I say, "I'm sorry you were stuck with the Larsons for so long."

Her expression says that isn't what I need to apologize for.

Ms. Sands lets us spend the rest of the class period in the library. We commandeer side-by-side computers, looking up scenes. It's not long until I find a site, *Scenes for One Male and One Female*, with links to scenes we could print out. Only three or four pages.

But this one won't work. This one is stupid. And this one is boring.

I tip my chair back to peer at Madi's screen. She's looking up scenes for two females. My cheeks warm. I don't say anything. Then, my skin starts to itch. How can she so easily dismiss me as male? Would she have done this before?

She clicks back to her search page where she has simply looked up scenes for two characters. Oh, good. She feels me watching her. "You don't . . . want to . . . Are you out to everyone?"

"Uh . . ." That was my intention at the talent show, but it doesn't seem to have had the effect I'd hoped for. Too many people in this school have known me for too long as Kayla who wears boys clothes and probably likes girls.

She keeps her voice down even though there aren't many people here in the library. "Do you want to play a male part?"

"I don't want to play a female part." I clench my teeth hard, so I don't say anything more.

"Okay, so we'll find you a male part." She pauses before returning to her search as if she knows I'll say more.

"If I'm in front of the whole class, playing a male part . . . I mean, these are people who've known me all my life . . ."

"What do you think would happen?"

"I don't know. One of them will talk to someone outside of class and then the rumors will start."

"Rumors about you doing a male role?"

"Yeah. Rumors about me wanting to be male."

She smiles too broadly. "But you *are* male."

I laugh, but I'm not reassured. "Of course, I am, but I don't think they understand. And what about Ms. Sands? She could call my parents."

Madi takes my hand in hers. "She wouldn't. I can't see her being bothered by you being a boy."

"My mom will freak out." And I'm not sure what my dad'll do.

"So what?"

"So . . . I don't know. It's really weird with her. She doesn't get it." I shiver when this truth comes out into the open.

Madi chews on the edge of her lip. "Okay. You want to play a male part, but you don't want anyone to overreact." Her eyes soften.

"Yeah."

She lays her hands on the computer keyboard, inactive. Then says, "Why don't you leave this to me? I have an idea."

Chapter 26

THE MORNINGS ARE SO MUCH less stressful since I've been changing in Coach's office instead of the girls' locker room. He was right that no one would bother me; I haven't even seen him in this office since he gave me the key.

Once I'm dressed and on the way to class, I see JT walking directly toward me. No one else is in the hall.

Hesitating about which way to go, I watch him for too long. By the time I turn to go back into Coach's office, he's there. His meaty hand stops the door from moving. "Hey," he says like we're friends.

I duck under his arm and start down the hall away from him.

"Kayla, wait. I just want to talk."

"Go to hell," I call over my shoulder. I'm too far from the weight room to save myself, and nobody else is here. His sneakers speed up to catch me.

Then something lands on my shoulder, like a tarantula in a horror film. It's JT's hand. I shove it off, but he's matched my pace now. I won't be able to get away.

"I need to talk to you about something." He reaches for my arm, but I dodge away. "Can you stop for a second?"

I stop, but every part of me says I'm making a mistake.

He holds his hands up. "I'm not going to do anything."

Glaring at him, I fold my arms over my bound chest.

After a little hemming and hawing, he mimics me by crossing his arms.

"Are you mocking me?" My fists clench.

"No, no, it's just that I don't know what to say."

Ha ha, you got the trans kid to believe you wanted to talk. So funny. I turn my back to him, heading for the weight room.

"Really, Kayla, wait." He jogs after me. His breath huffs out a nearly visual plume.

"It's Kay."

"Do you remember Miss Dischinger's class? Fourth grade." He smiles in a non-glaring way. "We made those puppets out of paper bags. She made us switch 'cause she said mine looked more like a bull and yours looked more like an antelope."

I remember his puppet with the large nostrils and mine that was clearly an antelope fail. "That was a long time ago." I don't like the direction this is going.

Like a moody breeze, Tiyana passes by, and the conversation is happily over. JT straightens up, flexing every muscle he can, and saunters away from me.

Tiyana looks back over her shoulder at us, her expression not quite as ornery as usual.

All through class, I find JT watching me. When I'm doing tricep presses, when I'm drinking water, when I'm talking with Danny. When I meet JT's eyes, I can't help lingering there for a minute. What does he want? He stares back, no gestures, no mouthed profanities, but no words.

Danny, weighted down by a barbell for squats, scoffs while I'm looking back at JT. "Ignore him."

"I am," I say while staring at JT.

"Not what it looks like."

I grab the barbell so he's squatting nothing, set the weights on the floor.

"Hey!" Danny straightens up.

"He's been following me around."

Now Danny stares at him too. "What for?"

I lower my voice. "He wants to be friends or something."

Danny snickers. "Don't fall for that."

"No, really—" I start to explain, but Danny changes the subject.

"There's a punk, alternative, new wave band that's going to be at my uncle's pub this weekend."

Danny's easy to be around, and he accepts me. Forget JT. "You want to go?"

He fist-bumps my knuckles. "That was the idea."

By the following meeting of the Drama class, Madi hands me a piece of paper, a back-to-back photocopy from a Shakespeare play. Everyone else has partnered up, exchanging already-memorized lines. The room fills with crisp word pronunciations.

I skim the first sentences on my photocopy. "Shakespeare?"

She rustles her own copy of the scene. "Why not?"

"The language, for one."

"You're in AP Lit with me, Nate. Do you think for a

second I believe you can't handle Shakespearean language?" She raises an eyebrow.

She just called me Nate. I focus on the paper. Act like it's normal. She delivers the first line. "Didst thou hear these verses?"

Clearing my throat, I reply, "O, yes, I heard them all, and more too; for some of them had in them more feet than the verses would bear."

Skimming the paper, I see it's back and forth between these two characters for about three book pages. Fine. I can memorize three pages. She reads her next line, "That's no matter: the feet might bear the verses."

Reading my reply, I feel my breath catch. The characters' names: Celia and Rosalind. Not remotely close to male. This is the scene she chose for us?

She waits for me to say my part.

More pretending. All the time. Everything about life is pretending.

"What is it?" Madi puts her hand down on my arm. She hasn't done that since *Earnest*. The softness of her fingers sends a tingle up my arm.

"It's . . ." I shouldn't have to say this again. I glance around the room at the other pairs. They're focused on each other. I wish I didn't care if they heard me. "Celia? Rosalind? Which one is supposed to be me?"

She drops her acting stance. "Rosalind." Her finger traces my next line. "The one you were reading. She's disguised as a man right now."

I meet her eyes.

"Celia's pretending to be a farm girl," she gestures to herself, "and Rosalind is Ganymede."

"So, Rosalind's a boy in this scene?"

Madi smiles, leaning close to my ear. Her breath tickles my neck. "And you know in Shakespeare's time, all the women's parts were played by teenage boys anyway."

Right. So I'm a boy playing the part of a girl pretending to be a boy.

"I thought that way you could be a boy in the scene, but everyone else wouldn't think much of it 'cause the character's pretending."

That's really smart. I want to hug her. I almost want to cry about how she actually understands me.

As her smile fades, her whole body seems to sink a little. "You don't like it?"

I do. I really do. "I do like it." I force the best smile I can. "It's such a great idea."

"Good. I'm glad." She touches my arm when she says, "Can you learn your first five lines for tomorrow?"

"Tomorrow?"

"We have to do blocking and gesturing and props. We've got to get our lines down now so we can make everything come together for this."

Something in my chest flips as she speaks. She's so sure of herself. I love the way she knows exactly how we should proceed.

While I wrestle with my inner romantic, Madi continues on with instructions for the opening of the scene, a vision she has. Then costumes. Mine will even have a sword.

"Are you listening?" She's partially amused, but partially annoyed.

"Just trying to wrap my head around it all."

Her expression goes blank as she looks past me. "Isn't that . . ." She doesn't finish.

I twist around to see what she sees. Shit. It's JT. "What the hell is he doing here?"

"He's staring straight at you." She stands as if to be my protector.

I laugh. "He can go to hell."

But there he is just outside the choir room door, waiting for me after the bell rings. Madi moves in front of me, which is fairly gallant of her, though she has no chance if he decides to be a douche. When she doesn't get out of the way, JT extends his ugly blond head around her and says, "Can we talk?"

"We have nothing to say." I hold Madi still while I step around her and make my getaway.

JT is undeterred. "I-I do. Even if you don't."

The hallway is nicely full of other students, so I boldly state, "I don't care what you have to say."

Madi throws him a death glare that he easily deflects.

With some quick maneuvers, she and I are able to lose him in a herd of freshmen with band instruments. I know he's behind us, but I doubt he'll be able to catch us.

After a flight of stairs and another hallway, I reassure Madi that I'll know my first five lines by tomorrow and get on my way home. When I glance back to see her one last time, she still stands in the same place I left her, giving me a little wave.

Chapter 27

ITRY TO GET MY HEAD around everything I have to do right now. The audition is in two days. And Troy texted me about Dakota's surgery. Dr. Wallin wants to operate on Dakota in two days. The same day as auditions. Why not today? Or tomorrow?

Even though April has brought considerably nice weather, I don't really feel like I can enjoy it. On my drive home from school, I see people outside. Light jackets, no longer bundled up for the winter, an elderly woman walks her Pomeranian, elementary school kids ride bikes, and a couple walks hand in hand. Their heads bow toward each other as they talk. Inadvertently, I slow. They're so happy together.

The SUV behind me honks.

Fine, fine, I'm going.

Inside my house, I gather a drink and a snack and my guitar and settle in on the couch. Mom and Dad won't be home for at least an hour. Until then, this is my house, my living room, my couch, my rules. I rest one foot on the coffee table as I get ready to play. I start one of the songs I wrote last week, but then I pick out the solo on "Livin' on a Prayer." We've got to be ready for prom.

I play through "Livin' on a Prayer," then "Thriller," secretly thanking the rock gods that so many mainstream male singers use their upper tenor range. As I start the leading riff to the next song, the doorbell rings.

I quiet the strings, waiting for whoever it is to go away.

When the doorbell rings again, my resting leg spasms. I am not answering that.

A moment later, it rings a third time. Surely this will be the last. But it's not. So finally, I get up and check my phone. Maybe Libby is here and she's texting me to let her in. Or maybe Madi. But no one has texted.

Slinking up near the entryway, I see a shadow move on the front step. Still here? The bell rings again. Seriously? Who is it that won't give up and leave me alone? I tiptoe to the door, hoping to be able to see out the window better. But when the bell rings again, I don't care who it is. I throw open the door to tell them to get lost.

It's not Libby or Madi. It's JT.

I swear too loudly and try to shut him out. But once the door is open, I can't close it again. His muscled hand shoves it toward me. "Just let me talk to you."

"I'm going to call the cops," I say. God, I don't want to call the cops. What do I tell them? That there's a boy who's harassing me? Embarrassing.

His white Nike high-tops step onto our welcome mat inside the door. "I have to tell you something."

"What are you doing here?" I'm considering letting him stay for a moment, which makes me doubt my sanity.

"Come sit down with me." He waltzes into the living room like he's a guest. Small mercy, though: he doesn't sit.

"Get out of my house. Now." I stay rooted by the front door.

His familiar yellow-toothed smirk appears. "Wow. This room has not changed one bit."

I stay by the door, keeping it open.

"This morning you said you remembered Ms. Dischinger's class and the puppets we made."

I roll my eyes. Sentimental kids' stuff.

"What about Mr. Lang's music class? We had that duet in fifth grade."

I forgot he can sing. Probably shouldn't vape so much then.

He puts his hand on his chest. "'Love Is an Open Door.' I used to sing my part to your yearbook picture." He begins to sing Hans's lines, accenting the words with his mango stench.

"No, no, no. Stop singing." I find myself directly in front of him, as if I'm going to physically stop him somehow.

He shoves his hands in his pockets sheepishly. "I thought it was perfect for us. Then."

Oh, no. He can't think . . .

He dips his head so he's not so tall. "We went for ice cream after that concert. You looked so great in that blue flowered dress."

God, don't remind me. My mother nearly held me down to put that thing on me. Every school presentation ever, my mom made sure I was wearing such a frilly dress. Humiliating.

"I was eleven," I say.

"You were beautiful."

I scowl at him. I never was beautiful. Cute, maybe.

His hands creep out of his pockets to grasp mine. "You could be beautiful again." His hand goes to my short, short hair. He strokes it.

I take a giant step back. "Whoa, whoa, whoa. What the fuck are you doing?"

His mouth opens. He stutters a few words then anxiously licks his lips. "We went out together."

"One time. Seven years ago."

"You can't say you didn't like me."

Did I? He wore a blue button-down shirt and khakis that I envied. Did he think I was looking at him when I was longing for his wardrobe?

"Why would I like you when you make fun of me?"

He explains himself. He elaborates. He confesses. All of it was meant to help me see the error of my ways, see that I was ridiculous to dress like a boy. He shifts his hips and I remember weeks ago when he and Dirk and Hunter all wore fake dresses and rude makeup. They accused me of trying to dress like a girl. When I point this out to him, he shakes his head.

"Maybe it was stupid. But that doesn't mean my heart wasn't in the right place." His sincerity is sickening.

"I can't do this right now." I march to the front door, opening it wide. "You need to get out of my house."

He raises his hands. "I will. I'm going. I just want you to ask you something."

Glaring at him does not make him move any faster.

"I'd like to take you to prom."

He has to be joking. "What?"

He grabs my forearm. "Think about it."

I'm about to yell when he finally steps through the door. He turns to me, about to speak again, but I slam the door and turn the bolt.

How can he be so clueless? He doesn't see me. He doesn't listen.

Danny's right. No one wants to be like JT. He's the ugly side of being a man.

A second later, the roar of the garage door sounds, up and down, and my dad comes into the room. "Was that JT?"

I can't look at him.

Dad opens the front door to look outside, but I slam it closed again. "It's fine," I say. I expect to see his protective daddy face, but all I see is concern.

"What did he want?"

"Don't worry about it, Dad."

He returns to his after-work routine, hanging his jacket, kicking off his shoes.

I remember we haven't talked about what we really need to talk about. Is that why he's home early?

He pops the tab on a can, returning to the living room. "I haven't seen that shithead around since you were a kid."

Apt name, Dad. I gather my things to move to my room.

"You don't have to leave," he says. "Why don't you play me one of your prom songs?"

"You don't want to hear that crap."

He pulls a kitchen chair into the living room and sits. "I'm all ears."

"Dad, really." I can't do this in front of him.

"Humor your old man."

I stand dumbly with my guitar in the middle of the living room. If he asks again and I refuse again, he'll be sad.

So, I sit on the edge of the couch, debating what to play, what sounds neutral or could be taken as androgynous.

Meeting his gaze, I hope to find boredom or distraction, but all I see is his proud dad smile.

I pluck out the beginning of "Time After Time." With each word, my voice shakes, but I find my way in the first verse. Libby would be pleased with my choice. At the end of the song, Dad cheers like he's in a crowd of thousands. I'm sure I'm blushing.

"Kay—uh." He keeps himself from saying my name. "That was fantastic."

My right eyebrow rises. "Yeah, yeah."

"I forgot how well you sing." He's in his own world for a moment, perhaps thinking of my past, my future. Then he says, "They better choose you and Libby or they're idiots."

Gingerly, I place my guitar on the floor, resting against the couch. "Dad, I need to tell you something." My heart thuds frantically against my chest.

Crossing his hands on his stomach, he sits back in his chair. Is he praying I won't say what he thinks I might say? He has to know already. My hair, my clothes, my ID from Wallin Animal Rescue.

I don't know how to start. I see my mother sitting next to me on the couch two years ago, acting like she'd listen when all she did was close her mind. Then I meet Dad's gaze. Here. Now. His small grin keeps his eyes alight as if he's trying to send me love from across the room.

I tear up. "You know that card you found?" I clear my throat. "The one with my picture. For the animal rescue."

Nodding, he leans forward.

When I'm at the rescue, they call me Nate. That's not what I want to say. Too unclear. And how could I tell him I've been impersonating a kid who might be dead?

"You know how I cut my hair . . ." I shake my head. This isn't the right way to tell him. I drop myself down on the couch. Think of something he'll understand.

Without an invitation, my dad joins me on the couch, taking hold of my hand.

Stupid tears fall down my face.

Gently, he squeezes my hand. "It's all right. Just tell me."

"I don't want to be a girl. I hate being a girl."

He lets out a breathy laugh. "I know that." He pulls me toward him so our shoulders touch.

"I don't feel like a girl. I never have."

"I know that too."

I pull back from him to see his expression. He's serious. "I'm transgender, Dad."

He nods. "I hear you."

"But . . . aren't you mad? Don't you want me to think about it?"

"Do you need to think about it?" he counters.

"No. I've known since I was little." I stand up and walk across the room. "You're okay with this?"

He shrugs. "It's not up to me, kiddo. You are who you are."

I come back over to the couch, but before I can sit, he stands and envelops me in his arms. "You're my kid, and I love you."

When my eyes get hot, I don't want more tears to come. I try to wipe them away, but Dad says, "Men cry sometimes too. It's okay." As if to prove it, he rubs the back of his hand against his own wet eyes.

I never thought he would be so cool about this. I allow him to hug me for as long as he's willing, and I allow myself to think over and over that he accepts me. My dad still loves me.

Chapter 28

THE NEXT MORNING SEEMS BRIGHTER than usual, which has nothing to do with the weather and everything to do with my dad. He gets me.

At school, Libby and I hang out by our tree near the student lot. At our feet are a few remaining splotches of snow and ice. All of the dirt from last autumn is revealed, and though it's not beautiful, it's wonderfully warm.

Libby takes a folded sheet of notebook paper from her jean jacket pocket, hands it to me, and says, "Tell me what you think of this."

It's an updated setlist for prom. She's written it out like she has no fear that we will be chosen. The gig is ours already. Start off with a fast song people can sing along to. Midtempo to get people dancing. She's even penciled in some breaks for us. I smile at the little drawings of punch cups and embellishments of swirls and stars. I skim down the list, checking each tune off in my head. I know this one, I can almost play this one, I like this one, wait a minute. "Fall Through" is listed along with all the covers and later "Blind Like the Night."

"These are my songs," I say. I can't believe she agreed.

She smiles. "I decided you had a good point. We should

play something original. Otherwise, how are we going to make a strong impression?"

I pull her into a hug. "You're the best."

"Whoa, whoa, whoa. Hang on there." She struggles a little—she doesn't like to be hugged—but gives in, patting me on the back. "Okay. You can let go now."

I step back to give her space again. "I was going to tell you that you were right. I mean, why would anyone want to hear songs they don't know when they're trying to dance?"

"Well, yeah, I'm more right than you, but we need to have both."

I jump in, "Except at the audition."

"Except at the audition where we play only covers." She takes the list from me for a moment, pointing out some of the patterns she created. "And here we have a few slow songs to get the groping going. But then it's back to dance time."

Pretty smart planning. Libby really has a gift for this.

"Tomorrow." She locks eyes with me.

I nod. Our audition is tomorrow.

"We're up fourth."

I say, "I'll be there," like I'm being sarcastic, but then I start thinking about it. Tomorrow is Dakota's surgery. If we audition fourth, that'll be like 4:30. What time did Troy say for Dakota? I check my phone. 3:30.

Libby's eyes darken. "What's the matter?"

I start to tell her, but I can't think of the right thing to say. "Nothing. Everything's fine."

What am I supposed to decide? If we're not on time for the audition, are we knocked out of the running? We'll lose our chance to play prom. Bekkah Ingram's dad will never hear of us. I'll end up working for the Wallins, cleaning up poop and vomit for the rest of my days under some other kid's name.

But Dakota needs me there. She'll be so scared by herself. I need to be there for her.

I'm sure there'll be enough time for both.

Throughout the day, I type into my phone the address of the school and of Wallin Animal Rescue, requesting the distance and driving time between them. Five miles, thirteen minutes. They're so close, and yet thirteen minutes is too long. I need to leave the rescue by 4:17 at the absolute latest. But I really want Dakota to see me when she wakes up.

If I don't leave by quarter after, I'll be late to the audition. The Student Council was very clear: Everyone has to be on time. But what if Dakota doesn't wake up right away? Or what if Dakota doesn't wake up at all and I wasn't there to say goodbye?

At dinner with my parents, Mom and Dad share bits from their days, more uninteresting than usual. Eventually they'll remember I'm here and ask about my day, and what do I tell them? Dr. Wallin doing the surgery is a huge deal, but I don't want Mom to know how things are with Madi. I could leave Madi out of the story.

Maybe I could tell just Dad. If I talked to him alone, maybe he could help me decide what I should do. Dakota or audition.

Not that it would help. Whichever decision he suggests, I'll question if it's the right one.

He's been eyeing me for a little while now. After chomping

through his last bite of peas, he raises his eyebrows at me. "Something bothering you, champ?"

Champ? That's his name for Sam.

"You haven't said anything since we all got home."

My mother stabs a piece of chicken. "Tell us about your day."

Swatting me on the shoulder, Dad says, "Hey, that audition is tomorrow." He already looks proud, and we haven't even played a single note for the Student Council yet.

Mom's expression is blank.

"To be the band at the prom," I fill in for her.

She waves a hand at me. "Of course." I don't think she remembers that I've told her about prom a couple of times now.

"You're going to do great." Dad winks at me.

Mom saws at her chicken with the side of her fork. "Maybe you ought to focus on getting a date to prom instead."

Dad and I both give her the same look.

"What?" The worry on her face makes me believe she has to know what.

"Why would K——, why would sh——" Dad can't decide what to call me.

"Why would I want to do that?" I drop my fork on my plate for emphasis.

Dad clears his throat and adds, "Yeah."

Mom's eyes flit from me to Dad and back. "Well, I don't know, but I wouldn't want to miss my senior prom."

"I'm not missing it."

We're all stuck. No one says a word. No one moves. For too long, no one even blinks.

I work up my nerve, sliding my chair back and standing. When I glance at Dad, his eyes are full of reassurance
and love.

Why did I ever think he wouldn't understand me?

When I glance at Mom, she's fixed on him, her eyes nar-
rowing as if she finally sees him coming into focus. I'd kill to
hear the conversation that's about to go down, but if I stay,
Mom won't say a word. She'll act like nothing is wrong.

Once I've stationed myself at the top of the stairs, in the
dark and out of view, I wait for the action to begin. Dad's
the first one to talk, and the way his voice carries, I can tell
they're still at the table.

"Do you mean to tell me that you have no idea what's
going on with Kay?"

There's nothing for a while.

"Since when are you so closed-minded?" His voice rises.

Again, there's nothing.

"Hey." Now I can barely hear him. He's consoling her.
"Hey, what is it?"

I bet she's making herself cry so he feels sorry for her.
Through tiny sobs, I think I hear, "What are we going to do?"

"About what? What do you mean?"

"She's not even our daughter anymore."

A chair moves and I assume he's holding her. I hear her
crying still, and his gentle, hushing sounds. I can't tell if he's
crying too, but I always imagined he would. So what was he
doing before when he seemed to be on my side? Was that all
an act?

I grip the railing at the top of the staircase, step down half
the flight and then I stop.

I hear something soft and low like the TV volume down too far. But no. It's Dad's voice, so quiet. What is he saying?

I gently set my foot on the next step down, then the next, and the next. I creep as close as I can to the kitchen. By the time I'm positioned where I can hear Dad talking, he's finished, and Mom is saying, "I can't. I won't," and still crying.

"You don't have a choice. This is who Kay is."

But that's it. End of their discussion.

Dad's words echo through my head as I piece together his tone. Apologetic? Angry? No, nothing like that. It was like he was telling her to get her shit together. I shouldn't have doubted him. I guess I'm just not used to trusting people who know the truth.

Chapter 29

UNCLE DOUG HELPS LIBBY SET up her drum kit backstage at the auditorium first thing in the morning. Libby's idea. With each move he makes, Doug adds a piece of advice about the audition. He secures a drum in place and tells her to keep her head up, confidently. He attaches the bass drum mallet and explains the importance of restrained enthusiasm. I nod at his words while I carry in a cymbal and attach it to the stand, but I have to get my guitar and amp in place.

We've commandeered the same rolling stand we had at the talent show, so we get everything just where we want it. Libby wants to be sure her drums are set, but I have to be able to come in from the parking lot after Dakota's surgery and be ready to play.

I can do this.

Libby smiles like a little kid. "4:30."

I run through the timeline in my head again then give her a fist bump.

I can barely make it through the day, thinking about Dakota's surgery. What if everything goes wrong? The tumor is so close to her heart and her lungs. I consider at lunch, between bites of cheese pizza, confessing it all to Madi, getting her opinion. Would she just hope for the best with Dakota and tell me to be at the audition? No way. Not with how she feels about Cooper. Madi knows how important dogs are.

Instead of asking, I stare at her, then at Libby, and say nothing.

Libby runs through the songs we're going to play today, keeping Madi interested by singing snippets of back-up vocals really poorly. When I don't laugh at her rendition of "Livin' on a Prayer," she snickers at me and says, "What's your problem?"

I could tell her now. I could be completely straight with her. But I say nothing. If it all goes as it should, Libby doesn't have to know.

In Drama class, while we're supposed to be rehearsing our scene, Madi sings the back-up vocals like Libby did at lunch. She wants me to laugh, but we need to practice. I know my twenty lines in *As You Like It* pretty well, but I still slip up near the end and miss my cue. We need to get this down.

We're in a practice room off the music hall. It has a piano and about four feet of space with a fake ficus. We nabbed one of these rooms so we could do our lines in peace, and now Madi's just goofing around. She twirls from one side of the piano bench to the other as if she's a rock star. I dodge her feet, landing partially in the ficus.

I would recite the first line, but it isn't mine. And I certainly don't want her to think I want to switch parts. My character is dressed like a boy, not hers.

When she twirls back around, I lean defensively into the ficus and say, "Tell me your first line again."

She laughs at herself. "Right, right. We need to be serious."

"Yes, we do."

"Didst thou hear these verses?" she says in a pseudo-British accent.

"O, yes, I heard them all and more too. For some of them had in them more feet than the verses would bear."

"I can't believe your audition is in less than two hours." She covers her face for a moment.

I pretend she's said her line correctly. "Ay, but the feet were lame and could not bear themselves without the verse."

"Aren't you nervous?"

"I was seven of the nine days out of the wonder before you came—"

"Nate, really. You and Libby could be the band for prom."

Something I've known for months now. The name rolls off her tongue so naturally now. Don't draw attention to it. It's not the first time. I continue with Rosaline's line. "For look what I found on a palm tree; I was never so be-rimed since Pythagoras's time, that I was an Irish rat, which I can hardly remember."

"Are you ready? Do you think Libby's ready?" She bounces like she's dying to know.

"Madi!"

"Are you?"

"Yes, and so is Gene. We're going to do fine."

While she watches me, the energy she had seems to drain until her face is serious. "Then what's bothering you?"

"We need to rehearse—"

"I thought you and Libby rehearsed like every day for the last three—"

"No, you and me. This scene. We need to rehearse."

"Once you tell me what's wrong." She slides over on the bench to make room for me.

Dakota's wet nose and smiling eyes appear in my mind with her thick black and white fur. I sit. "It's nothing."

"It's something."

The longer I stall, the less time we'll have to rehearse. "It's the dog at the rescue that I like."

"Dakota? What about her?"

"She . . ." I stop so I don't make an embarrassing sobbing noise. "Has a tumor."

"Oh, no. I'm so sorry."

"She's having a surgery today."

"Today?" She scowls a little. "But the audition."

"I know." I brush away a tear.

Madi takes my hand in both of hers. "It's going to be all right. I'm sure Dakota will come through it."

I inspect the fake leaves on the ficus tree so I don't have to look in her eyes.

"When I brought Cooper in, you helped me, even though we'd had that fight." She says this as if it's an aside. "Dr. Wallin took care of Cooper, fixed him up without a problem."

"Dakota has more than a cut. She has a tumor." I clench my jaw.

She tightens her hold on my hand. "Dakota will be okay." She squeezes my palm firmly, then releases it. "Let's rehearse."

When she gives her line, I respond, and we go back and forth without our sheets for a while. Then we mess up and have to use our copies of the play, but we continue back and forth. Until line 200, when I stop. I skim the rest of it in my head.

"What's the matter?" she asks.

"I can't say this. Rosalind is asking if Orlando will know she's a woman even though she's wearing men's clothes."

Madi says something to protest my concern.

I don't hear her; I'm reading more upsetting lines. "'Do you not know I am a woman?' You've got to be kidding me. I'm not going to say that in front of the class."

Madi lays her hands over mine, forcing me to lower the pages so I can't read any more. "We're going to switch parts." She nods. "Celia never says anything about needing to be a woman."

My face cringes, giving her the ugliest look.

Madi laughs it off. "Really. You'll be a great Celia."

I'm not sure about this. But I can't think straight. The bell's going to ring, and I need to get to Dakota.

"I have to go." I gather my stuff.

"Now?"

"The surgery's in half an hour." Pushing open the door to our little practice room, I hear a number of people talking, some chairs moving. I didn't realize the room was soundproof.

"What about the audition?" Madi calls after me.

I pretend I don't hear. I'll have time for both, but only if I go now. The bell to end the school day is barely ringing when I dart from the door to the student parking lot.

When did it get so cold? It's almost May, for Christ's sake, and it feels like it's not even thirty degrees. As I pull out of the lot, tiny ice drops clink against my windshield. I crank the heat up so they melt on impact, then send the wipers to smoosh them. This better let up. Icy roads will not get me back in time for the audition.

By the time I arrive at the rescue, I'm already late. It's only a few minutes, but how do I know those few minutes don't count? Parking causes my car's tires to slide a few extra inches, and my feet slip on the pavement all the way to the door, nearly taking me down.

Once I'm inside, I quicken my pace, rushing through the lobby and into the back. I cruise down the hall to the surgery room. The door's closed, but that doesn't mean they've started. I peer through the rectangular window in the door. Dr. Wallin is there, dressed in light blue scrubs with a mask over her nose and mouth. Two assistants are with her, and there on a table before them is my sweet furry dog. A tube is taped to her snout, an intravenous line in her front leg.

She's motionless.

Sedated. She's only sedated. Right?

I want to pet her, to tell her everything will be all right, to tell her I'm here.

She doesn't know I'm here. I push the door to go inside, but once it's moved a few inches, Troy slips his arm in front of the door as if he thinks he'll have to physically restrain me. "Don't go in."

I step back. "I didn't get to see her before . . ."

M. E. Corey

His hand against my back ushers me down the hall to the same room I spent hours waiting with Madi. He says, "You might as well take a seat."

"How am I going to know when—"

"I'll come get you." His eyes reassure me for the moment, but once he's out of the room, the positive energy dries up and I'm sinking in worry.

Maybe I should have told Dr. Wallin not to do the surgery. Maybe I could have changed Dakota's future. Given her a few more years. But how would I know? She could come through the surgery just fine.

My guilt and my anxiety pool together into a noxious secretion in my mouth that I try to rinse out at the drinking fountain. A dollar fifty for a Coke does nothing to remove it, either. Only time—obnoxiously slow-moving time—will help.

I check my phone continuously to see that the minute hasn't changed, and soon each time I check, I find a message from Libby. *Where are you?* And *Do you know we're on in twenty minutes?* Then it's fifteen. I have to go.

But nothing about Dakota.

I can't sit still. I pace the waiting room. Down the hall I peer in the door where Dakota is. Everything looks the same as when I came by the first time. I can't see what they're doing—thank God. I pace some more, then watch ice rain fall outside.

Libby's next texts are strings of swear words and threats. *Do you want me to go out there with Gene and see how it goes?! Where the hell are you?*

What do I expect her to do?

Shit. Shit. Shit.

I pace the hall again. Peer in the window at Dr. Wallin. How long can this possibly take?

The answer doesn't come for two hours. Far too late to make it to the audition, even with a last-minute Hail Mary attempt to persuade the Student Council to let us play. It's over.

Dr. Wallin, brow drizzled with sweat, emerges from the surgery room, stripping off a layer of protective clothing spattered with dark red. My heart invades my throat, thudding so hard I can't speak.

Removing her mask, Dr. Wallin reveals a cautious smile. "Dakota made it through the surgery just fine." Before I can jump up and down and celebrate, she cautions me, "She still needs to do some healing, and she hasn't come out of the anesthesia yet. But everything went as well as I could have hoped."

While Dakota recovers, she is in a warming blanket, still hooked up to the IV, which runs through one of the slats in her kennel. She lies on her side, taking shallow breaths. A lump of black, white, and gray fur. I stick my hand through the kennel slats and place it on her side, so she knows I'm with her.

The recovery room door opens behind me, and Troy comes in. Gazing through the slats of the kennel, he assesses Dakota. "She could be like this for a while." His voice is quiet. Squeezing my shoulder like he's my older brother, he says, "Are you doing all right?"

I nod. Without realizing it's coming, I feel a tear fall down my cheek.

Troy holds my shoulder like he's keeping me from splitting down the middle. "Why don't you go home? I'll call if there's any change with her."

Chapter 30

THE ONLY REDEEMING THING ABOUT the next day is that the ice has melted from the uncharacteristically freezing late-April storm. Everything else absolutely sucks. Mom's morning judgment of my clothes barely registers on the scale of suckiness compared to everything else.

Libby won't answer my texts. After the flood of pleas and insults yesterday, she's now completely silent. She's never stonewalled me before. Not even when my fist went through the head of her snare drum two years ago. I explain what happened with Dakota and why I didn't make it to the audition. I text and text and text, but nothing. I flat out call her three times, and she refuses to answer.

No news about Dakota, either. Troy texted to say there's been no change.

Christine is charcoaling yet another tropical tree. I roll my eyes. Maybe a strand of her beautiful hair falls across her sculpted cheek, but I'm not paying attention. Instead, I'm scouting out Libby's movements. She's everywhere in the room without pausing. She says a few things to Madi, then she's at Ms. Horvath's desk, then she's over near the kiln even though she isn't working on pottery.

Never does she glance my way. She is royally pissed off, and I don't blame her. I don't have any idea how I can apologize.

Madi checks on me a few times, but I don't make eye contact; I don't need her worried face weighing down my already-guilty conscience.

I have to figure out how I can fix this. The only thing I could do is get us a new audition so Libby will forgive me.

The solution becomes completely clear a moment later. I only have to find the right Student Council person. And that person, of course, is Hunter. I have an in since he's dating Madi, something she hasn't brought up and I can't make myself mention. When I puzzle through how I'll track him down, I conclude that I don't know any of the classes he's in. He certainly isn't in any of mine or any of Madi's.

Is that what she likes about him? She's smarter than he is?

The only thing I know about Hunter's schedule is that he has lunch when I do. Since Libby's angry and I'm not talking to her, I can find Hunter and ask him for another audition. Then I'll have a peace offering to bring her.

When lunch time comes, I chill over by the wall near the entrance, waiting for Hunter. A procession of teens passes, some face down in their phones, some talking with each other. Hunter arrives soon enough, trailing in after Dirk and JT. Why did that not occur to me? Of course, he'd be with them. Of course, if I want to talk with him, I have to go through JT.

Though instinct tells me to step back when I see him, I clench my fists and stand tall. Still, despite my bravado, I'm relieved none of them notice me. A few other students move by before I get in line behind Hunter. I slide my tray along, forgoing every food option, waiting for the moment to jump ahead of the people between us.

JT turns to talk to Dirk and catches me watching them. He winks. My hands shake, my empty tray slipping to the ground where it rattles before settling. I get a round of applause from Dirk and JT and seemingly everyone else in line. Everyone aside from Hunter, who stares at me like I've called him out as my closest friend, like dropping the tray released a mountain of his private information just because we have this awkward connection through Madi.

After two failed attempts, I pick up the tray and desert the line. I can't ask him now. Screw this. I'll find him later.

Across the cafeteria, Libby walks too confidently to our regular table as if everything is fine. But it must be a trap. No way she's going to let this wrap up so easily. Okay, I'll play. I saunter over without a lunch and without a ready apology and take my usual place across from her.

She's eating carrot sticks and doesn't hesitate to continue when I arrive. No acknowledgement that I'm here.

I fold my hands on the table. Should I tell her I'm sorry and it's all my fault? I mean, it is all my fault, but shouldn't she understand? Of all people in my life, Libby should understand why I needed to be with Dakota.

She sneaks a glance at me, one carrot stick suspended from her lips. When I try to make eye contact, she resumes crunching and looking across the cafeteria. She mutters, "I can't believe you didn't show up."

"I can't believe you don't understand why."

She scoffs. "You have this idea that you're the only one with difficult choices."

I shake my head at her.

"Like if you're suffering, you're the only one who matters." She crunches a carrot stick. "Everyone has shit they're dealing with, Kinkade. Everyone."

"I thought she was going to die," I mumble.

Her carrot hand thuds down on the table. "This was our big chance. This was our time to get a recording deal."

Without meaning to, I roll my eyes. "Just because Bekkah will be there doesn't mean she'll say a damn thing to her dad."

Libby glares at me like I've killed her future.

Through closed eyes I can still feel her stare. "I didn't mean that."

Libby whispers, "She tells him everything."

There's also the possibility that we won't be chosen, especially since we missed our original audition, but I'm not mentioning that right now. "I'll fix it."

"Oh, really?"

"I just have to talk to a few key people."

Madi appears beside us. "About what?" she asks.

"Uh . . ."

Libby butts in, "Kay needs to move a few mountains and fix what happened with our audition."

Madi sets her tray down, but before she can sit, I grasp her elbow and she picks up her carton of French fries before I lead her a few paces away.

Popping a fry in her mouth, she asks, "What's going on?"

"I really messed up yesterday."

"You didn't make it back for the audition," she deduces.

"Yeah, and Libby's really pissed." I glance back at Libby. She's out of earshot, but not out of range to wound me with her glare.

"Well, sure, she is."

My stare keeps her from continuing.

She scowls. "Blue isn't going to be the band at prom, then?"

"No."

She picks up a fry, looks at it for a second, then puts it back. "Everyone will be so disappointed."

I don't meet her eyes. "Unless I can get someone on the Student Council to help us out. Get us another audition. And I don't really know anyone on Student Council."

Her only response is to stare at me, as if waiting for me to continue.

"So . . .?" I don't want to have to say the words.

"You know I'm always willing to help you, but I don't know anyone either." She bites into another French fry.

"Your boyfriend?"

She stops chewing. "Hunter?"

I shake my head without wanting to. She doesn't know the first thing about him, but she's dating him.

She chokes down the fries in her mouth. "You want me to ask Hunter to help you."

I nod. It's a disturbing thought, but it is what it is.

Her face reddens. "I don't know . . ."

I turn back toward Libby and our lunch table. "Forget it."

She catches my arm. "I will. I just don't know . . ." She shakes off her thought. "Blue should be the band that plays prom."

It should be simple, really. Madi talks to Hunter who talks to the Student Council who gives us a new audition so we can play music at prom to impress Bekkah Ingram and make her tell her dad how fabulous we are and sign us for his record label.

Simple.

Like me, Madi doesn't have any classes with Hunter so the plan is to nab him after school at his locker.

I trail behind Madi a few steps, unsure if I want to be there when she talks to him. We've spent the past forty minutes pretending to be Shakespearean characters and pausing every now and then for her to say, "I didn't know you knew," too frequently. And me to respond, "I didn't know it was a secret." If dating Hunter is a secret, who is she hiding it from?

Now after school, we head to his locker to submit a proposal, only we have nothing to propose in exchange for the gift of a new audition.

Madi pauses before we get to his hallway. "I don't know what to say."

"To explain why you're dating him?"

"Stop that," she says, though her face reddens.

"Just tell him how great my band is and that we deserve to audition."

She doesn't look reassured. She glances down the hallway for him but doesn't see him.

"Why are you dating him?" I really would like to know. Right now, I'm just trying to get under her skin, but she's going to need to give me a reason at some point.

She lightly shoves me, and then she's walking away because there he is. Hunter Vetrelec in his pseudo glory. With her back to me, I can't see her smiling at him, though I know she is. It's got to be fake. Please let it be fake.

Upon seeing her, he grasps her arms and pulls her in for

a kiss, letting out a nauseating sound. He enjoyed that too much. "Hey. I didn't know we were meeting today."

"I hope that's all right."

I roll my eyes. Come on, Madi. Have a spine. I step closer to the wall, hoping to blend in more, but the opposite happens. Hunter spots me.

He drops Madi's arms like he's been caught, his eyes fixed on me as if he's about to speak, but then he speaks to Madi. "What's Kay want?"

Madi takes both of his hands and turns him around so she's the one facing me. Her smile, so tender, though, is directed at him. I'd prefer his accusing stare to having to see her look at someone else that way. I can't watch this.

I back up a few steps, trailing my hand along the wall so I know where I am. When I've gone far enough, I let my hands ball into fists. Just once, I'd like to punch him in his stupid face.

Instead, I punch a locker, allowing the hollow metal sound to echo down the empty hallway.

Chapter 31

THE HOLLOWNESS FEELS LIKE IT'S in my chest. I want to head for the animal rescue to see Dakota, but last I heard, she's still recovering from anesthesia. Home from school, I secure myself in my bedroom, tossing up my pillow so I can punch it into the wall. At what point does it become less about recovering from anesthesia and more about recovering in general? Troy hasn't said the word *coma*, but I can't keep myself from thinking it.

Paging through last year's yearbook, I skip over the seniors, the juniors, the sophomores, the freshmen, and I come to sports and clubs. Football, soccer, basketball, Spanish Club, Art Club, here it is. Student Council. I need someone who is not Hunter. Who the hell is in Student Council?

Person I don't know, person I don't know, ass-face Hunter, person I don't know.

I slam the book closed. This is hopeless.

I keep myself from throwing the book across the room. That kind of noise might bring my mom in here. I don't need her brand of bullshit right now. I need someone who has some kind of sway over the Student Council. It can't be that there's only Hunter Vetrelec.

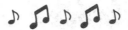

The next morning at school, I'm so tense, I almost talk to JT during Strength Training, ask him what Hunter found out from the Student Council. But I can't imagine he knows anything about what's going on in Hunter's life. He's too narcissistic. I mean, he only noticed that I've changed because of how it affected him.

I glare across the weight room at JT. Beside him, Hunter curls a dumbbell and Dirk says something stupid they all three laugh at. I could go over there and ask Hunter myself.

Instead, I meet Danny at the leg presses where we take neighboring machines. I lay out some of the details, wanting to tell him everything about Hunter and Madi, but I don't know if I can handle a confession right now. And I feel like the first one to know that I love Madi should be Madi, but frankly, I'm so pissed at her, I don't even know if I love her right now.

"You don't know anyone else on Student Council?" Danny's surprised, like he thinks I have giant masses of friends revolving around me at all times.

I press the weights instead of answering him, a trickle of sweat at my temple.

"I know a few people," he offers. His weights clang when he sets them down too fast.

"You do?" Why don't I know a few people?

"Let me talk to Lauren. She's probably bummed you didn't audition anyway. She's a fan."

I laugh. "A what?"

"A fan." He ends his set and comes to stand closer to me. "Blue is an underground cult phenomenon."

I roll my eyes. "Sure, we are."

"Well, sort of." He says this very perkily.

"I think someone would have told me by now if my band was a hit."

"All I know is there are some MP3 files floating around."

Wait. What? "Where'd they get the MP3's?"

"I don't know. Someone in the Tech Club got them from the mass recordings the school made of the talent show and you know, that other time you guys played here. The Battle of the High School Bands? Wasn't that in the fall this year?" He wipes his brow. "I know there are some videos too."

Ugh. Videos. I hope only after my coming out. I'm adding Battle of the Bands and the talent show in my head so I know what songs are out there. I shouldn't care, especially if people like them, but something about this concerns me. Maybe because I don't trust many people.

"There are a ton of people who'll be pretty unhappy if you guys aren't the band for prom."

I want to believe him.

"I'll talk to Lauren," he says, patting me on my sweaty back.

By Art class, my sweat has mostly congealed. I run a hand through my hair before I go inside in case Madi's already there. She's not. Probably avoiding me if she doesn't have an answer from Hunter yet. I plop down on my stool with a huff.

Christine brushes past me, dropping her bag to the floor. "What's the matter?"

I roll my eyes. To think if she'd only acted concerned months ago, she could have prevented at least one day of breaking my heart. Alas, now I care not.

"Long story."

She removes her art supplies, lining them up across her desk. "We're here all hour, and I know how to listen."

Madi wanders in just two seconds before the bell, throwing a smile to me, but I don't return it.

Christine brings me back to our conversation. "Come on. What's going on?"

Fine. Okay. I try to keep it simple—we simply missed the auditions—but Christine has to know why. She insists. So I end up telling her about Dakota at the shelter and how I work there and had to be at her surgery.

"That's so sad." She sucks in her lip. "And you still don't know how she is?"

I shake my head. Don't cry.

"Wow." She sets her charcoal down, which she never does. "I get it." She shrugs. "I don't see why you can't get a new audition. They have to understand things like this can happen."

"I don't know. They said one day for auditions and that's it."

This clearly doesn't sit well with her. "But your band should play at prom."

That's what I've been saying.

"Who did you talk to?"

"Madi's talking to Hunter, but I don't know anyone in Student Council."

She laughs. "Kay, that's so dumb." She cracks herself up. "I'm in Student Council."

I just about fall off my stool. "No . . . you're not. You aren't in the yearbook."

"I wasn't in it last year. Just this year. You know, for college applications."

I nod, but I would never join a group like that just to impress some college.

"I'll talk to Mr. Gerber. He'll want to give an audition once I'm done with him." She gives me a dopey self-satisfied smile and plucks up her charcoal. "Your band has to play prom, Kayla."

I ignore the name she's called me and choose to think of this as fantastic. If Madi talks to Hunter and Danny talks to Lauren and Christine talks to Mr. Gerber, they'll have to give us a new audition, right? Then Libby will forgive me, and Blue will have a chance.

Later in the hour, Madi strolls over to me. The smile she had before is gone, replaced by something much gloomier. She leans on my desk. "I don't know how to tell you this," she says. "Hunter doesn't think he can get the Student Council to budge."

Wait a minute. Danny said . . . and Christine . . . My heart begins to pound. I thought I had a solution to this mess. "Are you sure?"

Her eyes widen. "That's what he told me." She glances at Christine, who's obviously listening.

"Did he even talk to them?" I ask. Knowing what I know about Hunter, I doubt it. He walked away from his conversation with Madi and didn't think about it again.

A second of hesitation shows she doubts that he said any-thing, too, but she says, "Of course he did. According to him, they won't allow a second audition."

Christine looks over at us. She has to get involved. "Why not?"

She shrugs. "He didn't say."

I stare at Madi.

She stares back.

"You were too busy looking into his dreamy eyes to think to ask why?"

She scowls.

I cross my arms. "So what's the next step?"

She fidgets with her fingers. "I don't know what else he can do."

"Fine, whatever, Madi." I engage myself with the drawing I've barely begun.

Though she loiters for a while, she thankfully says noth-ing more. What could she say? Her stupid boyfriend is a waste of time, a waste of space. That should make me somewhat happy, but it doesn't.

Now it's on to Plan B. Danny and Christine. They both sounded so sure of themselves, but that doesn't mean they'll be able to persuade the council to break the rules for us. I thought I just wanted this for Libby's sake, but now prom seems like an opportunity for me too.

Christine waits until Madi is back at her own desk, then she whispers, "Don't worry."

But worrying is all I have left.

Chapter 32

WORRYING LEADS ME TO TEXT Troy about Dakota while I'm in my AP Lit class. The AP exam is coming up soon, but instead of reading the practice multiple choice questions on my desk, I envision Dakota's gray and black fur, IV stuck in her leg, eyes closed. Shit. I wish I could have been with her before they put her under. I might never see her awake again.

A half an hour later, I still haven't gotten a response from him, so I text again. This time he replies: *She's awake!*

Thank God. It's been days. I thought for sure . . . but forget all of that now. If she's awake, I need to see her, let her know I'm here for her. I ask for a pass to the bathroom and walk out of the building.

Once I'm at Wallin Animal Rescue, I make a plan to avoid Jeanie in the front room as much as possible. I'm not giving her my driver's license. It's never going to happen. I wait until she's on the phone, and I slip past her with a menial wave.

No one's in the hallway, so I go unimpeded to the last room I saw her in. Dakota's still in the recovery area, but her IV is out. As the door closes behind me, her eyebrows twitch, eyes opening. She sniffs at me for a second, then lets out a quiet bark. I unlatch her kennel without a second thought, gently touching her side and petting her. Once I can clearly see where her incision is among a patch of pale shaved skin, I lean in a little, so I can rest my head on her, safely. As long as she lets me. She takes little short breaths almost like she's purring at me, her eyes closing. I talk to her, little encouraging phrases, feeling the warmth of her soft, soft fur.

I'm not sure how long I've been there when Troy comes in. He steps cautiously closer to me and whispers, "You probably shouldn't have your head in there."

I laugh to myself. Even though he's wrong, I pull my head out. "She's going to be okay."

He nods once. "Looks like it. I'm hopeful, anyway."

"If everything works out, do you think I'd be able to adopt her?" I haven't made a plan for this at all. The words just come out of my mouth.

He grimaces. "There's something I need to tell you."

Why does he look so sad? I stand up straighter, preparing for the blow.

"We got lucky when we did some x-rays of Dakota."

I laugh. "Lucky. So what's with the face?"

"Lucky for Dakota, or actually Luna. We found her ID chip."

No. "I thought she didn't have one."

"Sometimes they migrate and they're not at the implant site. It's not that common, but we really should have scanned her more than once."

I stare into her dog face. Her eyebrow whiskers twitch as she looks from me to Troy and back, seeming to know something's going on. "So now what?"

"Now, we're checking the ID number we found with the

registration center. We'll probably know who her owner is some time today."

When I get home later that night, I can't stop thinking about Dakota, and then Danny and Christine and Hunter and Madi and Libby. And now Dakota's real owner. They all run around my head like I'm supposed to corral them somehow.

Dad has convinced me that I should hang out more with him and Mom instead of hiding in my room. While I think that's a horrible idea, I humor him tonight, hoping they will keep me from thinking too much. Hoping to find a way to bring up the idea of adopting Dakota. Maybe I can find a picture of her on my phone. Only, all they want to do is watch CNN where for the past hour the reporter has been talking in circles about the same thing. I've stopped listening. Mom and Dad recline on the couch together, both occasionally checking their phones for emails or texts or whatever it is they do. I'm a chair away by myself, not texting Danny.

I could text Danny. What does he know? What did Lauren say? If he talked to her and it was good news, wouldn't he have texted me? I think myself out of it. I'm desperate, but I don't want to seem desperate.

I could text Christine. Of course, I don't have Christine's number, which is a good thing. Who knows how often I would have texted her in the past year if I'd had it? That would have been embarrassing. But now, I wish I could ask her what she found out. Did Mr. Gerber say they'd make an exception for us? Is there even any way to make an exception?

Finally, the news story changes, but this story is worse. "Recent news from several southern states reveals legislation that will unfairly discriminate against an already vulnerable population: transgender youth."

Time stops. The reporter goes silent. My parents freeze. At the same moment, my stomach ices over. Are they staring at me? I can't look away from the TV. Is Mom giving me the evil eye?

Time begins again. The reporter continues, "Gender-confirming hormone treatments for minors. That's what's on the chopping block in all of these states"——the map of the south lights up——"where doctors will no longer be allowed to prescribe these treatments for anyone under the age of eighteen."

My mother scoffs. "Why would anyone under the age of eighteen want to——" She realizes she is about to put herself in the minority in this room.

"Some people want to be who they were supposed to be before they go into the real world. Some kids are lucky enough not to go through puberty for their birth gender," I say. My voice isn't nearly as loud as I want it to be, yet I can't believe those words came out of my mouth to my mother.

She shifts toward me too quickly. "What does that mean?" But she realizes what it means as she's asking.

It means I wouldn't have had my period for the past five years. It means I wouldn't have grown extra parts I don't need. I can't make myself say this out loud. It's like now that Dad knows, Mom knows again, as if I've told them both for the first time.

Dad stretches and gently says, "I think it's a mistake to

make a law like that." He gestures toward the TV at the politician who signed the bill into effect in Tennessee. "Who is he that he gets to speak for transgender kids?"

Mom digs her nails into her thighs, attempting to restrain herself.

"Go ahead," Dad tells her.

"How does a kid know they want to make a change like that? It's unnatural. What if they regret it later? These legislators need to protect the children from themselves."

Dad peers around her to me where I'm sorting through the swear words in my head to find my point. Right now, they're wrapped together too tightly.

"Mom, do you remember when Sam and I were little, and you took us over to your friend's house where they had a pool? Sam went out wearing his swim trunks and jumped into the water. Started splashing around. Having a great time. I went out to do the same thing and you stopped me because I was only wearing the bottom of my swimsuit."

"Of course, I remember. I was so embarrassed. You were half naked in front of everyone."

"How old was I?"

"I don't remember. Five, maybe."

"I wanted to be like Sam."

She doesn't get it.

"Do you know that when I went away to summer camp, I made friends with the boys and didn't tell them what cabin I was in so they wouldn't think I was a girl?"

She seems to pick up on what I'm trying to say. "That doesn't mean—"

"Do you know how upset I was when one of them found

out?" I remember that Sam was at the same camp, but because we were two years apart, I didn't see him too much. One day, though, one of my friends was messing around and Sam thought he was harassing me. Put him in a headlock. Told him to leave "his sister" alone. That was the end of the masquerade.

Mom looks at me. Her eyes have softened. A little. "I don't see how you can think that you were born the wrong gender. It's not like there was anything I could do about that."

What? "Of course not."

Dad puts a hand on her knee. "Why would you say something like that?"

Is she as delusional as those stupid legislators? They all think they're somehow in control of how other people live.

Mom purses her lips. "I don't want you to think that I did this on purpose."

"This has nothing to do with you," I say.

Her eyes widen. "How could it have nothing to do with me?"

"What do you think you did, Mom?"

"I don't know. Obviously, I must have raised you wrong. I let you play with Sam too much. I let you play sports when I should have shoved dolls in your room."

"I hate dolls."

"Yeah, well, maybe you wouldn't have if I made you play with them."

Dad stands up. "All right. That's enough. This isn't going to help anything."

I swallow hard, forcing down the suggestions of where she can put the dolls and dresses and any other feminine things she wants to recommend.

Dad's hand closes around Mom's wrist. "You need to get past this."

She's hopeless.

"I'm going to my room," I say.

"Kayla . . ." She doesn't continue.

"It's Nate, Mom."

She says nothing in response, but to my surprise, she doesn't look disgusted. It's a start.

Chapter 33

IN THE MORNING, MOM TALKS to me like nothing has happened, though she doesn't ever use my name. Not Kayla, not Nate. Still, silence is better than something false.

Once I'm at school, I close myself inside Coach's office and make sure to relock the door. Can't get distracted and forget. I change so quickly for Strength Training that I nearly trip over my shoes when I put them back on. But I need to know what Danny has found out. I can't believe he hasn't texted me.

Danny isn't in the weight room yet. I stretch a little, my heart pounding. I don't know that my heart has ever raced like this when I've been waiting for a boy.

The look on his face when he finally comes in, nearly when the bell rings, is not one I had hoped for.

"Not good?" I ask.

"Not sure yet. Lauren said she'll see what she can do."

I laugh. "So what's the matter?"

"She made it pretty clear that there's not a good chance. They've already chosen a band."

Of course, they have. I hadn't wanted to think about that.

"Who is it?"

Danny rolls his eyes. "The Mastor Gators."

I groan. "They're horrible."

"I know, right? They scream lyrics that make no sense."

"They're, like, death metal. Why would the Council pick a death metal band?"

Danny stretches his deltoids. "They're not all death metal. They play at their church on the weekend."

I nearly choke when I laugh. "No way."

"Yeah. I guess they know some pop music too." Danny strolls over to the dumbbells. "I'm sorry, man. I thought she'd really go for it."

"So much for being a fan of Blue."

"Oh, no, she's still very much a fan. She had a list of insults for the Gators. She's pissed as hell that Blue isn't the prom band." He selects fifteen-pounders and moves to a bench. "She'll put in a good word for you, but . . ."

"I get it." I have really screwed this up.

But, there's still Christine. Maybe she'll have good news. Art class can't come soon enough.

Even though I've changed out of my gym clothes, by the time I run all the way to the art room, I'm nearly as sweaty as I was before I changed. But I can't care about that now. I need to talk to Christine.

I catch my breath in the hall before I saunter in, so I'm not heaving and sweating, but there's no Christine. Yet. Just because she always beats me here every day is no reason to panic. Everything's fine.

Though she's not the girl I'm waiting for, Madi arrives before Christine.

Madi says hello, and I want to smile and talk with her, but I need to see Christine, so I respond with, "Any news from Hunter?"

She glowers at me.

Inwardly, I smile. Can't help it.

Libby comes in, pausing by my desk. "Hey." She surveys the empty stool beside me. "Where's Christine?"

"Your guess is as good as mine."

She checks over her shoulder for Madi and then says to me, "What did she find out from Hunter?"

"Well, she hasn't found out yet that he's a douche."

Libby controls her laugh until she can completely suppress it. "You need to fix this."

"I'm working on it. I don't think Hunter has talked to anyone yet," I tell her honestly.

The bell rings, almost drowning out Libby saying, "Asshole," under her breath. Me or him? Probably both. She gives me a little wave before heading for her desk, but I really don't think she's done being mad at me.

Christine could still come through for us. Of course, she can only come through for us if she shows up.

Don't panic. Focus on art.

I can hardly remember what I've been drawing with all that's been going on, which is ridiculous, since I only ever draw Sasha. I slide the top drawing out of my portfolio and discover the beginning of a picture of Dakota. Oh, yeah.

Her beautiful eyes and cute ears bring a smile to my face. Only a few seconds later, I'm lost in the sketch with her. Such a great dog.

Ten minutes or more go by before I realize that someone

is now sitting in the desk beside me. Christine. "When did you get here?"

"Should I say ten minutes ago?" She laughs.

"When?"

"Just now."

I try to show restraint. I don't want to seem like I'm using her—which I am. So instead of demanding to know what she found out, I put myself on standby, hoping she'll be forthcoming.

Opening her art case, she begins to lay out charcoal and erasers. "I talked to Mr. Gerber."

I sit up straighter. I can take it no matter which way it goes.

Distracted with taking out her paper, she says nothing more.

"Well?"

She smiles. "He wouldn't give me an answer, but he said he'd talk to you."

My throat constricts. I don't know him. What could I possibly say to make him let us audition? On top of that, he'll probably think I'm strange. I hate meeting people. Hate it.

"That's a good thing," she said. "I think he wants to hear about why you didn't come to your first audition."

Though my heart breaks into a sprint to get out of my chest, I keep my voice steady. "Of course. No problem."

"Don't look so disappointed. Tell him the truth like you told me, and I'm sure he'll understand."

The rest of the day, I take sight-seeing tours of Mr. Gerber's hallway, even passing his door a few times. But I can't get myself to go through his door. After school. I'll go after school.

After school, I loiter in Gerber's hall, still unable to make myself go in. Cursing myself in my head does not help. Daring myself to just do it doesn't help. I hover around there so long that Mr. Gerber comes out into the hall with his keys in hand, bag slung over his shoulder. He's no taller than me, which usually makes me feel a bit better, but this time does nothing to appease me.

He locks the door and nearly runs into me. "Oh, hello. Are you here to see me?"

"Uh . . ."

He checks his watch.

I'm keeping him from something. "I wanted to talk to you about prom auditions."

"Right. You're the kid Christine and Lauren mentioned to me."

I try to smile. "Yeah. My band missed the first audition." I'm not sure how much Christine told him, so I tell him more. "We were hoping you could give us a chance to make that up."

He leans against his closed classroom door, crossing his arms. "Christine tells me you have a good excuse. Let me tell you up front, though, I can't just give you the spot."

"No, no, of course not."

"We've already chosen a band. The only reason I'll even consider doing this is if you have a legitimate, reasonable excuse."

I'm about to tell him. Really. But where do I start? I prioritized my dog's surgery over the audition? I stupidly thought I could fit both things into my schedule?

He raises his eyebrows. "And . . . the reasonable excuse is . . .?"

I explain as best as I can how important Dakota is. How she could have died. I tell him how I let Libby and Gene down and wasn't even decent enough to tell them I wasn't coming. How Libby has already made lists of songs we could play. How she's made us rehearse constantly like we're the chosen band.

Mr. Gerber doesn't respond while I'm talking—no head-nodding, no encouraging words—he just stares me down like it's an interrogation and he's trying to get the truth out of me.

He's still staring when I finish. The hallway is silent except for my thoughts, which are going wild. Say something. Tell me we can audition. At least blink.

"All right. That's a legitimate, reasonable excuse." He straightens his bag on his shoulder. "How about you come to the auditorium after school tomorrow."

"3:30?"

"3:30."

"We'll be there. For sure."

Chapter 34

RIGHT AWAY AFTER SCHOOL THE next day, I rush to meet Libby and Gene backstage at the auditorium. Madi hustles along with me, giving me two thumbs-up as I go in. Once I'm backstage, Libby is securing her cymbals. Behind her Gene straps on his bass, glaring at me from beneath his thick eyebrows.

"Don't start," I say.

Libby twirls her drumsticks over and over. "You ready?"

"So ready." I can feel my hands shaking a little, but I'm not scared. I can't believe we get to be on stage again. Sure, the crowd will only be like twenty to thirty people but still, we'll get them moving. We'll make them cheer.

I sling my guitar over my shoulder, test the strings. Do a quick tuning. My amp's plugged in and already reverberating. Hope it doesn't short out.

Gene runs out to the stage only to return a moment later. "Do we have microphones?"

Libby ignores him. "We'll do Aerosmith first," she says.

"I think we should do Fall Out Boy. It's up tempo."

Immediately, she's shaking her head. "No, it's better to start with Aerosmith."

"This is our chance to show them what we can do."

276

She jams her sticks into her back pocket. "And we will. We'll play Fall Out Boy second."

My fingers clutch the guitar too tightly. "Fine."

Gene swears.

From out front we hear a girl yell, "Are you back there?"

Libby considers answering them, then wants to know if I'm okay. Not that she has any inkling of changing her mind.

"I'm sure you're right." I take a step toward the stage.

"Hello?!" comes the call from the audience.

We roll out the drums and amps.

The moment we're on stage, everything is strange. The house lights are up, the stage lights are dark. I feel dizzy. In front of us are rows and rows of empty seats. I can't even see the girl who yelled to us a minute ago, then I spot her off on the side of the performance center. Rachel something. She's conferring with another girl. It's just the two of them? Two people in the audience?

Where's Mr. Gerber? Where is the "council"? Isn't the principal coming?

I meet Libby's eyes. She shrugs. I'm not sure if she's thinking what I'm thinking or if she's just shrugging off our disagreement. Libby hits her sticks together with the beat of our first song, and we're off. Gene thrums out the bass line. Only a few chord changes in, two more council members arrive. Hunter is one of them. They take seats in the front row and are joined by Rachel and the other girl.

I'm about to sing the first verse until I remember there's no microphone. When I miss my queue, Libby opens her eyes wide to me. I make a quick gesture about the microphone to which she only shakes her head like it's not a big deal.

Seriously? Vocals matter more than drums, Libby. But she doesn't stop, so when my queue comes around again, I take it, straining my voice to be heard above the amp and drums. Then static from my amp floods over the stage as the circuit is disrupted. Shit.

Rachel stands up, waving her arms. "Stop, stop, stop!"

My last chord dies out with Libby's last snare hit.

"What song was that? I can't hear you singing."

I look at the four members of the Student Council below me, letting my guitar riff peter out. Hunter stares straight at me. Maybe he's here to see if I'm on to him, if I know he had nothing to do with this. Or maybe he's here to psych me out.

Won't work.

Libby comes out from behind the drums to the center of the stage, crossing her arms. "Was someone supposed to set up mics for us?"

Rachel doesn't seem convinced that it was their responsibility, but she sends Hunter on stage to fix the problem.

He jogs backstage. For far too long, nothing happens. I can't hear anything backstage; I can't see anything happening out front here. The only thing I do finally hear is a hugely audible huff from Rachel. We're wasting her time. God, I hope she doesn't have the final say-so about our audition. Finally, finally, Hunter returns with mics and stands. When he sets mine up in silence, his eyes meet mine as he adjusts the height for my vocals.

Rachel calls out, "Thanks, Hunter. All right. Start over, please." Her *please* is anything but cordial.

Libby starts up again, and I catch up when I can, and then I'm singing, "I'd miss you, baby, and I don't want to miss a thing." The lyrics always make me wonder if I'm missing things I'm not even aware of. When I sing the chorus the second time, instead of seeing Christine's smile, Madi's face appears. Soft blue eyes. Tender lips.

Rachel gets up half way through the song, waving her arms again. We stop. "All right. That's pretty good. What else can you play?"

Rude. She could at least let us play the whole thing. I check Hunter's reaction, sure he must be snickering or leering at me. But he's only sitting there, hands folded, listening.

Gene starts our next piece, picking out the notes for "Time After Time." We're getting to the chorus for the second time when Rachel stops us again. My amp buzzes like it's exhausted and needs to short out. I jiggle the cord jack on my guitar to no avail. Then the buzzing stops on its own.

Rachel's pattern continues for a while—playing half a song then stopping—until we've gone through about ten pieces. I was not prepared for this. Truthfully, when we get to Fall Out Boy's "Dance, Dance," I feel like I screw up more of the chords than I get right.

Of course, with "Dance, Dance," Rachel insists we play the whole thing, as if she wants to note each misstep.

When we finish, she writes on a clipboard, talking to the council members beside her. The girl next to her with long green and purple hair animatedly waves her hands around when Rachel permits her to talk. She has some sway because Rachel's tense face untightens a bit as she nods. More move-ment from the green/purple haired girl. She's clearly a fan. Maybe this is Danny's friend Lauren.

Hunter, notably, says nothing at any point, even when they

turn to him for a response.

When I can't wait any longer, I finally say, "Well. What did you think?" As the words leave my mouth, I can feel my face flush. I don't want to look at Hunter, but that's exactly what I do. He stares back. For too long, there's nothing there, no judgment, no opinion.

"Here's what we'll have to do," Rachel says. Then she's quieter again as she confers with the council. "We'll have to talk with Principal Eckert," she says to us.

Does that mean we did well? Or does that mean we didn't?

Rachel passes a clipboard around to each of the members of the council, and then says, "We'll let you know."

Lauren leans over toward Rachel. I can almost hear what she's saying.

"All right." Rachel stands, spreading her arms like she'll envelop us in an embrace. "As far as we're concerned, you're our band for prom!" She spins around to face the council members. "And we can say goodbye to the Mastor Gators."

Libby and Gene and I fall into an awkward three-way hug and pat each other on the back. I can't believe we got the gig. Of course, that means putting myself in front of the whole school again, letting them take free shots at me while I have no way of taking cover. But it's worth it. If we can get Bekkah Ingram to talk to her dad, it's worth it. And, anyway, no one's going to bother making fun of me; they'll be too busy dancing.

I look around for Madi to see what she thinks, to see her smile at me. Did she listen to our audition? I don't see her anywhere. "I gotta go thank Madi!" Libby smiles and waves me off so instead of putting my instrument away or helping

Libby with her drum kit, I push through the side door of the auditorium to find Madi.

And I do. With Hunter.

I hear her thanking him. "I can't tell you how much I appreciate you getting them another audition!" She's using her excited voice, the one she uses when she's talking about theater or her dog.

He has his arm around her waist and seamlessly pulls her into his chest with a little laugh.

She steps back from him so she can finish what she was saying. "Aren't you glad they'll be the band at prom?"

He shrugs. "Sure." He pulls her closer again.

For a moment, I consider interrupting them, but then I see she's smiling.

Chapter 35

LIBBY'S WAITING FOR ME WITH my amp and guitar when I return to the auditorium. She fights a smile. "We're going to rock that prom!" She's still back in the glorious mindspace I was in five minutes ago: Our band is going places.

I try to get back there, too, mostly for Libby's sake. "We will be epic," I say, but my voice is monotone.

"You want to bring Madi?"

I scowl. "What?" Then I remember. The plan is to go get a pizza and celebrate. I look around to see if Madi happens to be there, and if she happens to be sans-Hunter, but Libby and I are alone.

I shake my head. "Nah. We should bring Gene, though."

But, Gene's already left with his dad and Libby's drums. He's going by our old rules that he's too young to hang out with us, but that has to change now that our band's doing so well.

At Emerald Isle Pizza, Libby and I find our favorite booth and settle in with refillable Cokes and a cheesy thick crust original.

Libby asks for the waitress's red pen and makes a list on the back of her paper placemat of the songs we should play for sure. "Okay, so you want everything from the soundtrack for *Hannah Montana*."

I throw my straw wrapper at her, which travels two inches then drops limply to the table. "Another list? I thought the last one was fine."

"'Livin' on a Prayer' is a must," she writes. "And 'Time After Time.'"

"Seriously? I sound like a total girl on that one."

She whacks me with the end of the pen. "You don't and it's a great song."

"Fine, but no Michael Jackson," I say.

"You told me yesterday Michael Jackson was okay."

"I changed my mind. He sings too high, and I don't want that reputation."

For a moment, she glares at me, and I wonder whether she's thinking what I'm thinking. It's inevitable that I'm going to sing too high. Right now. But she's kind enough not to say it.

"I'm just going to write down Aerosmith and Green Day."

"Agreed." I grab a slice of pizza, strings of cheese connecting it back to the whole.

"Justin Timberlake, Bruno Mars, Ed Sheeran. These are all ones you're awesome at."

I love how she says that in passing, like it's just a given in a geometry problem.

With each of these, she makes eye contact to get approval. "Panic! at the Disco." Absolutely. "Taylor Swift." Reluctantly. "Lady Gaga." Do my best.

Libby becomes uncharacteristically quiet. She doesn't take a bite of pizza; she only stares at her hands. "I was thinking we could add another Cyndi Lauper song."

Weird. "All right. Which one?"

"'True Colors'?"

I groan. "You have got to be kidding. It's so sappy and——"

"It was my mom's favorite song."

I close my mouth. She so rarely mentions her mom. I should have just listened. "I'm sorry."

She laughs. "You're sorry it's my mom's favorite song?"

I know she wants me to laugh, too, but I feel like a shit. "No. Not at all."

"This is such a big thing, you know?" She lowers her eyes. "I wish my mom knew we were doing this. That she was here and I knew she was proud of me."

"Of course, she's proud of you."

Libby shakes her head. "I know I'm blessed. My aunt and uncle are great. They support what I'm doing with music and make me feel like I'm their own kid, but sometimes I wish I had my mom again. Just for an afternoon or a few hours, so she could tell me that I've turned out all right, you know?" She's wearing her mom's jean jacket, as usual, but I notice for the first time in a long time that one of the band buttons is Cyndi Lauper.

"For what it's worth, I think you've turned out all right." I offer her my hand to hold.

She grasps it for a moment, giving it a thank you squeeze, then lets go.

It's not the same for me. I know that. But I wish my mom was proud of me too.

After about a half hour, we have a list of what we'll play and the possible order we should put them in. Libby has scheduled periods of all-out dancing frenzy and sustained, relaxed embraces. This is something I never pictured her doing. When she told me she was taking the class in music production, I wasn't sure she'd like that aspect of music, but she's completely absorbed herself in it.

I can feel my foot tapping, my fingers drumming. I want to play them all. Even Katy Perry. The stage. The lights. The crowd. I'm absolutely psyched about this.

Once we're stuffed with cheesy goodness, we go to Libby's basement, call Gene down, and give him three slices we had left over. Libby talks him through the set list as he eats, while I pick through a few riffs. Then we practice as many of the songs as we can. Maybe it's psychosomatic, but I keep messing up the Taylor Swift song, so much so that Libby finally says we should just move on. We'll need to skip that one entirely on prom night. More tenor guy songs. Fewer soprano girl songs.

This is going to happen and it's going to be epic.

Decidedly un-epic is the way I was bursting with so much of everything—but Madi was with Hunter. She didn't even say anything to me.

It's one thing for her not to love me, but to not even be my friend during something so important is something else entirely.

I'm sure he told her the Student Council only let us audition because of him, like he's the reason they chose us for the prom, as if he'd done it himself, as if he had the sole vote in the decision.

Now, this morning, sitting in my car in the school parking lot, waiting to go inside for class, I can't get Madi out of my head. If she likes a dickhead like Hunter, she's hopeless. She could never see me for what I am.

I slam my fist down on the steering wheel, then throw open the car door, heading for first hour. At least I won't have to see Madi until second.

No sooner am I inside the school than a dozen or so people singularly or in pairs come up to me, wanting a high five or fist bump or to give me a nod of congratulations. The captain of the lacrosse team winks at me from under his blond curls and says, "I was hoping it would be your band."

Something about those words from that guy puts me on cloud nine. He knows me and my music, and he wants us to perform. The rest of my steps don't touch the floor. In the main senior hallway, two girls from Student Council hang a series of flyers, one every tenth locker or so:

Prom. Dance to the music of Blue.

This is really happening.

Passing the girls locker room, I close myself in the coach's office, sliding the hook lock closed. This morning feels different, though; a weird sense of belonging undercuts the usual dread of the door opening as I change. Pulling on my gym shorts, I realize I'm smiling. When my little toe snags on the leg of the shorts, I'm amused instead of annoyed.

I meet Danny in the loser free-weights area. We nod hello, and as I grab the twenty-five-pound dumbbells, Danny is still nodding. "I saw the flyers."

I can't help but grin like an idiot.

He claps me on the back. "It worked out! That's so great."

He reaches down to grasp weights he can almost lift.

"It's pretty great, yeah." I curl my dumbbells one at a time, trying not to obviously out-lift him. "I'm sure Lauren had some influence."

He nods a little. "She's pretty pleased."

So cool.

Grumbling and sputtering, he brings up his weights, attempting to keep up with me rep for rep. He side-eyes me and forces his arms to work more quickly than they want to.

Without considering it, I slow a bit. No sense giving him a heart attack. When I finish a short set of eight, I set the weights down so he can rest. Once he's caught his breath, he says, "Are we still on for Saturday?"

I give him a blank look.

"Cool band. My uncle's pub."

"Right, right. Of course."

"I can get you in for free."

I laugh. "I know. You're a celebrity there." That's the kind of happy look that gets a kid beat up. I glance across the room, but JT is nowhere near.

"We'll hang out. My uncle'll set us up with some wings."

"Sounds great."

Coach Wendell wanders over to us. "Did I hear right?" he asks me.

Danny wants to hang out on Saturday? Can't be that.

"Your band is playing the prom this year?" He rubs his hands like he always does, as if he needs to warm them up.

"Yeah, that's right."

He shakes my hand like I'm one of his football players. "You'll knock 'em dead." He laughs reassuringly. "I heard you at the talent show back in January. You have a great voice, kid."

I thank him. He's such a cool guy. I love that he called me "kid" instead of the name on his class roster.

Behind him, I see JT watching, hands on his hips, like he's scrutinizing the stripes on a very odd zebra. He stares for too long, continually checking back as if assuring himself I'm still there.

All the way to art class, JT stays five steps behind me. No idea why he's following me, especially if his cronies aren't with him. He must have something rude to tell me about my band, but we reach the art room without a confrontation. He doesn't even care whether I know he's behind me. So strange.

I watch to ensure he doesn't follow me into the room. He doesn't. I pull out my stool, but before I can sit, Christine gives me a smile. "You did it."

I try to see if she has that look, the one she gave me the night of the talent show, but she's looking away. I'm stupidly drawn to her like she hasn't broken my heart a thousand times.

I want to say something witty about how I won't be able to dance with her if I'm playing the music, but I remind myself that those words won't impress her. But that's fine. I don't think I love her. She's beautiful, of course, but she's not the girl for me. And she doesn't love me. But she doesn't know me. I've been sitting next to her in this class for months without our getting the tiniest bit closer.

Across the art room, someone drops a hot glue gun with a thud, but I don't see who; my gaze stops at Madi, animatedly talking to Libby. I could have sat next to either of them this semester. I could've learned so much about Madi by now. Shown her so much more about me. She wouldn't be dating Hunter if I'd sat with her instead of Christine.

I've been such a fool.

But my music, that could catch her attention. She wasn't at the talent show. She hasn't heard us play. The music at the prom—

Shit. She'll go with fucking Hunter.

Closing my eyes, I make myself think of something else. All around the school are flyers for the prom and our band. It's so great to get our name out like this, like we're actual celebrities. We're the band playing the gig that the whole school will hear. We'll make their prom a night to remember.

And I really hope that's the only thing that makes it a night for Madi to remember.

Madi doesn't congratulate me. I wait for her to arrive for lunch, to say she's so glad she helped us get the audition, that we're doing the music. But nothing. Instead, Madi doesn't even show up.

Libby relays that Madi has to make up a test in Math and won't be at lunch. So instead of Madi talking about our awesomeness, Libby tells me about the prom setlist, only this time she adds something new. "I've been working on an application to a music production program for next year."

"What? That's amazing."

"I don't know; that class I took this year and working on the prom setlist has made me see music in a really different way. So I'm putting together a portfolio with the modifications I've made to some of the pop songs, showing how I can take one music genre and change it into another."

I think about the changes she's made to the songs we're playing. I've thought all along about how genius it is that she can do this. Right now, I don't know what to say to tell her how cool this is.

"I think I have a real chance of getting in."

"Of course you do," I say.

"No, you don't get it. This is a really elite music academy."

"Libs, I do get it. You're going to get in because you're amazing at this."

I've forgotten about Madi's absence temporarily, and the absence of her compliments for us. The moment of congratulations, apparently, won't be until Drama. Not until we're alone in the band practice room, working on our scene. What will she say? What will she do? If Hunter got a hug, what's in store for me?

I get to class a little early. And maybe that's a mistake because she's a little late. But soon enough, we're in the practice room with the fake tree and the upright piano. Her compliments are still forthcoming. I tinker around on the keys as she meanders through a few of her lines, holding her sheet up for help. I glare at her. "We should be off book, don't you think?"

She swats me. "I'm reviewing."

I spew out my first line, then the next, and the next until she swats me again. I try to keep my tone civil, but there are mitigating circumstances times two. "We have to present at the end of the week." I can't believe she doesn't know her part.

Her smile vanishes. "I'm reviewing."

I lay my forearms down on the piano keys. I imagine my fingers on the keys, playing her favorite song—whatever that is—like I wrote it personally. Perfect rhythm. No slip-ups. In real life, though, I take a moment to line up my fingers before tapping out a few hesitant notes that sound out of tune.

Madi makes a sound of sarcastic disgust, exaggerating rubbing her ear like it's been violated.

I close my eyes. Clear my head, calling up the song I was working on a week ago on the guitar, transposing guitar chords and lyrics into notes on the piano. It's awkward at first, for sure, but after only a few playthroughs, I have the melody down with a simple accompaniment. That's when I feel the warmth of Madi's arm against mine as she sits beside me on the piano bench.

"That's beautiful. Do I know that song?"

I almost confess I wrote it for her, that I was just working on this yesterday because I was thinking about her, but I don't. "Probably not." I go back over the same keys again, teaching my fingers the melody.

"I really like it."

I let myself smile. "I'm not sure what to call it yet."

Her hand returns to my arm. "You wrote this?"

I give her a strange look.

She stammers. "I know you and Libby have a band, but I didn't know you wrote music like this?"

"There's a lot you don't know about me."

She smiles as if I haven't just tried to make her feel bad. "The Student Council chose you because you're actually good."

"What?"

"Hunter made it sound like he tried to influence their decision, but a bunch of people today have been saying how glad they are that it's your band."

They have, but I didn't know they were saying it when I wasn't there. Underground cult sensation. "Hunter's a . . ." I can't think of a suitable insult for him. Instead, I say, "I can't see what you like about him."

Her eyes search our tiny rehearsal room for an answer. "He's a gentleman."

I scoff at her.

"What?"

"He lied to you. He never talked to the Student Council about the audition."

She hesitates. "You don't know that."

"Come on. I've known him for years."

"I don't believe you." But it's plain she partly believes me. "How did you get the audition, then?"

I lock eyes with her, hoping to make this sting. "Christine."

Her face falls. Maybe it stings too much.

"Listen." How do I walk this back now? "I don't want you to get hurt."

She's mulling it over.

"Let's just rehearse, huh?"

Absently, she nods.

"Didst thou hear these verses?" I say, and when she doesn't speak, I say her line too.

She laughs a little at my taking over for her and replies with my line, "That's no matter: the feet might bear the verses."

And for the entire scene, we do the other's role. She

exaggerates how manly her words can sound and I pretend to be a total ditz. It's very satisfying in light of our previous discussion. With the last line, we fall into a fit of laughter together. It's hard to stop when she's so clearly happy and I'm so clearly not unhappy.

I read the first bunch of lines again. "Rosalind seems desperate for Orlando to love her, but Celia, why doesn't she want someone to love? It seems like she's pushing love away."

Madi snorts. "If you know anything about her family situation, it makes total sense." And then just like that, her thoughts are forever away from here. She shakes her head as if dismissing them and says, "If you could change anything about your life, what would it be?"

Dumbest question ever. I give her the look.

She groans. "Besides that."

There is only that. "I guess get a dog."

"Right. Dakota?" She joins me on the bench, forcing me to slide down a few inches. She seems about ready to tell me what she would change, but instead she chooses a completely different road. "Can I ask you something? I've known a few other trans people, but I've always wanted to ask . . . Have you ever thought about just being a girl?"

I cluck my tongue. "Why would I want that?"

"I don't know. It would be a lot easier, wouldn't it?"

"No doubt." I play the melody of her song again, but my answer doesn't satisfy her. "I don't know how to be a girl." I laugh. "I've tried."

She laughs too. "That's true. But it would be easier than changing everything about yourself."

"Well, I'm not changing anything about myself, really."

"Oh." She lightly gestures to my body. "So you're not going to . . ."

I move two feet away from her, what the room allows. "First of all, that's not your business. Second, yes, that's my hope."

She nods, but it's clear she's processing something.

"What?"

"So you're changing the outside, not the inside."

I shrug. "The inside is a work in progress too."

She laughs, no doubt remembering our conversation about what kind of man I'm trying to be. "Just so you know, I was right about you."

"What?"

"You've been acting a little different at school since we talked. You're—I don't know, more real. Not so shut off from everyone."

"I don't want to be shut off from you." The words rush out of me, followed by warm icicles of embarrassment. I cover my eyes.

"That's sweet."

"You're the most interesting person I've ever talked to." I don't know what gives me the courage for it, but I know she'd rather hear she's intellectually stimulating than hear that her eyes are deep pools of blue. "You're just real. No acting."

She raises an eyebrow at me.

"You know what I mean. No pretending. It's how I think I would be if I had just been born . . . you know, the way I should have been."

Madi nods. "Sometimes I wish I knew how to put up a façade. 'Do you not know that I am a woman? When I think, I must speak.'"

Her quoting from the play makes me laugh.

Something between us is so powerful that I feel pulled toward her, compelled to kiss her. But I stop myself. This could be the beginning of us, but it's not yet the beginning of *us*.

Chapter 36

AFTER DRAMA, I FIND A dozen messages from Troy and half a dozen missed calls. I start skimming the texts, but it's clear I have to get to the animal rescue right away. That's almost all he's texted. *You need to get here right away.* Later messages are clearer: *Luna's owner is on his way here. If you want to say goodbye . . .*

This is a nightmare. I can't lose this dog. But there's nothing I can do to stop it.

I drive too fast all the way there and into the parking lot and can't catch my breath before I open the door. There in the lobby is Dakota, only she's not Dakota anymore. Her tail is wagging, and her mouth is open in a panting smile. Someone's dad stands over her, talking to her in a doggie voice. "How's my little Luna? How's my good girl?"

And her tail creates a gale-force wind with her enthusiasm.

I don't recognize the guy, but it's clear who he is.

Dr. Wallin, Troy, and Jeanie stand nearby with hesitant smiles on their faces. They look up as I rush in, and the smiles disappear.

Troy comes over to me, grabs my arm, and says quietly, "This guy's name is Jason Ashur. Is he your dad or something?"

I don't understand. "Of course not."

"Is Dakota actually your dog this whole time?" Troy is confused and he isn't making any sense.

Jason Ashur roughhouses a little with Luna, laughing, and says, "My son will be so happy to see her again." He looks at Jeanie and then over at Troy. "I can't thank you enough."

Troy perks up. "Son?"

Jason nods. "He was trying to get her to come inside when she got loose. Remember that blizzard back in January? Luna didn't want to come in. She loves the snow. So Nathan went out in his boots and jacket to try to pull her inside, and she got out of her collar. Took off running."

Nathan Ashur lost his dog Luna, who's my Dakota. This can't be happening.

"He's been so upset with himself. He thinks it's his fault she got away, and until you called, he thought she'd wound up dead somewhere." Jason becomes overly serious. "He's been so broken up all this time, thinking he'd let her die because he'd given up looking for her." He crouches down to pet Luna. "He was out in the blizzard for hours. Nearly died himself."

Troy looks at me. His fingers still wrapped around my arm; he thrusts me forward a little. "Is this your son?"

I gasp, scowling at Troy like he's insane. Bad timing, dude.

Jason Ashur assesses me, his gaze up and down. "Uh . . . no. Why would you ask that?"

Troy has let me go. "Funny coincidence. His name happens to be Nathan Ashur too."

Jason frowns. "What?"

I laugh. "Terrible joke, Troy. Why would you think that would be funny? I'm Nathan Kinkade." I shake Mr. Ashur's hand.

Dr. Julia Wallin, Jeanie, and Troy glare at me. I ignore all of them and move over to Dakota. Kneeling down in front of her, I hug her head and say, "You're still my dog." My tears are trapped behind my tense embarrassment. "I'll miss you." I ruffle her fur.

I get up, looking Mr. Ashur in the eye. "You should get her home to your son."

He's confused but his relief is obvious when he says, "Thanks again. We were lost without her."

And with those words, Dakota disappears from my life.

And the four of us are left in a silent lobby with my questionable identity.

Dr. Wallin crosses her arms. "I think you better explain yourself."

My heart beats so hard that it moves my body back and forth as I try to come up with the words. "I never meant to lie to you."

Troy raises his eyebrows.

"That first day I came in, Jeanie thought I was Nathan Ashur." I sound like I'm blaming her, but that is what happened. "I thought if he hadn't shown up, maybe I could be Nathan Ashur. I've always wanted to be accepted as a boy."

Troy turns to his sister and says, "I told you."

I close my eyes. I thought Troy knew, but it still hurts. "I came in that day to see if I could adopt a dog, and then you let me be Nate." I smile in spite of fearing their response. "I liked being Nate."

"Is that why you wouldn't give me your driver's license?" Jeanie is entirely unamused.

"I didn't want you to know I wasn't who you thought I

was. And the longer it was that the real Nathan didn't show up, the harder it was to tell the truth."

None of them meets my eyes. They must hate me so much.

"This is a great job. I really liked working here." I can feel my eyes filling with tears, so I head for the door.

No one says anything to stop me.

Chapter 37

EVERYTHING IS IN LIMBO AS the next few days meld together. Lifting weights with Danny, Art with Christine, Shakespeare lines in Drama, song rehearsal with Blue, missing Dakota and the animal rescue. I don't even have the slightest relief knowing that the real Nathan Ashur will never make me lose my job. I did that all on my own by lying to them. And while finding his Caring Bridge site back in January made me astoundingly happy, knowing he almost died only makes me ashamed.

Prom is mere weeks away. Our Blue-ified versions of these songs have improved even since the audition. I think I might love playing cover songs. Libby occasionally tweaks something here or there, jots a note in her little book, and we try it the new way to see if it gels.

JT has come up to me for a heart-to-heart twice since he popped up at my house. Both times, he wanted to walk down Memory Lane, rekindle our paltry, childhood romance. If he hadn't been so detailed about the fifth-grade music concert, I'd think this was a semi-elaborate plan to humiliate me; but he seems serious. Like seriously interested in me. Prom is coming. He needs a date. He must know it can't be me.

As deadlines go, though, Drama class is more serious. In two days, Madi and I have to perform our scene from *As You Like It*. Two days. We have our lines down, but our blocking is pretty sparse, mostly because we rehearse in a room the size of a shoebox. Major dramatic movements cannot be developed in a shoebox. Some groups have props. There's even one with swords and fake blood. They could be the best of all of us. My money's on Madi and me, though. We aren't relying on special effects or flashy objects; we need only our voices.

Then on Friday, everything changes. We're performing our scene today. But that's last hour. So all day, I have to think about how I can mess things up. Which line will I deliver wrong? When will I forget to take a step or make a gesture?

Thankfully, I don't worry long because third hour, I'm called down to the principal's office. Something completely different to worry about. I have never been summoned to the principal's office.

To my surprise when I arrive in the main office, Libby is here waiting.

Oh, no. Did something happen to her aunt or uncle? Ignoring the principal's secretary, I go straight to Libby. "Is everything all right?"

"I don't know." She shrugs. "What are you doing here?"

The principal's door opens. He looks from Libby to me and back to Libby. "Come on in, ladies."

My eye twitches. *Ladies.*

Libby snorts at him, gesturing toward him with her thumb like he's ridiculous.

"Take a seat," he says, closing the door behind us.

His chair behind his giant principal desk places him directly in front of me. As he assesses me, I try to think of any time I've ever spoken to Principal Eckert for more than a sentence or two. Only after the talent show.

Awkwardly laying his hands on his desk, he says, "Before we talk, I should congratulate you girls on being chosen to play at prom."

We adopt his awkwardness when we thank him.

"Unfortunately, a situation has been brought to my attention."

I sift through recent memories. What has happened that could be considered a situation? It's not like JT harassing me after the talent show or JT and his friends humiliating me wearing "dresses" and makeup was ever brought to his attention. I can't recall anything that traumatic recently.

He isn't talking, so I say, "What situation?"

His lips purse. "There's been some concern."

When he doesn't continue, I shift in my seat. If there's concern, it's likely about me. "What concern?"

At the same moment, Libby says, "From who?"

He removes his glasses, setting them on his desk. "Well, as you may know, our district has a fairly large group of conservative families."

This is starting to sound really bad. "Mr. Eckert, what's going on?"

"I'm afraid a few families have expressed concern over your band performing at prom." He puts his glasses back on.

"We'll play a huge variety of songs. They don't have to worry." Libby sits back in her chair, knowing she has this completely under control.

Principal Eckert says, "That's not the reason they're concerned—"

Libby interrupts him. "I know what I'm doing with music."

"The issue has nothing to do with the music. I'm sure your band is very good. But—" He gets louder when Libby starts to talk. "It has to do with the way Kayla . . . dresses."

My entire face gets hot. "How do I dress?"

Mr. Eckert gets up. "Now, I need you to understand, this request isn't coming from me. But I have to represent every student here, even those I might not agree with."

Libby squirms in her chair.

"What does it matter," I say, "how I dress?" Of course, I know very well why it matters, and if I forget, I can always consult my mother for the answer.

His eyebrows rise. "Indeed," he says, so very quietly.

Libby pushes against the arm rests that hold her in place. Standing, she says, "Are you telling us we can't perform at prom?"

The principal moves to his door as if he's showing us out. "No, no. Of course not." But he's positioned to herd us back in should we decide to bolt.

"Oh, good." The heavy weight on Libby's shoulders evaporates.

"But you'll have to wear appropriate attire. Formal attire." Now, he opens the door for us to leave.

I stay seated, looking over my jeans and T-shirt. "There's nothing inappropriate about what I wear."

"Appropriate for a—a young lady attending prom."

My disgust bursts from my mouth in a slew of words that

don't string together. "That's not fair. I don't have to . . . I mean I wear what I . . . I follow the dress code."

Eckert closes the door in a hurry as if I swore. "I'm afraid that's not good enough. The parents have threatened to take this to the school board if I can't convince you."

"I don't see why it matters." Libby clears her throat. "There's nothing wrong with these clothes." She picks at my T-shirt.

Principal Eckert sighs. "These parents believe young women need to dress in acceptable ways, and the compromise we reached was prom attire."

Libby tuts. "We're a rock band, Mr. Eckert."

I stand up in a huff, trying to flip my chair over, but it only rocks back a few inches. "I'm not changing who I am. I'll perform as me, or I won't perform at all."

Mr. Eckert opens his office door so we'll leave. "Please just think about it."

Libby grabs my shoulder and moves me out into the hallway, murmuring under her breath all the way. Once we're safely past adult ears, she spits out a string of swears, adding to the end, "How ridiculous am I going to look playing drums in a prom dress?"

I'm so amped up I can't speak. *Think about it.*

Like I won't be thinking about it every second of every day for the rest of my life. How I lost my chance to impress Madi Sayer with my voice and to show this stupid school that I'm worth more than they could ever imagine. How it all happened because of bigots who want everyone to fit into a perfect little gender box.

Every face I see, I have to wonder, was it her? Or him? It

could be anyone. It could be half the senior class. The juniors. It could be the whole school.

On our way back to our third hour classes, Libby and I have to split up. Spotting a prom flyer on the wall announcing what would have been my greatest accomplishment, I tear it down and shred it, letting the pieces fall from my hands like water flowing through my fingers. But then there's another. And another. All of these flyers saying Blue is playing prom.

All of them must die.

I rip each one down, scratching my nails against the gray stone wall. This yellow one, this green one, this blue one. Down they go. After a dozen or more, two of my nails have torn, but I don't care. And I don't care that my fingers are scratched or that the back of my hand prickles with blood, a rash burn.

I grab another yellow one and a green one. A classroom door opens wide, and two freshmen lurch into the hall mere feet in front of me. When they see me, their eyes widen. One grabs the other and pulls him back in the room.

Two lives saved.

I continue my remodeling spree.

It's discrimination. Flat out discrimination. If anyone in my stupid school had any idea what a transgender person was, they would know they can't do this. They can't dictate who I can be or how I can dress.

I move from hall to hall, needing to find every single flyer. Every mention of my band's name. Most I only tear in half or fourths, but some get the full confetti treatment. No classroom doors open. No one can hear me fuming through the halls, consuming papers like I'm a conflagration of calamity.

None of it assuages my rage. If anything, each new paper adds literal fuel to my discrimination fire.

The main hallway has a poster-sized prom announcement with our band's name written in Sharpie. Oh, that's coming down. That whole damned thing is coming down. When I reach for the glossy poster, the edge slashes into my palm just above my thumb. I wince. My skin burns, and for a moment I stall, clenching my wound with my other hand and swearing. Then I rip the poster down in strips.

Ahead I spot the trophy case where prom flyers have been taped up in front of past years' awards. These I tear down, too, until I uncover last year's prom king and queen with their court. Boys and girls in their *appropriate* formal attire, smiling without a care in the world. Their little lives are perfect. Beside them is the photo from the year before, then the year before that. Next shelf down is a series of the same but from Homecoming. They might as well be the same people every year. Preppy, smiley students with clear genders.

Why do I want to be part of this?

Out of the corner of my eye, I can see a few people approaching me: the assistant principal and the dean of students. They slow when they see me, and as the AP says something into his walkie-talkie, the dean puts up his hands like I'm holding a weapon instead of a prom flyer. Or maybe he can see flames billowing from my fingertips and blood dripping from my palm.

I hear the AP repeat into his walkie-talkie, "We found Kinkade."

They're here to handle me. Take me back to the principal. Assign me detention. Screw that. I shred the flyer I'm holding, then take another down, inching closer to them. The dean's hands are still up. "Take it easy."

I rip the paper in half, in fourths, in eighths. Before I grab the next one, I hesitate as if he's making me rethink another hostage. Instead, I mangle the next one, spiking it to the floor like a football. Barely makes a sound.

The AP holds back, static clicking from his radio, leaving the dean alone with the psycho. "We can talk about this."

"What are we going to talk about?" My voice surprises me; I expected something less civil.

He doesn't know. Nothing registers on his face. "Whatever you want."

I prolong the agony of the next prom flyer, letting the sound fill the hallway as I rip it from the wall. "I don't want to talk. I want all of these down."

This momentarily pleases him. "Good. Okay. I can help you with that."

Static from the AP's walkie-talkie interrupts.

"Taking them down?" Interesting idea. It would go much faster if he helped me.

"No, no. I mean, that's somewhere to start. Tell me why you want them down."

Our band cannot be associated with this place. I can't tell him that. How could this cis-gendered white male possibly understand? I fake like I'm going to remove the next flyer, but at the last second, I run toward the closest staircase, fleeing the scene.

Around the next corner, I slow to catch my breath, and as I do, the bell rings. Students and their noise fill the hallway. This is the last thing I need right now, to be surrounded by the people responsible for my misery.

My fists clench so tightly that the soreness of my broken nails screams out against the pressure. Maybe the pain will distract me from making a bad choice.

Directly ahead of me is a kid with long dark bangs, ripped jeans, and a black The Clash T-shirt, black nail polish, and eyeliner. Danny.

His smile is so genuine I forget I'm furiously angry. For a second. And that's when his smile fades anyway.

"What happened? You look—" He doesn't have the words.

All I can do is shake my head.

He gestures for me to follow him to the space under the stairs. We can still see the countless people mulling about, but they pay little attention to us.

"What's going on, man?"

"They won't let us do prom." I visibly spit when I form the words.

"Who?"

"The principal just said we can't do prom unless I wear a dress." My shoulders move up and down as I breathe far too laboriously.

His lips tick up like he's going to laugh, but instead he says, "That's absolute crap. He can't do that."

"It's parents," I say but I'm biting my lip.

"It's what?"

"Parents. He said parents complained."

"No way. Whose parents would complain about—" He stops himself when he realizes how plentiful the options are. "They want you to wear a dress?"

I nod.

"Maybe they should meet you. You know? They could see that what they're asking you to do is-is . . . just stupid."

The bell rings to start fourth hour, and here we are, nowhere near where we should be. Like Pavlov's dog, I make a move to go to class, but Danny stays completely still.

He puts his hands on his hips. "I can talk to my dad. He knows someone on the school board. We'll tell them it's discrimination. It's illegal."

"No, listen. Forget it. I don't even want to do it if I have to fight them to allow me to. Thanks, but no."

"We can't let this happen."

"It's happening."

Chapter 38

THE DAYS FOLLOWING ECKERT'S PROM mandate and Dakota's departure barely exist. They're clipped scenes of walking to my classes and getting into bed at night, of questions about prom and quandaries about homework.

I have to meet with the assistant principal and my counselor about destroying the flyers, an event they're calling "disturbance of the learning climate," but because of my good record, they let me off with a warning. They call my parents to be sure my family knows I'm becoming a delinquent. Mom attributes it to being trans.

The only thing on my mind, though, is Dakota.

Libby no longer asks me to practice, no longer gives me her producer's viewpoint on how we're going to perform. She has accepted reality, and each day at lunch, she's content to sit with me in silence as she mourns the death of prom and I mourn the absence of Dakota. We both know prom's band has quit, but no one else in the school is privy to that secret except Danny. Not even Madi. It's too embarrassing to explain to her. I don't want to put an image of me in a prom dress into her head, or worse, have her suggest that I simply do it so Blue can play prom.

When I can get my thoughts together, I talk with Ms. Sands

about when Madi and I can make up our assignment for *As You Like It*. Seems like every time I have some important task to do, I avoid it and make the situation worse. Ms. Sands is completely accommodating. I need to complete my work, focus on the end: graduation. Only a month left.

But it's more than that. We've been working on this scene for almost a month. It's going to go well. Performing with Madi might be the only good thing that happens the rest of this year.

Madi and I huddle at the front of the room, skimming through our lines. Behind us, the entire class waits in their tiered rows. Ms. Sands sits nearby, foot wiggling, keeping time to a song no one else hears.

Madi grunts. "We never did any real blocking," she whispers. She puts a finger down on one of her lines. "When I say this one, I'm going to grab your arm and then move over there. You follow me and spin me back around to face you."

Before she's half-finished, I'm shaking my head. Not following. My mind is too cloudy. "Let's do it how we rehearsed it."

She sets the script down. "Just follow my lead."

Ms. Sands gets to her feet as Madi discards the script. "All right, everyone. They're ready to do their scene." She gives instructions about some evaluation sheet they're all supposed to have. They're grading us?

Everyone cheers, but their applause makes no sound for me. My thoughts are swirling with Dakota and destroyed prom flyers and the principal calling Libby and me *ladies*. When Madi touches my hand, though, my mind clears. I rattle off my first line. "Didst thou hear these verses?"

"Yes, I heard them all, and more too," comes her familiar response.

After a few more lines, she turns her back to me, crossing the room. I follow, and we continue our back and forth, the words coming easily to my lips.

When she says, "Do you not know that I am a woman? When I think, I must speak," I remember our conversation in the rehearsal room, and I laugh. My character would respond with humor as well. Inside, I'm so glad we changed parts. And I'm so glad Madi chose Shakespeare, for I am simply a young man traditionally playing a woman's role.

With Rosalind and Celia's last lines, we are on bended knee in the center of our stage, our arms outstretched as if Rosalind's love Orlando approaches.

There is too long of a pause before the mandatory clapping begins. Though our classmates are only mildly inspired by our rendition of *As You Like It*, Madi and I are astounded. We made it through the entire scene without a dropped word or line and without having to ask for a cue from Ms. Sands. She, in contrast with the class, cheers quite enthusiastically, saying, "Bravo! Bravo!" like she's in an audience at an opera.

Still kneeling, Madi looks into my eyes. For just a second I think her blue eyes look—but no. I imagine producing an engagement ring from my pocket; the look on her face is an enthusiastic *I do*.

Breathtaking.

Then suddenly, we're both on our feet, taking a meager bow to applause that has trickled out already. But we made it through the scene. We did fantastic.

Standing on her tiptoes, Madi wraps her arms around my neck. She breathes close to my ear. "Nate, we did it." I can feel her chest against me, my hands on her back, and for a moment, everything beyond her is gone. There is only Madi.

When she lets go, she grasps my hand before gathering up her books and finding her chair. I smile after her, completely unconcerned that anyone might see I love her.

Before I can take my seat beside Madi, Ms. Sands steps between us with a pass to the office.

This ruins everything.

No doubt the principal wants to express the importance of gender conformity in our community. Coldness rushes through me when I look down at what I'm wearing. Very boyish. But why does that make me nervous? This is who I am. I don't need to answer to anyone.

Libby and I arrive at the same time. Her permanent frown momentarily lifts. "Guess we both know what this is about."

Some stupid part of my mind makes me hope Mr. Eckert will say the parents dropped their complaint or that he himself will stick up for us. But I've lived too long as Kayla Kinkade to think that's how this part of my life's story will work out.

Inside his office, we all take our places in our assigned chairs from last time. He's blathering on about being the principal for every student and not allowing political views to influence what happens at the school.

But that's what you're doing.

It takes too long to realize I haven't challenged him out loud; I've merely thought something brave.

I sit up straighter. "How can you say this isn't political?"

"I'm sorry?" He's honestly confused.

"You're letting those parents decide how I dress."

Scowling, he says, "That's not what I'm—"

313

"Of course, it is. Did anyone on the Student Council ask me to dress differently?"

He tries to think.

"Anyone from the Choir or the Band?"

He stands as if he has something to say. "Now wait a minute."

"The Art Club? The Drama Club?"

"What exactly is your point?"

"My point is that you're listening to a handful of bigots and you're letting them make decisions for the whole school."

"It's only clothes."

Libby stands when I do. "We're not doing it," she says.

This is idiotic. I hold the door open for Libby to pass through. Eckert calls after us, "It's one night. One outfit."

I spin on him. "It's not one night. It's not one outfit. It's every night, it's every*thing* that you and the *normals*"—I make air quotes—"take as yours. When do I get to choose? When do you all have to accept what I want?"

He releases a mirthless laugh. "You're doing what you want right now." He gestures at my clothing.

"How would you like to wear a dress to run graduation?"

"It's not the same for me," he splutters.

I'm braced with another retort. Instead, I take a deep breath and say, "You just don't get it."

Outside the office and around the corner, Libby and I pause. My heart is beating so fast. I can't believe I said those things.

"For the record," Libby says, "I hadn't gotten too far along on my prom dress."

I blink at her.

She smirks. "I was making it out of black duct tape."

"That would've been cool."

"Yeah." Her eyes go far away for a moment.

I close mine tight, then meet her stare. "Now what?"

She grins. "Now we hold our heads up high and say we didn't give in to the man."

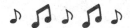

Word has gotten around school that Blue will not perform at prom. That honor is going back to the Mastor Gators, the death metal band that knows some hymns. New flyers in a single color—pink—have replaced the multi-colored flyers for Blue. Libby says nothing about the new band, the new flyers, but I know she's fuming underneath.

I want to be relieved but I'm not. I don't care if Lakeview High has a prom. I don't care if all of these idiots get dressed up and grope each other. I care about making an impression on Bekkah Ingram's dad, and I care about performing.

During study hall, as if he knows my schedule, I get a text from Sam about prom. *Dad said you and your band were supposed to play the music at the prom this year. What happened?*

A chill races through me when I consider what I have to explain to answer this question until I remember that Sam is fine with my being trans. I don't have to explain that part.

I keep it fairly simple. *Eckert wants me to wear a formal dress if I want to play prom.*

Sam returns rolling-eye emoji and *That's what Dad said. Eckert is such a jackass.*

Sam and I message back and forth for a while until he tells

me I better do my homework because college is hard, as if he's going to sign off.

Then he adds, *I have a big test to study for, but if you want, I'll come home this weekend. We can hang out.*

I'm tempted, but I'm too busy as it is. *I'll be all right.*

He sends a thumbs up. Then when I think he's gone back to college life, he texts again: *Just because I'm not home doesn't mean I'm gone. I'm not that far away.*

I roll my eyes. *I know.*

If you need me, I want you to call me.

Instead of responding to that, I consider how that might look. I could call Sam to tell him I'm feeling like everyone is judging me and no one understands. What would he do?

He texts again: *I'm serious. I've got a little brother vacancy in my life that I'm going to need filled from time to time.*

I laugh out loud. *I'm going to need some advice on girls.*

He sends a laughing emoji.

And how to bulk up more.

Thumbs up emoji. *We can work out together.*

Yeah. We can work out together. I wish I'd realized how supportive Sam would be, so I would have told him about myself instead of telling Mom. I could have had him help me with boy stuff. I could have talked to him that night after I embarrassed myself at the mall. I could've told him I wanted to die. He was right down the hall from me almost like he was waiting for me to come talk to him, like he knew I needed him.

I text him a heart emoji. Because boys can love their brothers.

Only a few hours after the pink flyers are up, I see one with the word *boycott* scrawled across it. I notice a few more in between classes, and later I see another one. The handwriting is not the same. Capital letters, lowercase letters, a combination. One has a *k* in boycott instead of a *c*. Possibly in German, possibly misspelled. My skin prickles with the sheer idea that this many people are angry that Blue won't be at prom. I let myself imagine they're on my side—up with trans rights—but I shouldn't let myself get carried away.

Libby finds me in the hallway, grabs my shirt sleeve, and pulls me over by the drinking fountain. Her eyes shine with excitement. "Do you know what's going on?" She cranes her neck around, performs a sort of semaphoric dance. "There's an underground rebellion."

Ridiculous. "You're crazy."

She grabs my arm before I can walk away. "People are pissed off, Kay. They wanted Blue."

I've trained myself so well to think that other people don't like me that I refuse to believe her, despite what Danny told me before. Despite what happened when we originally won. Despite what I was pondering moments before. "Guess that doesn't matter. We aren't going to do it."

Her elation dims. "No, but isn't it great?"

"Graffiti on flyers." I pull down a Mastor Gators at prom paper with *boycott* scrawled in blue Sharpie pen and shake it at her. "Real impressive."

I shouldn't have said it. Why can't I let Libby be happy about this? I force a smile and pat her shoulder. "It's actually pretty cool."

She's skeptical of my mood swing.

"There were a bunch in the other halls too." I gesture back the way I came.

She smiles. "And there were some downstairs."

"I bet there are more we haven't seen yet."

Full-on Libby glow is back. "We've got fans."

"We've got fans!"

The beanie-wearing kid and the blue-haired girl have props for their scene, and they've set up a table and chairs to simulate a kitchen. No one else has had anything but costumes.

Beside me, Madi digs into her bag and pulls out a piece of pink paper. In a whisper, she says, "Have you seen this?"

At first, I think she means the band for prom that's playing instead of us. But no. She's pointing to the handwritten word *boycott.*

I rouse a smirk for her, but that's all.

She closes the paper again as if it's a secret. "I've heard a lot of people say they don't want to go if your band isn't playing."

I won't tell her that I don't care if other people aren't going to the prom.

In front of us past three rows of chairs, the beanie kid fakes eating something while the girl rants about the manipulation of the communist party.

Madi scooches closer to me and whispers, "What happened?"

I shake my head. I don't want to tell her what the principal wants. Then she'll picture me in a prom dress. That would be worse than the night at the mall with Christine.

She places a hand on my leg, sending a shiver through me.

"It must have been pretty serious."

"Why?" I want to sound nonchalant, but I only sound ticked off.

"After everything you did to get a second audition. After how upset you and Libby both were." She tries to make eye contact with that look she gets.

"After class," I say.

Before much longer, the blue-haired girl has worked out her issue with the communist party and the bell rings.

Neither of us says anything. Madi matches my movements, step by step, until I stop outside at the tree Libby and I like by the parking lot.

I try to put together the right words in my head to make her understand without creating an image I don't want.

"It's okay, Nate. You can tell me."

It's strange but I feel I can trust her more than anyone else I know.

I hit my foot absently on the ground, kicking up dirt. "The principal said he got complaints from parents about me, and if we wanted to play, we'd have to dress appropriately."

"What does that mean?"

I catch her gaze and hold it. "Prom clothes."

She looks confused. "So wear a tux and play your guitar. Why is that such a big—"

I cut her off. "No. Appropriate clothes. He wants to make me wear . . ." I trail off, not wanting to say it.

She doesn't pick up on my meaning at first. Then suddenly she does. "Oh."

My shoe has made an ugly divot in the grass. I keep my focus there instead of on her reaction. I'm already seething in anger with a little twinge of embarrassment.

"That's the most ridiculous thing I've ever heard. What does it matter what you wear?"

"That's what I said, but he won't go against the parents."

She shakes her head, seeming as incensed as I am.

I wish she would hold my hand like she did in Drama class. Her anger on my behalf is almost enough. Almost.

I take hold of her pinky and ring fingers, gently, and she doesn't pull away. I need to be connected to her if I'm going to be real with her. "I didn't realize how much I wanted this, you know? I thought it was Libby's thing, and I'd do it because she wanted to."

She slides her hand into mine without a word.

"But I really thought this was going to happen. I'd be on stage singing to our whole high school, and everyone would cheer. And I wouldn't be . . ." I pull back the sob that wants to come out. "I wouldn't be a joke to them anymore."

Madi squeezes my hand. "You're not a joke to them."

I let out a brittle laugh.

"Really. If anything, you're a mystery to them. There are a lot of people who've never thought about gender or questioned their own."

That's probably true. And most of them have no idea that I've never questioned mine either. I've always known my birth gender is wrong.

In weightlifting class the next morning, Danny and I spot each other on the bench press. I'm getting close to another weight increase, and Danny is all encouragement. No more envy. With him cheering me on, I lift one-hundred and forty-five pounds almost six times. When he slaps on another five-pounder on each side, my muscles tremble. One hundred and fifty-five pounds.

Danny swats the bar with both hands. "You can do this. It's only ten more pounds."

"Ten pounds is a medium-sized cat. Ten pounds is enough bananas to feed a whole troop of monkeys. Ten pounds is——"

"Lift it already." Danny commands.

I wriggle my head under the bar, putting my feet flat on the bench with bended knees. Curling my fingers around the barbell, I keep my arms loose until I have to brace them against the increase. Then I do it. One hundred and fifty-five pounds not once, not twice, but three times. My arms will be Jell-O the rest of the day, but it was worth it.

Danny slaps me on the back. "Nice piece of work, Kinkade." He uses a thick Irish brogue.

"You sound just like your uncle."

He's adjusting the weights on the barbell. "You bet your sweet arse——" Danny stops moving. He stops talking. Slowly, his lips curl up into the smuggest grin. "I've got an idea."

It's hard not to smile back at him. He's quite pleased with himself. "Well . . .?"

"Well, you and Blue have a setlist, yeah?"

"Libby made a concert-length, mega-list, yeah."

He leans against the barbell all cool-like. "How'd you feel about playing at an Irish pub?"

Returning to Wallin Animal Rescue, knowing that Dakota is no longer there, feels completely wrong, but I have to talk to Dr. Wallin. I feel sick about deceiving all of them for so long, and whether they understand who I am and why I liked being Nate is beside the point. I have to do this for me.

I suppress the nausea I feel as I open the door and step into the lobby. I shake off the images of the last time I was here and Dakota was a happy, smiley dog, and everyone knew I wasn't Nathan Ashur.

Behind the counter, Jeanie looks up as she sees me approaching. For an instant she smiles, then her memory erases her happiness.

"Hi, Jeanie." I stop a few feet from the counter.

"I'll get Dr. Wallin." Her tone isn't hateful but it isn't kind either. She disappears through the back door.

For a moment I worry that when she says "Dr. Wallin" she means Troy and Julia's dad, but Dr. Julia Wallin enters.

Jeanie lingers for a bit, then decides she doesn't want to be a part of this conversation and leaves.

Dr. Wallin allows herself a cursory smile. "Hi there. Is it Nate still?"

I nod. This is harder than I thought it would be. "I wanted to let you know how sorry I am. I know I said that before, but I need you to know that I never was trying to deceive anyone."

She nods in acknowledgement.

"The days I spent here were some of the best days I've had this year. I love being with the dogs. And all of you were so kind." I sigh at myself. I can't get these words right. Maybe I should have written it down. "Coming here and being Nate was important to me. I appreciate having the chance to work here."

Dr. Wallin waits for me to say something more.

"I hope you all can forgive me." And then because I don't know how to end the conversation, I give her a wave, and head for the door.

Each step feels like an eternity; I know she's staring at me.

She calls out, "You have a way with dogs, you know?"

I spin around. "Yeah?"

"When you're ready to show us your ID, we can get you paid for all your hard work and write you on the schedule officially."

"You mean it?"

She smiles. "The way you were with Dakota shows how much you care about animals. I talked with Troy. We both think you belong here."

My shoulders untense a little. Troy doesn't hate me. "What about your dad?"

She shrugs. "He's mostly retired. He only comes around a few times a month. I'll tell him what I need to tell him."

I laugh to myself. I should've asked that question weeks ago.

"Come back in a few days and we'll get you set up."

Chapter 39

IT'S BETTER THAN I EXPECTED. Danny and I talk to Libby and Gene about going down to O'Sullivan's to speak with Uncle Brian. We'd like to play a Friday or Saturday night, ideally the night of prom, but I don't want to get too hopeful. Libby has her hair in a pseudo-mohawk that makes her look dangerous. I'm wearing my black leather jacket that I can only hope makes me look just as intimidating. And Gene, well, I think his chin has at least three more hairs poking out. He's smartly worn his black jeans and a Jimi Hendrix T-shirt. Danny's make-up is prominent, which tells me his uncle must be a cool guy. The four of us sit together, talking about which songs we'd do if we had an hour to play, which we'd do if we had a second hour.

Uncle Brian joins us with a tray full of Cokes, hands one to each of us. He looks us over, then says to me, "Danny gave me some of your songs." His eyebrows rise. "A little rough."

My stomach ices over.

"But you've got fierce promise there. Lots of emotion."

I think that's good, but I'm not certain.

"You could do with a bit of familiar music, of course."

Libby, who's been eyeing her Coke, says, "We have a number of popular songs prepared with our own personal spin."

Uncle Brian chuckles. "You do, now, do you?"

As she names a dozen or so, he turns to Danny at his left elbow and whispers something.

Danny grimaces. "I don't think so."

Libby, Gene, and I stare at them, waiting, though neither of them says anything right away.

Uncle Brian breaks the silence with words to his nephew. "Not even 'With or Without You'?"

Danny checks with me. Am I supposed to know that song?

Libby clears her throat. "Not currently in our regular rotation, but we do have an arrangement for 'One.'"

This appeases Uncle Brian. "I think I have room for you kids to play some night."

Some night? We want a very particular night. We have a statement to make that will fail to gather any steam if we don't get the right date. I know Danny understands that. He must've told his uncle.

Uncle Brian opens a green ledger. He flips through a few pages before he comes to the page he wants: May. His forefinger trails down and he says, "I have this one free."

I'm poised on the blunt edge of asking for the fifteenth. Does he know how much we need this?

"Saturday, May fifteenth."

Prom night.

"I'll give Danny some posters to hang around your school," Brian says. "We always put up a few around town too."

I wonder if O'Sullivan's posters will draw an audience. Maybe. Maybe not. But Danny said the pub brings in quite a few people for the free live music. Fingers crossed.

A day later, Danny finds Madi, Libby, and me in the

commons area. He rolls out a poster on the table—the background is a starry night sky with letters that say: LIVE! Blue. May 15 at 8:00 p.m. with O'Sullivan's Pub logo at the top.

Libby slaps her palm down on it. "Perfect!"

Madi smiles as broadly as the rest of us. "That's amazing! You're playing a real show!"

I meet Libby's eyes. It's better than prom, and we both know it.

Madi says, "That's the same night as prom."

"Exactly," I say.

Realization crosses her face.

"It's all right if you don't come," I say, even though, more than anyone else, I really want her to be there.

"Why wouldn't I?"

"Aren't you already busy that night? With Hunter?"

Madi smiles as her face reddens. "I was only going to buy a ticket to prom if it meant that I could see you."

I close my eyes. She's too kind sometimes. "You should go to prom. I just wish you wouldn't go with one of JT's friends."

She's about to defend her choice when I hold up a hand in apology and stop her. "You can date whoever you want."

"Thank you for your permission," she says.

"No, no, that's not how I meant it."

She touches my arm gently. "I know how you meant it."

The O'Sullivan's posters are up around the school before lunch, and people are already talking about it. I get a few acknowledgements in the hall—smiles, nods, fist bumps.

When Christine approaches, I panic. I want to disappear. But she's beside me before I can take a detour.

She's seen the posters, of course. "I didn't know you played out in the real world." She chuckles at her own joke.

My breath comes easily now that she's here; she's not intimidating anymore.

Her face becomes concerned. "Isn't that prom night?"

"I'm not going." Why would I?

She nods. "Of course not. Maybe I'll have to change my plans that night."

My mind trips through any guys I've seen her with, wondering who's been planning to hold her close at prom, but before I figure it out, my thoughts drift to the chords for "Time After Time" and then Gene's face when I told Libby to slow down the tempo. He nearly spit he laughed so hard.

When I come back to the present, Christine's waiting for a response.

I give her my school photograph smile. "I hope you make it." I can't recall what she said.

Our instruments are set up well in advance, but then all we can do is wait. O'Sullivan's boasts the best burgers in the Twin Cities, but I don't have an appetite. Probably never eat again. There's no backstage, so we're just hanging out in the same booth we occupied when we first met with Uncle Brian. Gene and Libby share a giant basket of *chips*, but Gene has slowed down considerably in the past ten minutes as a few people have come in.

Danny's there to be our cheerleader, bursting through my

nerves and Gene's nausea.

Quite a few people are here already for the dinner hour, talking easily and laughing loudly. I look past them at the framed pictures decorating the walls: famous Irish people, newspaper articles about the pub, clippings about a football team—which is, of course, a soccer team.

A few couples stride up to the bar and call out for drinks, causing Gene's face to change; it looks green.

Libby swats him. "Knock it off. You're making me tense." She snags another fry and munches it down.

"There are so many people here." He puts his fist near his mouth so he can bite his knuckles.

"What's the big deal?"

He doesn't answer me, but it has to be because we've only played at school, not in a real venue before. I don't see many teenagers, just a lot of adults.

I should have known it was foolish to think they'd boycott the prom because of me. No matter what students scribbled on the flyers. It could have been the work of a single person for all I know.

Catching my reflection in the mirror behind the bartender, I don't recognize myself at first. Maybe it's the dim lighting or maybe I've been too up in my head worrying about appearing female, but the kid in the mirror looks like a pretty cool guy. Almost like the one I want to be.

More people arrive, but I stick my chin up a little higher. I can do this.

Brian appears at our table side with his cheery smile. "Well, lads." He glances to Libby. "And lasses. It's about time. I'll go up and introduce you, then you come on up and play."

Libby wipes her greasy fingers on her jeans. "Showtime."

I glance around the room at the adults engaged in conversation, drinking, and eating. They're not here for our band. This is going to be a giant flop.

Libby shoves Gene to make him get up. "Let's go."

Brian O'Sullivan talks to the audience from the stage, which is raised little more than a few feet from table level. I'll be able to look directly into their faces.

"Tonight we have a special treat for you, directly from my nephew's high school. If you haven't heard of them before, you have now, and you won't soon forget them. Put your hands together for the band Blue!" Brian claps with the rest of the people, slipping off the stage as we step up.

Libby safely secures herself behind her drums while Gene slings his bass over his shoulder, solidifying his stance off to the side and far from the audience's accosting eyes.

I hesitate as I turn on my amp and it gives off static. Stupid piece of crap. Don't you dare ruin this for me. I make myself laugh it off and grab the mic. "How are you doing tonight?"

A number of them are having conversations again, but the majority either clap or yell out. "O'Sullivan's has some pretty awesome food!" I add, hoping for some free applause.

It works, and some random guy adds, "And beer!"

He gets a bigger laugh than I got applause, but so be it.

Madi. Madi is near the stage, standing. Thank God she's here. She gives me a little wave. I give her a goofy smile. She's just wearing jeans and a shirt, but she looks absolutely lovely.

"Our first song is our take on a hit from the eighties. 'Don't Stop Believin'.'" Gene and I have worked out guitar and bass parts to replace the missing synthesizer. As I strum my first chord, I spot a few people from Lakeview High. Someone came.

My amp crackles for a moment but stops.

The talking picks up for a bit, but then when we come to the chorus the second time, a number of people sing along, which quiets down the whole room. Libby speeds up the tempo until it feels like we're racing. My fingers falter but no one seems to notice since my amp crackles again.

O'Sullivan's stage lights are green, red, and blue intermittently with yellow. The blue light comes on most frequently, perhaps as an homage to our band. Perhaps in my imagination.

Tiyana and some of the basketball team are mixing in with the audience. And singing. Tiyana's hair surrounds her head in a magnificent corona of dark curlettes. Her bronze prom gown makes her look like a celebrity. She holds hands with a boy in a tux who follows every move she makes.

I check on Madi, smiling and moving to the music.

Libby and Gene signal to each other and then to me that we're going to do the chorus one last time. Blue light pours over the small stage. Even more people sing with us, and even more people from school arrive. Some are in full prom attire with fancy hair and corsages, some in jeans. The pub has filled as we've played the opening number. There have to be more than fifty people here. No, more than eighty. I locate Danny with his dark, spiny hair talking to a girl with purple and green hair who's wearing a multi-colored dress like nothing I've ever seen. Lauren.

I find Madi among the mass of faces again, dancing with the music. She looks so happy. As she sings, our mouths are completely in sync.

Before the last note, the room erupts in applause. It's louder than I'd expected. So many people. Gene's eyes are wide, shocked by the response. Libby, though, spins a drumstick and bangs out the rhythm for our next song. She knows not to waste any time, or we won't get through the whole setlist. That's her goal.

In between the verse and chorus, I look for Madi again, dancing alone.

I wink at her.

Once we've played about five songs, I swear there are more people here than before. I can barely see to the door, but it looks like more are waiting to come in. I spot Christine with her date. Don't know him. He's in a tux, but she's dressed down. Seems he thought they were going to prom, but she'd already decided to come here. Even just a month ago that would have meant so much to me. Now, I guess I'm glad they're here, but I don't care if she stays.

Someone awkwardly waves a hand above the crowd, and I assume they're trying to meet up with their friends, but then I get a closer look. It's my dad. Waving, waving. How embarrassing. But how great that he's here. I give him a tiny nod back, but only so he'll stop flailing around. Dad isn't the least bit upset that I tore the flyers down at school. He said something about a lawyer and my rights being violated, but I shut that down. I don't need the prom gig; I have this.

As Dad grows closer to the stage, I see Sam is with him. Sam, though, is cool enough not to wave. He makes eye contact for a second to say hello, but that's all. I feel like jumping down from the stage and running to hug him, but I stay professional.

We close the first part of our show with "Dance, Dance" by Fall Out Boy. Challenging for my hands to keep up, but the lyrics flow out perfectly. As the last notes fade out and blue light illuminates the stage, I thank them all for their applause. "We're going to take a little break. Order another Coke and try the fish-n-chips." I hope to sound charming, but the noise from my mouth has grown obnoxious.

Brian meets us at the edge of the stage and escorts us toward the kitchen. It's the only place behind the scenes. Amid the savory smells, he sets us up with ice water and leads us down a short hallway to an office.

"You kids are brilliant," he says, gesturing for us to sit.

We crowd together on the couch while he paces in front of us. "How do you manage to get three instruments to sound so . . ." He waves his arms. "You sound so brilliant."

All three of us thank him at once.

"Did you see all the people?"

Libby cackles and says, "There's so many!"

Brian punches a fist into his palm. "We're turning people away. We're full to capacity."

"Is that a big deal?" I ask.

Brian laughs. "We've had big shows before. Usually about half this many on a Saturday." He paces back the other way.

He stops in front of me. "Tell me something. Are you available next Saturday?"

I'm not clear what he's getting at.

Libby stands up. "Of course, we are!"

I check with Gene to see if he understands, and then it hits me. "Seriously? You want us to come back?"

He claps me on the back. "You're good for business, boyo."

After checking with us on how we're feeling, Brian leads us back toward the dining room. He leans in toward me. "You have to know how skeptical I was. Do you mind swapping out your broken amp for the house amp?"

I can barely hear him over the voices from the other room. How will my guitar sound on a real amp?

"When Danny said he knew about a band—" He laughs, and I don't hear the next words he says.

Then suddenly, the whole place quiets. We're still beside the kitchen, semi-blocked by people in aprons with onion rings, when a man's voice comes over the speakers. "Everyone having a good time tonight?"

The crowd whoops and cheers.

"I have to say," the man continues, "the music sounds mighty good."

The voice sounds so familiar, but I can't place it. Whoever has the mic must be up there to psych the crowd for our second set. Only, Brian's brow is furrowed, and he's trying to see around the servers into the dining room. The servers push through a throng of people and we follow after them.

"Too bad they couldn't play prom tonight at our school like they were supposed to."

I get ahead of Brian and Libby and Gene, though I can't quite get to the stage through all the people. It's some guy in a tuxedo, loosened bow tie. Tall, muscular, blond crew cut.

Shit.

It's JT.

Why would he even come here? Shivers rush through me. Something is not right.

"You know why, don't you?"

My throat closes up. Though I want to check the crowd's reaction, my eyes stay fixed on him. He'll tell them why we couldn't do prom. The truth. They'll know I ruined their night because I wouldn't wear a dress, because I refuse to be a girl.

I pull my eyes away from him to the murmurs near me. What are they saying about me? They won't get it. There are probably plenty of them who would wear whatever someone asked and not think anything of it.

"It's my fault, really." JT steps to the side of the mic, as if he might step down. He doesn't. "I got my mom so paranoid that when this band played their music at prom, it would turn everyone gay." He laughs too much.

The murmuring increases a little, tinged with confusion.

"Mom got all her friends to complain to the school."

Holy shit. JT is the one who ruined prom for me? Is this some twisted scheme from the evil powers that be?

"'Cause there's not much my mom hates more than gays." He puts up a hand. "No offense."

I try to get through the few people between me and the stage to punch him in the throat, but I can't get through.

"You know that Kay's a girl, right?"

The room stills. No one breathes.

He jumps down into the crowd right in front of me. "This guy. Right here. Your lead singer." JT reaches out his baboon hand, grabs my shirt, and pulls me up on the stage with him. He balls up my shirt in his fist. "Girl." The offensive word vomits out of his mouth with accents of mango.

The entire pub becomes staring eyes, grimacing faces, and furrowed brows. My stomach fills with frozen shards; I'm going to throw up.

They could rush the stage. They could attack me.

Sam would help. So would Dad. Danny too.

Where's Brian? Still stuck back by the kitchen. He's

signaling to someone at the back of the pub. Then someone else from over by the bar.

A voice calls out from the back of the pub, "Nobody cares!"

The air, brimming with JT's bitterness just seconds before, now floods with a thousand nos. Pockets of laughter erupt. Someone cries, "Get off the stage," which is clearly directed at JT and not at me.

JT lowers his hand, loosening his grasp on my shirt. When I'm free, I shove him hard into the crowd. They catch him, but they have no interest in keeping him and let him drop to the floor. Other groups in the crowd move aside so Brian's guys can get through. Bouncers. They seize JT by the arms and drag him to the door. Next to these guys, JT looks like a child. A smile spreads across my face.

Someone in the crowd says, "Where's the music?"

Libby and Gene, now behind me on the stage, set up a steady beat and a bass riff for one of my songs. We're sure to run out of cover songs if we keep playing. Grabbing my guitar, I blend in the melody line and begin to sing. The audience cheers. Radio tunes, my songs—they seem to like it all.

Blue melds its instruments into exquisite musical waves while the crowd falls into step with the beat and dances. Without the bursts of static from my cheap amplifier, everything comes out pure. The stage lights pool green all around me, then yellow for the briefest moment, and green again. The house lights dim as couples in tuxes and beautiful dresses press against each other. I check on Madi who closes her eyes as she moves her head gently to the rhythm of the song. Everyone seems to be smiling.

Even me.

Chapter 40

LATE INTO THE NIGHT, PROM-GOERS stay at the pub, swaying back and forth as we play love songs. Low lights cast the whole room in shadow. Brian O'Sullivan pays us extra to extend our set, and we have no trouble agreeing. With every song we play, I gaze at Madi, singing the words only for her. The stage lights continue to alternate between yellow and green. Strangely, through the green, I see everything so much brighter.

Especially Madi. She stays until the bitter end when my fingers are permanently dented in by the guitar strings and my voice is husky and low like I wish it always was.

It's nearly midnight when we're packing up our instruments. Brian has the house lights turned up a bit, but the stage lights glow green, staining my arms.

Madi strolls up beside me as I zip up my guitar bag. "You were amazing." Her whole face seems to glow as she beams at me. "You have such a great voice."

Any attempt to retain my cool fails; I smile like an idiot. I doubt there are too many other things I'd rather hear her say to me.

Behind us, Gene and Libby carry her drums out the back door.

Madi takes hold of my hand, startles and examines my fingertips. "Wow."

"Hey, at least they aren't bleeding."

She presses them between her palms. "All the great ones suffer for their art."

I roll my eyes. "Come on."

Laughing, she continues to examine my fingers. "You were truly wonderful tonight."

"Thank you very much." I bow slightly.

"You seem so different here."

I swallow. "Good different?"

"Great different." Her hand drifts through the green light, as her other hand continues to hold mine. "I need to ask you something."

"Okay."

"It might sound strange after some of the things I've said, but I——" She stops herself. "You have every right to say no."

"What is it?"

"Can you forgive me for going out with Hunter?" She continues, "He wasn't who he pretended to be."

I raise my eyebrows. "I'm sure."

She gives me a little shove. "And I didn't know he was so awful to you." She grasps both of my hands. "Besides, I like a different boy."

"What do you mean by 'different'?"

She shakes her head at me. "So? Do you forgive me?"

"I suppose I'll have to if I'm going to ask you out."

"Are you?" Her smile lights up her face and sets my heart pounding.

"That's the plan. But it would have to be a real date. Not

one where we pretend it isn't a date, but it really is."

"I'd like that."

If I knew anything about girls or about dating or about relationships, I'd know whether I could kiss her right now, and if she'd be okay with it. All of my instincts say she will be.

I touch her chin, gently tilting it as I inch toward her. Her eyes close. Before I close mine, I imprint her tender smile on my memory. She loves me.

When my lips meet hers, it's simply the most wonderful thing. Wonderful, wonderful.

Chapter 41

I 'VE MADE AN APPOINTMENT WITH the Institute of Human Sexuality at the University of Minnesota like Dr. Behmann recommended. I guess he only wanted me to be strong enough, prepared enough to face the seriousness of the road ahead. My plan is to take hormones and change my driver's license and come out to all of my relatives and friends who don't already know. Maybe I'll even talk to a surgeon.

Daunting. All of it.

But this is what I want.

♪ ♫ ♪ ♫ ♪

It's a warm and beautiful May morning, a week before graduation when I start the project I've been wanting to do for years. It's only now that I've completely accepted my future, now that I've fallen for a girl who has also fallen for me, now that I've started down the road to musical success and a job working with dogs. All of it has prepared me for this moment.

I dress in old jeans and a T-shirt, and I lay out sheets of plastic, making them hug the place where the carpet meets the floorboards. Then I dip my roller in, evening out the paint before I apply it to the nightmarish pink. The more I cover, the more I smile. The more I smile, the more I don't care that my mother is glaring at me from the hallway.

I'm waiting for her to yell. To tell me that I didn't get permission to change my room.

She opens the door to my room despite the fact that I wanted it closed.

"The fumes aren't good for you," she says, fanning her hands as if she can fan away the toxins she believes are in the air.

Seconds later, a short-haired, copper-colored dog slips by her, prancing right up to me with no concern about the paint.

"That's why the door was closed, Mom."

I lay down the paint roller as deftly as I can before Chloe bounds over and jumps up on me. I grab hold of her, playfully moving her off the plastic sheets. I kneel down to contain her, so I don't have paw prints forever on my carpet.

"Sorry," Mom says, almost audibly. "I'm glad you've decided to live here next year, Kay—I mean, Nate."

Every time. She does it every time. It's as if she means to remind me that Nate is not actually my name. But really what she should do is remind herself that it's my life.

"Chloe!" I hear from down the hall. "Come here, girl." It's my dad's voice.

Chloe's ears perk up, and she's off and running to find him.

"Thanks, Dad," I call.

"Not a problem, Nate," he calls back, loudly enunciating my new name.

Mom purses her lips but says nothing.

I resume painting. A while later, I'm nearly done with the

first coat when Dad arrives.

"I like the way this looks." He inspects my work. "You're going to do a second coat, aren't you?"

"I'm not an idiot." I roll my eyes.

"All right. All right." He crosses his arms. "Why don't you finish up this coat and we'll go."

I nod.

I'm laying down the paint roller when I hear him again, calling me to get going. I wash what I can from my hands and rush down the stairs to meet him.

He has a spring jacket on and widens his eyes when I appear with only my T-shirt.

"Fine." I turn back, find my black leather jacket, and return to him.

"You're going to need it," he says.

"What?"

"How can you pick out your own rock 'n' roll amp if you aren't wearing your rock 'n' roll jacket?" He messes up my hair.

Shaking my head at him, I say, "It's just an amp, Dad. There's no such thing as a rock 'n' roll amp."

"I know what I know."

I put the jacket on as we get in the car. He's right; it is my rock 'n' roll jacket. And I feel like me in it. I am Nate Kinkade, the lead singer and guitarist of Blue, performing Saturdays at O'Sullivan's Pub.

acknowledgments

THIS BOOK AND EVERYTHING ELSE in my life would not be possible without my soulmate, Māra. She has been patient with my anxiety, my depression, my hopelessness, and my definitive feelings that no one would ever want to read my writing. More importantly, she has helped me with the completion of all my novels by finding plot holes and problems, as well as crying in the right places and laughing at my sarcastic humor. She has encouraged my enrollment in writing classes and workshops and my participation in writing groups. Of course, she horned in on my classes, workshops, and writing groups until she was part of it all with her own novels. Still, I'd rather have her with me in everything than not. There's no one I'd rather be with every day of the week, on every trip overseas, in all the adventures life continues to throw at us because when it comes down to it, my love, I hate you less than I hate all the others.

Maybe it's cliché to say that my editor Tamara Grasty was heaven sent, yet it's true. She was able to see the value through the darkness and note the need for a lighthouse. Her insights, enthusiasm, and understanding of my vision for these characters have helped me make this Nate's story instead of mine. The book could only be as deep as it is today with her help. A million thank-yous to Tamara, Rosie J. Stewart, Laura Benton, Krystle Green, Cas Jones, Elena Van Horn, Elliot Wren Phillips, Lauren Knowles and everyone at Page Street for your support, direction, and encouragement throughout this process.

A special thanks to Heather Taylor for finding all the problems that stayed hidden in every rewrite and for suggesting ways to make the confusing parts clearer.

My agent, Tina Schwartz, immediately saw the possibilities for my book. She was inspired to find a publisher and respected my work enough to start with the Big Six. Flattering, to say the least. Tina, your guidance to publication with continued encouragement and excitement has made this experience easy to manage despite the anxiety and stress. Thank you for being so supportive of my work. You are an outstanding cheerleader and liaison.

I owe the last fourteen years of my writing growth to Laurel Yourke. By far my most significant, inspiring mentor, Laurel has led me on a journey from weekend classes to week-long intensive workshops about maximizing tension, varying sentences, developing hooks, having the inciting incident on the first page, avoiding useless stage business, creating verisimilitude, and worshipping Aristotle. Thank you for reading my worst and my best, for keeping my secret, for sharing the old run-down cabin with me (I think the candles are still in my car), and for listening to my repeated confusion about sweet space. You see fiction more clearly than anyone else. Your friendship and your mentorship have made all the difference in my life and have led me to create writing that is actually going to be published! Thank you for leading me down this path.

Kat Falls, mentor and friend, I absolutely love how you construct stories. Your guidance has helped me keep my work young and fresh, and it's because of you that my library of Tarot cards has grown. So many possibilities. I would take a class from you anywhere in the country. Name the date and place, and I'll book my flight. Your suggestions created the conclusion for this book, and your help with my synopsis and query are what got my foot in the door. Finally. Thank you for your encouragement with my writing.

Throughout my writing career, I have had the privilege of working with many talented writing groups. The Madison and Rhinelander group helped me with the bulk of this book. They saw the early incarnation with dual narration that seriously didn't work. Countless suggestions strengthened this story, and I owe wholehearted thanks for your patience and your encouraging words that always showed such deep respect for my work. John Walsh, George Peters, Marisa Hirsch, Jane Banning, Michael McGovern, you are all incredible people and incredible writers.

Love and thanks to my writing colleagues Laurel Osterkamp, Heather Zenzen, Ann Quiring, Brett Carter, and Carrie Bender. You've saved me from embarrassing plot turns and improbable character traits.

A fabulous writer, artist, and person, Theo Nicole Lorenz has developed one of the most sympathetic books for trans-people with The Trans Self-Care Workbook. I'm proud of your art in all of its forms, but so impressed with the empathy shown in your book. Thank you for the inside look into what it's like to be trans now instead of in the eighties. It's the update I needed to keep Nate relevant.

On that note, I must also thank Ren Ford for explaining the scope of meaning of trans these days. You are uniquely brilliant and will find a place where you can be you. I have.

To Ashley Mercer, you were right that I had to get this story out of my system. Thank you for listening and understanding even when I wasn't always intelligible. You have been a crucial support for me through all of this.

Finally, I would be nowhere if it weren't for David Bowie. You were the first to say you didn't care if I was a boy or a girl, that I was wonderful all the same. Your music saved my life, as did your ability to be whoever you wanted for whatever reason at whatever time. I admire your talent, your strength, and your compassion. You made the world a better place.